COCKED AND LOADED

Lucas Brothers Book 4

JORDAN MARIE

By: Jordan Marie

Linda D. Jones... thank you so much for letting me turn you into a pyscho in my book. I love you lady!

Jenn Allen my beautiful friend. Thank you so much for all of your help, no matter the time or hour. I can't thank you enough lady.

Emily Smith-Kidman and the entire team at Social Butterfly. I'm so blessed to have found you. Thank you so much for your help.

Pauline Digaletos I love you and your anus above and beyond. Thank you for everything.

And finally my sister from another mister, Dessure Hutchins you're my ride or die, my bff, and my sanity. I love you.

xoxo
J

STAY CONNECTED

Want to keep up with Jordan and NEVER miss a sale or a new release?

Follow me on these platforms!
Newsletter
Books & Main
BookBub
Facebook Page
Facebook Readers Group
Jordan's Blog
Text Alerts (US Subscribers Only—Standard Text Messaging Rates May Apply):

Text *JORDAN* to 797979 to be the first to know when Jordan has a sale or released a new book.

When I slap the handcuffs on her
I'll be taking her to bed, not jail.

Getting involved with the wrong woman can destroy your life.
   I had to move back home and lose my position as Detective to
get away from one.
   The last thing I need is to repeat my mistake.
   I finally have what I want.
   Deputy in my home town, surrounded by family and friends—
   Life is good.

Then she crashes—literally crashes—into my world.

Adelle Harrington is a pain in my ass.
   She's way too high maintenance for my tastes.
   She's sassy, opinionated, and stubborn as hell.
   She's also the Mayor's only daughter.
   Which means she should be completely off limits.
   When she forces my hand and breaks the law, all bets are off.
   She picked the wrong cop to tangle with.
   I've got her in my sites, she's not getting away
   And I'm definitely not shooting blanks.

Chapter One

BLACK

"How does it feel getting used to a small town again?" Luka asks as he perches his ass on my desk. I frown up at him. He might be married to my sister, and I like and respect the man, but I don't need his ass-cooties on my desk.

"Do you mind?" I ask him, frowning and looking at him sitting there with annoyance on my face, clear for him to read—I should have known it wouldn't matter.

"Normally no. I like it better when I make women mind... Well more to the point one woman—Petal. She likes it too. Just last night—"

"If you start talking about having sex with my sister I may have to pistol whip you... *to death*."

"You've gotten so pissy since you moved back from Dallas. Have I mentioned?"

"You're starting to sound like, Petal," I grumble.

He's not wrong. I mean, I like being back and I'm actually enjoying the job. But, I'd be lying if I said I didn't miss the excitement of the cases I got back in Dallas. Being home has been a big adjustment. Not to mention, I've been forced to live back at home with Mom and Jansen while I find a good place to rent. I had one...

only to discover it was infested by mice. So back to mom's I went. Mason isn't that big and finding a decent place is not easy.

"She must be rubbing off on me. Which reminds me of last night, we were in bed...

"That's it!" I growl... *loudly*. "I don't know why you and my mom ever had problems because you're just alike! I'm out of here, there's no way I'm listening to you go on about schtupping my sister."

"Schtupp? That's so crass. I'm a cop so I like to call it pounding the punanni pavement."

"Is this what I've been resigned to? Is this my life now? Living at home with my mother listening to her talk about having sex with Jansen—whom I love but probably has balls that look like prunes—only to come to work and listen to my boss talk about having sex with my sister?" I moan, sounding pitiful. But fuck, right now I feel pitiful.

Luka—the bastard—just laughs.

"Eventually probably not, but for now I find I'm enjoying it. Especially after finding out you are the fucker who gave Petal that damn dress she wore out to see that fuckwad Craig."

"I don't actually think *fuckwad* is Craig's first name, even if that is what you call him all the time."

"It fits," Luka shrugs taking a drink of his coffee. "I can't believe you gave her that damn dress."

"It worked to get your attention, now didn't it?" I remind him. The bastard should be grateful. I was a genius with that plan, man. People never fully appreciate me.

"Petal always had my attention, asshole."

"Whatever. My plan was golden. If you think about it, I'm the reason you have little Rain now."

"Oh, now you're just being delusional. The reason we have my daughter has nothing to do with you and everything to do with the power of my—"

"And I'm out. I'm going to go on patrol and find a jaywalker or something. I can't sit here and listen to you talk about your dick like it's the hammer of Thor. You know, you complain about my mom... well you used to, but you're only proving you're as wacky as she is. You're naming your kids after water," I grumble. I actually like the names of Luka's kids, but I like to remind him that he's like a male version of my mother as often as I can.

"Petal talked me into it. I can't resist her when she's on her knees and begging—"

"La-La-La! *I can't hear you!*" I call out, jumping up and reaching into my desk for my weapon. I won't need it. Nothing happens in Mason, but I get it just the same.

"Since you're leaving, can you run these papers by Mayor Harrington's house? He asked to see the budget proposal for the year before the next City Council meeting."

"This all has been a trick hasn't it? Your way of getting me to do your dirty work because you hate dealing with the Mayor?"

"Well, no. I really am pissed you dressed Petal up for fuckwad Craig. Plus, you're too damn fun to annoy. But, I really don't want to head out to the Mayor's place. Petal is bringing River and Rain over and we're going to lunch at the diner."

"Can't you send Danny-Boy?" I whine, really not in the mood to deal with bureaucrats.

"He's out with the flu today and besides I hate to play this card, but he has seniority."

"Fuck you," I grumble. "Give me the file and I'll go."

"He's not that bad, you know," Luka says going to his desk and picking up a file. "He's much better than the last Mayor," he adds with a shrug, giving me the file.

I look at him. The last Mayor was his father, Roger, and there really are no words to adequately describe that piece of shit, still he died and the way he did was fucked up and I know that has to mess with Luka's mind.

"Luka, man—"

"I'm good, Black. Better than good. I have everything a man could want. Except a deputy who does what I ask and doesn't give me shit."

"Fine, I'm going," I mutter.

I take the file and put on my hat. I'm almost at the door when Luka calls out from behind me.

"And play nice. Mayor Harrington might be new to the job, but he seems to have the best interests of Mason at heart."

"He had a three story house built high up on the hill over-looking the town, Luka."

"So?"

"He put a damn elevator in it. He spent more on that house than most of us will make in salary the rest of our lives. You want to fit in, in a small town, you don't lord money over people and show them constantly how much you have. He owns the town bank and—"

"Black, come on. You need to give him a break."

"Like he did Joey Dawson's widow?"

"Black—"

"All Tina asked for was an extension on their mortgage so she didn't lose the house along with that fool husband of hers. The good Mayor wouldn't even hear her out. He foreclosed on the house and served her with eviction papers the same day they were burying Joey. Poor Tina got everything dumped on her at once."

"Black—"

"Save it. In my book that makes Mayor Harrington a fucking prick," I grumble.

"Just play nice, okay?"

"I will. Doesn't mean I'll like it," I mutter, closing the door before Luka can say anything else. Nothing he can say will convince me to like the guy anyway.

Chapter Two

ADDIE

I pull my thick blonde hair up and wrap the band around it pulling two parts of the hair in opposite direction to tighten it. It's ninety out here today, but I'm ignoring it. It's a gorgeous day and the yard needs mowed. Dad will have a cow. He hires a service for this very thing. But we have this huge expensive lawnmower in the shed for this very purpose and I still need to work some things out in my head. Okay, sure... the lawnmower looks like it hasn't been started in years and maybe it hasn't. Dad always hires a firm that has their own equipment.

I've been studying abroad. Coming back stateside has been a shock to my system, especially if you consider the fact that I've practically been living in Paris for the last three years. It's been nice and I've learned a lot about a different culture and it's helped me become a better chef, but it's time for me to be home—past time really. The thing is, I didn't expect to find my home was no longer my home. I guess that was silly. I expected my father to move on with his life, it was inevitable after Mom's death. I didn't expect him to have sold the family home and moved to Mason, Texas. He owned a bank here, sure. But, Dad owns lots of banks. The fact that he decided to move to a new town, sell the family home, and put all of my stuff and my mom's stuff in storage boggles my mind. I mean, it's not that I felt like he needed to clear it with me, but he could have *told* me. I had no idea until three days ago when I told him I was coming in. Then he gave me his new address. I've always called him on his cell so I never even knew the house phone didn't work anymore. Plus, he's always made a point of coming to Paris for the holidays to see me, instead of me coming home. He said we both needed memories away from the house and the sadness of Mom... I never questioned it, but I guess I should have. Dad will never understand how much it hurt to call the house after he told me and not getting our answering machine—just a recording saying the number had been disconnected.

I wonder what he did with the old answering machine... the one with Mom's voice. Did he erase the message? Throw the machine away?

I have all these questions and yet, I can't seem to voice them to my father. I've only been back a couple of days, so maybe I'll work up to it—right now, I can't seem to vocalize anything with him. It doesn't help that he's not been here either. Last night it was business meetings and today he had to go out of town to meet with the Governor of Texas. I'm used to my dad the banker. Dad the political figure is going to take some getting used to.

I put on my earphones and click my phone, finding my favorite playlist, then tuck my phone in my bra. Once the music begins blaring, I do my best to shake off some of the stress while I start the lawn mower. The front yard isn't overly huge, but it's much bigger than our home in Houston. I let the music take over, trying my best to still my mind and not think. Ever since I talked to Dad and he told me he sold the old house, I've been in turmoil. Those walls held the memories I had of my mom. The late night movie bingeing, baking cookies together, planting flowers, the times we played in the pool together, family Christmases... *Everything.*

I can't get those back, and now I can't even walk into the rooms and remember them. It's my fault I guess. I should have come back sooner. I needed to heal, and my dad and I had never been particularly close. He's a good guy, he really is. He's just married to his career... and apparently that's even more true now that he's in politics. I've barely been home and he's already leaving...

Surprisingly the lawnmower started up with just a pull on the choke and cutting the grass is helping if only because it's giving me something to concentrate on. The smooth melody of a love song comes on and I sigh.

What would it be like to find love like that?

I never have. I seem to have an internal pheromone or something that draws all losers to me like a kid to candy.

I spend the next hour—or at least close to it—mowing the lawn. I feel sweat running down my back and along my neck. I look a mess, I'm sure, but it's the first time I've felt semi-normal in a week. I'm completely zoned out...

Until the moment a yellow jacket comes hurtling at me at the speed of light. That's probably an exaggeration, but it seems like it. I see it coming and I jerk to the side to miss it. I swat and flail like someone trying to dance the twerk without rhythm. Then the worst that could happen, happens. The damn thing falls into my shirt. Panic hits me like it hadn't before. At least when I could see it, I could fight it off. But now I just feel it crawling around in there and I scream. I don't want to be stung. I'm not allergic—I don't think—but just the thought of being stung is enough to terrify me. I hate bees—of any kind—and I hate pain. Put the two together and I lose it. Which is unfortunate because I'm no longer paying attention to mowing the lawn. I'm no longer even looking. I'm pulling my shirt way out while trying to find the bee, I can't see anything, so I rip the shirt over my head, throwing it to the ground slapping around on my stomach and back trying to find it.

I can't find it. I didn't see it fly away. It must have gone somewhere else. I pull off my head phones, I wear the large ones because I've found the smaller ones can cause me to get a headache and I'm afraid maybe the bee went up to it and will crawl in my ear.

I saw a documentary once about this guy who had a bug lay eggs in his ear. That shit legitimately left me emotionally scarred. I didn't even know that was possible. He had like hundreds of these bugs in his ear and they would just randomly crawl out. The thought of a million colonies of bees taking up nest in my head is freaking me out so bad I'm screaming every breath. I stand up stomping on the mower, trying to shake my head back and forth. The mower is supposed to die when you stand up. This one didn't get that memo. It's sputtering but it moves forward and stalls out, but only after it crashes into something. I stumble back against the seat. For a second I think I'm going to save myself, but then I fall backwards and my ass hits the ground.

"What the hell is wrong with you?" I look up to see a guy in a police uniform standing over me. He's got dark hair with hints of dark blond in it and even with the long sleeves and high collar of his shirt there are tattoos visible on his neck. In any other circumstance I'd have to stop everything I was doing and just stare. I've always had a thing for a guy in uniform and this guy is hot as hell. That's not what would get a girl's attention though—at least not all of it. That would be those piercing blue eyes he has. Blue eyes which are currently staring at me like I'm crazy. He's furious... and with good reason. Dad's lawnmower has just plowed into the side of his squad car.

Crap.

That's the exact moment the bee makes itself known. I'm convinced it's probably a demon from hell only taking the form of a bee, because it appears again out of nowhere and is diving, aiming right for my face. I scream—loudly again—and swat it away.

Unfortunately, I swat it directly at the man who is already pissed at me. He tries to dodge it, but his reflexes are obviously not as great as mine and the bee lands on his face...

I can only surmise by the stream of curse words that it stings him right between the eyes.

I stand up, intent on helping him when I realize I'm in my bra and have no shirt on.

Double crap.

I scream again—for no real reason unless you count that I'm half naked and search for my shirt. I finally find it and bend down to grab it just as the guy is and our heads slam together.

This time it's a tie as to who is cursing louder. Me or him. But there's really no mystery in the fact that ole' blue eyes is looking at me like he wants to kill me.

Triple crap.

Chapter Three

BLACK

I hold my head while steadying the woman who apparently is trying to kill me. I look down at the lawnmower with a crumpled front end, the huge dent to the door in my squad car and I feel my face go tight. If I hadn't jumped out of the way, the crazy woman would have run right over me. And on top of all of that, she swatted a yellow jacket right at me and the damn thing stung the fire out of me. I haven't been stung in years.

Christ.

"Are you out of your mind?" I growl.

"There was a bee," she says, like that explains the chaos that just erupted. She puts her shirt on while she responds and some of the words are muffled. If I wasn't in pain from clanging heads with her *and* the bee sting, I'd probably take time to enjoy those full breasts that are overflowing in her bra. I don't even blink as she covers herself up. Women are trouble, I learned that the hard way in Dallas, and it's clear that this one is even more trouble.

"You can't tell me you don't run into bees every day in your line of work," I chastise, because really that's no excuse.

"My line of work?" she asks, blinking.

"I assumed you were the Harrington's gardener."

She's silent for a minute.

"It's 2018," she says. "The proper term these days is landscaper."

"Oh..."

"There's much more to maintaining a healthy lawn and trees than you realize," she begins to lecture me.

"Like jumping around like a lunatic and stripping naked for the world to see?" I prod her. If she wants to have an issue with me, I'll just remind her of why we're even talking in the first place.

"I told you," she huffs. "There was a *bee.*"

"What happens when you see a snake?"

She ignores my question. If it wasn't for the annoyance and a spark of anger that goes over her face, I'd think she didn't hear me.

"I'm sorry about your car. I'll just get your info and contact—"

"It belongs to the town of Mason. We can tell the Mayor and he can sort it out, since you are working for him."

"Oh... Yes, we can do that. Although, he's probably going to want to kill me."

"What you did was very foolish," I tell her honestly. "You could have been seriously injured or injured me. You need to be more aware of your surroundings. You also will have to contact the owner of your company so they can warn their insurance carrier."

"Oh... I own the lawnmower actually."

"You own your own landscaping business?"

"Is that so hard to believe?" she asks, her tone sharp. It's clear she's going to get pissed off. I know I sounded condescending, but landscaping seems like a job where lots of muscles would come in handy, plus there is the fact that she's clearly a train wreck. How she can run her own business could possibly be one of life's greatest mysteries.

"It's just that most landscapers are..." I trail off because with each word her face gets tighter. The only woman I've ever known whose face is so animated that I can read almost every emotion is my mother. I take a step back away from this woman, taking that as a warning more than anything else.

"You can go ahead and say it, you know," she responds, crossing her arms across her chest, just below her breasts. The stance is like a challenge and it's a really bad time to notice her tits now. You would have thought earlier they would have caught my eye more when they were just hanging out—but nope. I don't have the slightest urge to look at them until this moment. When the girl looks pissed as hell at me.

I apparently am still an idiot when it comes to women and the whole mess in Dallas taught me zip. At this point, I'm as angry at myself as she obviously is with me.

"Say what?" I ask, just needing to get the hell out of here.

"That you expected me to be a man," she almost snarls at me. This is clearly a sore spot with her.

If it were possible there would be a large neon sign over her head at this point flashing, "Danger." I back away a little more. I didn't come here for this crap and the last thing I want to do is tangle with Harrington's gardener—landscaper—crazy as a Bessie bug—don't call her a woman—person.

"Well I did. Is that so wrong?" I ask, sounding and feeling defensive.

"I run across guys like you all the time in my industry. You think if a man doesn't do it, it can't be done. I got news for you buck-o, a woman can do anything a man can do and most times do it a hell of a lot better!"

Now, coming from a single mother, who raised a large family on her own for the most part, I happen to agree with her. That and the fact that my sisters are all strong, loving women, I get it. What I don't like is the fact that this woman is jamming it down my throat. She clearly has issues and this is not my battle, plus I'm getting *really* tired of going on the defensive when it was *her* that tried to kill me and I'm not even mentioning the fact that my head is really starting to kill me. It must have been so long since I've been stung that I don't remember the pain, because right now my face feels hot, tight and it's pulsing with pain. With that in mind, I just walk away.

I've turned away and gone a whole five steps when I hear her calling out behind me.

"What? You don't have anything to say to the argument? Did you suddenly realize what an ass you sound like?"

"Lady, I don't have time to fool with you. I'm going to drop these papers off with the Mayor and then I'm getting the hell out of here. You've done enough damage trying to kill me, I don't need to stand around and let you chew my ass out over the injustices of the world on top of that."

"What a typical male response!" she yells.

"I doubt you know what a typical male response is like," I mutter. I didn't think she could hear me, but apparently she decided she wasn't going to let me walk away because the next thing I know she's standing beside of me. I do my best to ignore her while walking to the Mayor's front door.

"What is *that* supposed to mean?"

I sigh, reaching up to rub my forehead and I can tell that the bee sting has swollen. I've got a golf ball size knot on my damn head. Fuck, maybe I should go back to Dallas. At least I knew to watch out for the crazy women back there. Here they just jump out of nowhere—or come riding in on a damn mower.

"It doesn't mean anything," I mumble, knocking on the door.

"Oh come on. You expect me to think you didn't mean anything by that snide remark?" she snorts.

I knock again and there's still no answer.

"If you're going to say something, you should at least have the balls to explain what you mean," she nudges, snidely.

"Lady, you don't know shit about my balls. I doubt you've seen any man's balls in a hell of a long time—unless you were wearing them around your neck as a trophy."

"Oh my God! You *did not* just say that to me!"

"In fact, I did, Ball-Busting-Barbie," I snarl and bang on the door again. "Where in the hell is the Mayor?" I ask, more to myself —definitely not to her.

"He's not home!"

"You couldn't have told me that to begin with?"

"You didn't ask!"

"Who can ask you anything? You're too busy trying to kill me or scream me to death with that high-pitched voice of yours."

"There's nothing wrong with my voice," she says, putting her hands on her hips.

"Maybe not if it wasn't constantly yelling," I growl. "When the Mayor gets back tell him Sheriff Parrish—"

"I'm not your messenger boy either."

"Fine. Lady, I swear you take the cake. You think you'd be sorry for trying to kill me."

"You think you wouldn't be able to walk because you're such a caveman!"

"That's it. I'm out of here. Best of luck in life and in explaining how you nearly demolished a police car."

"That wouldn't have happened if you hadn't parked where you did!"

"I parked in the damn driveway!"

"But only so far. If you had parked in front of the garage, it wouldn't have happened, now would it?"

"You're unbelievable. For the sake of your business, and every male that gets within ten feet of you, here's hoping you get laid soon. Maybe it will get the stick out of your ass and put you in a better mood."

"I... You... *Oh. My. God!* How dare you say that to me!"

"I bet I'm not the first, I just said it where you can hear me."

I give my parting shot as I get in my car. I peel out of the Mayor's drive leaving a trail of burnt, blackened rubber in my wake. The mower turns sideways as I leave, as it disengages with my crumpled passenger side car door.

Luka's not going to be happy about that. Hell, if the Mayor's *landscaper* blabs about what I said to her, I probably won't have a job anymore.

Fuck it.

I'm not sure I care anymore. Maybe that old saying is true and you really can't go back home again. It worked for some of my brothers and sisters, but it's definitely *not* working for me and I'm getting tired of trying.

Chapter Four

ADDIE

"You okay, Princess?" Dad asks over the phone.

I flop back on my bed and close my eyes. I'm lying on the bed, wrapped in a towel with another smaller towel around my hair. I soaked in the tub for hours, adding hot water until there was no more hot water to be found. I've finally calmed down and now I just feel like an idiot. I shouldn't have reacted the way I did to that officer. It all just exploded and got out of hand. I don't even think he meant anything about me being a landscaper. After all, it is a male dominated field—much like being a chef is these days.

Which is exactly the problem.

I'm touchy about it. I know. Living in Paris was amazing, but most of my classmates were males. Growing up you have this mindset that your mother does the majority of the cooking and that's how it was for me—until she died and I took over. But, once I decided to pursue the culinary field it became clear that the most successful chefs that I wanted to emulate were males. Then, I enrolled in school. That was an eye opener for sure. Being in Paris, it became apparent that to succeed I had to try twice as hard, work twice as hard and never show weakness. That's been forged inside of me over the last few years and I reacted badly to the officer. I should have held my tongue—

"Princess?" Dad says again, drawing my attention back to the phone and our conversation.

"I wrecked the lawnmower, Dad," I tell him, starting out with the easier part of the story. I'm not sure how much I'm going to tell him, honestly. But, he needs to know about the police car and the damage.

"The lawnmower? What in the hell were you doing out on the lawnmower, Adelle?"

"I wanted to clear my head and working outside usually helps."

"Clear your head. I can guess what about. You're going to have to forgive me for selling the house, Princess," Dad says softly and I can't stop the tears that boil up out of nowhere and begin seeping from my eyes.

"You should have told me," I whisper, keeping my eyes closed and ignoring the hot tracks of tears running done my face.

"You would have asked me not to."

"So? It was our home, Daddy. It was *her* home."

"But she's not here anymore, Princess. I was alone in that home. You weren't there, she wasn't there. The silence was killing me. Maybe what I did was wrong to you... but, I had to do it to survive."

"Daddy—"

"Your mother was a special woman, Adelle. I loved her with all of my heart. I always will, but I had to keep living. Being in Mason feels right. I think your Mom would be happy for me and I hope you will too."

I think over his words and although I know he's right, my heart breaks just the same.

"You okay, Addie-girl?"

I know he's talking about me being upset over Mom. Honestly, I miss her so much I don't feel like I will ever be okay again. It's like a piece of me is gone. So, instead of lying to him, I play dumb.

"The lawnmower's not. I hit a cop car."

"A cop car?"

"A bee flew down my shirt and I panicked. There was an officer that came by to leave a file for you."

"Who was it?"

I think for a minute. I know somewhere in our shouting match with each other he gave a name. It finally comes back to me.

"I think he said Sheriff Parrish, or something like that."

"Yeah, Luka. He's a good guy I think. What did you think of him?"

A good guy?

"Well, he wasn't really happy with me, Daddy. I just ruined his car..."

"I suppose so, but he'll get over it. I really like Luka. He's nothing like his father, and trust me when I tell you that in this case—that's a good thing. Are you sure you're okay?"

"Yeah. I'm okay, Daddy. I promise."

"Okay, Princess. I'll be home in a couple of days and we'll spend some time together, just the two of us."

"That sounds good."

"For me too. Night, Addie-girl."

"Night, Daddy," I whisper as we hang up.

I lie there staring up at the ceiling for a little while. I'm still crying, but I ignore the tears. I've found that wiping them away just makes them fall harder.

"I miss you, Mommy," I whisper out into the room.

Only quiet answers me and I didn't think it was possible, but my heart breaks a little more.

Chapter Five

BLACK

"What in the tarnation happened to you?"

I look up to see my mom standing at the front door and I love her, but I was really hoping she'd be gone when I got home.

"Nothing why?" I ask. I'm bone tired. I just want to crawl into bed with a bottle of Ibuprophen or Jack, whatever I find first that might help this headache.

"You look like you've been hit by a baseball bat," she complains, coming down off the steps and meeting me at my car.

"Just a landscaper," I mutter under my breath.

"What?"

"It's nothing, Mom. I just got stung by a bee."

"Stung by a bee? I've never seen one make a goose egg that big."

"I'm just lucky I guess. I just want to take some pain meds and go to bed."

"Bullshit. You're going to the emergency room. That sucker is huge. You could be allergic."

"Oh for fuck's sake! I'm not allergic. I just need rest."

"I know you did not just use that tone and those words on your

Mama? You're not too big to yank a knot out of your tail, you know, boy."

When I don't immediately respond, she grabs me by the ear and harshly pulls me down to her. It's kind of humiliating to be treated like you're an eleven-year-old by your mother. But, if I think about it, I know I probably deserve it.

"Sorry, Mom. It's just been a fucked up day."

"Come inside and let me put some crap on your head and tell me about it."

"What kind of crap?" I ask, suddenly afraid.

"Just never you mind. It will make you better and that's all you need to know. You got a slight allergy going on, boy. You're lucky you didn't get stung in your throat, it could have killed you. I've got to get something on you to draw the venom out."

"Nothing you use is going to make my sperm super human so I knock up sand rocks or something right?"

"Sand rocks? Just where in the hell are you sticking your willie at these days, Black?"

"Sadly, nowhere."

"That's good enough for you after that coo-coo bird you were living with in Dallas. I still don't know what on earth possessed you to let that woman in your bed."

"She had big tits," Cyan answers as we walk through the door.

I flip him off. He's not wrong, but he's too much of a damn know it all about it.

"You boys. I tried to teach you. The good Lord knows I did. Those things are meant to give sustenance to babies. That's it."

"They're a lot more fun than that, Mom," Cyan mumbles over a full mouth. Looks like I made it home in time for dinner—not that I feel like eating any of it.

"Hate to break it to you boys, but those women you chase after with the tits the size of cantaloupes might look pretty right now, but one day those tits are going to be ankle warmers," Mom mutters. "Pull up a seat Black and let me find my medicine bag."

"What happened to you?"

"Got into a fight with a damn bee," I tell Cyan, reaching over and grabbing a cucumber slice off of his plate.

"Try that again and I'll stab you with my fork," he grouses. "Hate to break it to you, but I think the bee won."

"It was probably a female. It was definitely mean enough to be one."

"Women aren't mean, brother. You just have to know how to pet them the right way."

"Tried that, nearly got my *"pet-ter"* chopped off. I'm pretty sure I'm done."

If I sound bitter, it's probably because I am. Losing a job you loved, a condo you really liked in a town you loved, will do that to a man. I mean, a lot of it was my fault. I'll admit to that. I'm a trained detective. I should have somehow seen Linda's crazy. There were signs, I was just too busy enjoying the perks of the relationship to see them. If anything can be said about Crazy Linda, it's that she is a *major* pro in the sack—which, looking back, should have been a warning sign all on its own.

"Not all women are looney-tunes, big brother," Cyan responds as Mom comes hustling back in carrying an old leather bag, which is sure to be full of home remedies.

Shit. Fuck. Damn.

I have *got* to get my own place.

"Well not all women are mean when they're looney-tunes anyway," Cyan says with a wink, his eyes shifting back to our Mom.

"I never spanked you enough as a kid," she mutters to Cyan, proving her hearing is still the best of any of us in the household.

"You did Mom and I like spankings. I just like to be the one to give them now," he says with yet another wink. Mom shakes her head, but she does it smiling. Of all of us, I think Cyan could sweet talk Mom into anything. It's always been that way.

"Now, let me see if I have that cream for bites in here somewhere," she mumbles, shuffling through the contents of her bag.

"Wait. Black is actually agreeing to a home remedy? What the hell for?"

"Didn't you notice the baseball he's sporting around on his head?"

"No. I was busy eating and you know how I am when I'm hungry... Holy shit you do have a knot on your head. Crazy Linda find you and take a bat to you?"

"Believe it or not, no. I was stung by a bee."

"Christ man, it must have been hung like a gorilla," Cyan mutters, shaking his head.

"What are you talking about?" I ask, my brain too tired to go where Cyan's goes—*ever*.

"The stinger. They sting you with their dick," he says, like what he is saying is straight up gospel.

"Sometimes I feel like I'm the only sane crayon in this box," I answer with a sigh. "Mom you swear this shit has no side effects?"

"What do you care if you plan on retiring your coc—"

"Cyan, watch your mouth at my kitchen table. It's holy ground," Mom chastises, causing me and Cyan both to look at each other and hide our laughter.

"If you plan on retiring your *petting utensil*, then," Cyan jokes.

"There's nothing in this that will help or hurt your wiener," Mom mumbles, slapping some of the cream on my face. It's cold at first, but it almost instantly starts feeling better.

"My *wiener* is fine the way it is," I answer before Cyan can say something smartass about it. "Mom, that actually feels good," I tell her, but I think I've spoken too soon. Because a fowl stench the likes of which I've never smelled in my life starts hitting me. That's saying something too, because as a detective in Dallas I've done my fair share of dumpster diving.

"What the fuck is that smell?" Cyan asks, almost gagging as he says the words.

"Well the remedy works, but it does have a little *stank* to it," Mom defends.

"A little stank?" I cry and I mean cry, because there are literally tears in my eyes from the smell and now it's starting to burn. "What's in this crap?"

"Nothing for you to get your boxers in a twist over. It's all natural, aloe, homemade cow butter, a touch of lemon juice, some cinnamon..." she trails off.

I relax a bit, because that can't be too harmful, but there's no way those ingredients can make this smell either.

"What else?" I ask, because I know there has to be something else.

"Just a few more natural ingredients, I swear. You guys worry over everything. It's feeling better right?" she asks and I think about it for a minute.

"It's either better, or I can't feel the pain because I'm too busy dying from the smell."

"Oh my God mom! I thought I told you never to use that crap again while I'm in the house?"

"Well you weren't in the house until just a few seconds ago, were you, Marigold? Besides your brother had to have it. He was swelling up like a balloon from a bee sting and was having a lot of pain," Mom mumbles. She's apparently satisfied that she has enough on me because she's already putting her things away. I'm holding my nose, but I'm at least grateful the burning seems to have stopped.

"He must have been in a lot of pain to agree to put that crap on," Mary murmurs, shaking her head at me. She grabs an apple and instead of turning around, she backs out of the room toward the door, her gaze locked with mine. There's something in her look, something that tells me she has knowledge that I don't.

"You know what's in this junk? Am I going to get a woman pregnant by looking at her?"

"Pregnant? No. No chance in that. Heck, once they find out what you've been soaking your skin in, they may never want around you again," she says, still backing away. She takes a bite out of her apple, and I know she's waiting for me to ask more questions.

I know it and now I'm afraid.

"That sounds like something he should show Crazy Linda,"

Cyan replies and everyone laughs—except me. I've lost my ability to laugh where Linda is concerned.

"What's in it?" I respond, my voice quiet.

"I told you it was all natural!" Mom says, instantly offended.

"What's in it, Mary?"

Mary looks at Mom and then at me. Something makes her hesitate.

"Mom's right. It *is* all natural," she says with a shrug.

"Told you. Fudge-sickles and handlebars, I get zero respect around here when Jansen is out of town."

"What's in it, Mary?"

"Relax, Black. It's nothing really," she says with a smile that I do *not* trust.

"Tell me, or I'll make sure Teddy Ray down at the station knows you're sweet on him," I warn her.

Her eyes go hard.

"You wouldn't dare. I can't stand him!"

"I know that, you know that, but Teddy has no idea if you do... or if you don't. He's been looking for a good woman to take out frog gigging with him on Saturday nights."

"I hate you," she mumbles. "Fine. There's nothing in it but a muffin or two," she says turning around and starting up the stairs.

"Mom, I thought you said there wasn't any of your home cooking involved that would make me knock a woman up?" I ask, thoroughly confused now.

"She's not talking about that kind of muffin, Black."

"What? Then what kind—"

"Meadow muffins dear," she says, calmly. Then she picks up her bag like she hadn't just dropped a bomb on me. "Now you keep that on for a good hour and then wash it off. If it's not better in the morning we'll have to try something a wee bit stronger," she says, ruffling my hair and then she leaves.

"A meadow muffin?" Cyan asks, sounding confused. He grew up in the country, but honestly he spends very little time at the ranch in any useful form. I stand up immediately, grabbing a dish towel and wiping this shit off my face. I start walking because I'm going straight to the damn shower and then I'm going to find that bottle of Jack, because the good Lord knows I need something to get me through the rest of today.

"Hey! Where you going?" Cyan asks. "What's going on?"

"I'm going to shower."

"I thought Mom said you needed to keep that on for an hour. If you've gone this far you might as well stick to it. Mom's remedies are strange as fuck, but they always seem to work," Cyan defends.

"Meadow muffins are slang for cow shit," I hear Mary explain. The little witch obviously came back down the stairs. I ignore their laughter and head out to the front of the house which is where the living room and the bedroom I'm using are located. If I ever manage to get this smell off of me, I may kill them both.

I really need to get my own place.

Chapter Six

ADDIE

"Can I help you?" a lady at the front desk asks. I take off my sunglasses and blink as I adjust from the transition of coming inside after the bright sunlight outside. I look around the small lobby area that claims to be the home to the Mason County Sheriff's office. It's rather confusing because Mason County has only one real small suburb which is also called... Mason. Honestly, I'm not even sure how that works, but I'd venture to say a man was in charge.

"I'm looking for a Sheriff Parrish?" I respond, pulling on my dress. I've been feeling guilty about the way I treated the man. I mean, I don't know him and I kind of jumped down his throat when I really shouldn't have. I've just grown so accustomed to being made to feel inferior because I'm a woman chef that I leaped before I thought and took it all out on him. It doesn't change the fact he was kind of an ass, but maybe if I extend an olive branch, he can too. Dad thinks we will like each other and because I want him to be happy, I'm willing to bury the hatchet.

Hopefully Sheriff Parrish doesn't piss me off so that I bury it in his head...

"I'm sorry he's not here right now. I'm afraid he's gone to

lunch. I can take a message or you're welcome to come back. Or maybe someone here would be able to help you?"

I breathe deeply, more than a little disappointed. I kind of wanted this out of my way. Check it off and be done with it, really. It doesn't look like that's going to happen now—

"What are you doing here?"

I'd know that loud, grouchy snarl anywhere. It's been two days since our fateful run in. I guess it was too much to hope for that he would have developed a personality.

This was probably a bad idea.

"I was looking for you. Oh wow you look better. I guess you weren't allergic after all!"

"Uh... yeah. What do you want? I told you I'd turn the paperwork in. Your boss could have handled all of this," Mr. Grumpy says and I fight to hold onto my temper. That won't help the situation at all.

"Oh, this wasn't about the little incident," I say, waving off his words before he annoys me again. "I wanted to talk with you, I think we started off on the wrong foot the other day," I begin.

"It wasn't an incident! You tried to kill me."

"I did not!"

"Uh, yeah. *You did.*"

"Listen buddy, if I wanted you dead, you wouldn't be here yelling at me right now!" I huff.

"Did you just threaten an officer of the law?"

"What? Of course not!"

"You did!"

"Oh my God! Why did I think you'd actually be sane today! I just came here to ask if you wanted to have lunch together."

"Why on earth would we have dinner together?"

"Not dinner, *lunch*. I thought since you would be working with my... boss that it'd be best if we get along well with each other."

"Why?" he asks and it was question I wasn't expecting.

"Why?"

"Yeah, Princess, why?"

"What did you call me?"

"Princess."

"My dad calls me that…"

"That explains a lot."

"I'm going to ignore you said that. Are we going to lunch or not?"

"You realize I don't have any need to hire a landscaper? Especially one that is a menace to society on the back of a lawnmower," he replies.

He's so infuriating. I really want to slap him. At the same time, I'm only human—and a female human at that, one who hasn't even seen a man who clicked all her buttons at once. This guy does that and then some. He's hot. I can't pretend he's not. He has these buttoned up uniforms—that hide way too much. Not to mention, this Texas heat has to be a killer in those long sleeves. I think I'd break protocol and roll them up. *I wish he would.*

Still, around the collar of his neck and on his hand I can see hints of ink and even when I find myself screaming at him, I want to see the ink. Shit. *Who am I kidding?* I want to lick it. Then, there are those blue eyes of his. They're like these pools of crystal blue that make a girl do all over body shivers. Maybe that's why I ignore the urge to kill him, and put my sunglasses back on, and poke the bear.

Who knows?

"I didn't realize you were *that* type of man," I say with a disappointed sigh.

"What type is that?"

"The type to let fear make his decisions for him," I say with a shrug, like I'm unaware I've hit him below the belt and exactly where I needed to, to get him to do what I want. No man likes to be looked at as weak. I might be young, but even I know that.

"I'm not afraid of you, Princess. Why would I be afraid of you?"

"I'm not sure, but it's okay. I'll go to lunch by myself," I tell him, giving him an understanding smile. "I'm so sorry to have bothered you. You have a good day—"

"Fine we'll go to lunch. But, we're going to the diner. We can *walk* there. I'm hoping you won't kill one of us just walking across the street."

"How many girlfriends have you had?"

"What? Why are you asking that?"

"I'm just assuming it must be a staggering number with the way you sweet talk a girl," I quip. He looks at me for a minute like he doesn't understand what I'm saying and then he frowns at me and does this little growl under his breath that for some reason makes my nipples hard.

I'm probably playing with fire, but if I'm honest, the reason I sought this man out today has nothing to do with my father and everything to do with me. In fact, I'm not even going to tell him who my dad is. I don't want it to change how he treats me. I want him to change how he treats me because....

Well I'm not going to think about that right now.

Chapter Seven

BLACK

This woman can get under my skin quicker than my damn brothers. I had no intention of fighting with her this morning, but it's like she opens her mouth and I can't help myself. I was an ass in there however, I know that. It's just lunch... *what could be the harm?*

Those are my thoughts when we first start walking across the street. After that, I'm watching her walk in front of me, her ass swaying in a tight skirt. She has a loose silk shirt on too and the hem of it rises as she moves her arm and flashes a small strip of skin between it and the back of her skirt. My gaze lifts from the sway of that bouncing ass, to that piece of flesh. I become obsessed with it. What does it feel like? What would it taste like if I run my tongue over it... *bite it?*

Or look with my name inked on it...

That makes me jerk my head up. *What in the hell is wrong with me?*

"Are you okay?"

"What?" I ask, not about to admit that I'm not okay. I'm not okay at all. That thought came out of left field. Did Linda not teach me anything? I need to stay away from crazy-ass women and this woman is *crazy*. She nearly ran me over with a lawnmower, went ballistic over nothing and probably has trophies made out of men's balls hidden in her bedroom.

"It's just.... Wait!" she yells, but it's too late.

I walk right into a damn light pole.

"Motherfucker," I groan, holding my nose. My head *had been* feeling better.

"Are you okay?" she asks again and I wonder how many times a damn woman can ask that, when it's clear I'm not.

"If you'd quit talking to me while I'm walking, I'd be great," I grumble, rubbing my damn nose wondering if it's going to swell now and Mom will want to put cow piss or something on it to match the manure she put on my forehead.

"Wow. You really are a grouch. I was just wanting to tell you to watch out for that light pole. I was afraid you were still suffering from blurry vision or something because you were walking straight for it..."

"Let's get this lunch over with," I mutter under my breath, putting my hand on her back and leading her to the diner. I open the door and guide us to the back, waving or saying hi to a few people as we go. Mason is a small place and everyone basically knows everyone.

"You're like a celebrity."

"What's your name?" I ask her, because it suddenly occurs to me that I have no idea what it is.

She leans up on the table and gives me a grin and I really shouldn't like how that smile makes her eyes light up and dance —*but I do.*

"I thought you decided it was Princess?" she says, grinning even more.

"If you're Princess, what does that make me?"

"Hmm... I may need to think on that," she responds as if giving it serious thought.

"Here are your menus. Can I take your drink order?"

"I'll have sweet tea please," Princess says and for some damn reason my eyes are glued to her lips as she speaks. It's probably just because I'm hungry. Like the commercial says, I'm not myself when I'm hungry.

"What about you, Black?" she asks. I've known her since we were kids and her Mama first built this place. Susie all but runs it now, but Wednesdays are usually slow days in town in general and she keeps her wait staff to minimum.

"Coffee is good, Susie."

"Do you guys want to order? Or do you need a few minutes?"

"What are you having?" Princess asks me.

"Same thing as I always have on Wednesdays—"

"Mom's famous enchiladas. That seems to be the consensus today," Susie laughs.

"Well then I guess that's what I'm having," Princess responds, closing her menu and handing it back. I do the same and it's after Susie leaves that she turns the smile back on me.

"Does everyone call you Black?" she asks, surprising me. It's a strange question, but I guess we haven't really introduced ourselves —especially since she's refusing to give me her name.

"Most everyone," I shrug. "Some call me asshole..."

"At least you admit it," she laughs.

"My name is Addie, although I kind of like you calling me Princess. I can always call you my loyal servant."

"*Annnnd*.... Addie it is."

"Spoilsport."

"Whatever," I laugh, she's a firecracker. I don't know if I've ever met a woman so quick to give me shit—unless it's my sisters or my mother. I shouldn't like it... *but I do*.

"What made you decide to go into law as a career?"

I think on the question. I'm not sure how to answer—at least to someone I barely know, so I turn it around on her.

"What made you decide to get in the landscaping business?" I ask instead.

She looks surprised for a second and then she gets a sweet blush on her cheeks that I wasn't expecting. Her eyes dart down as Susie brings our drinks and for a minute I think she's not going to answer. I watch as her fingertip moves over the rim of her glass. Slowly she looks back up at me and her eyes, which I've just figured out look almost gray come back to me. The way she looks right now is mesmerizing. Her gaze has an intensity that I can feel and she's beautiful. I vaguely noticed it the last time—I was too aggravated, but right now she literally takes my breath.

Damn. When is the last time that happened? Has it ever before? *I don't think it has.*

"I love what I do. I could spend hours creating and planning and never get tired. Before my mother got sick, we used to spend hours together... now it's like she's with me in some ways."

"I'm sorry about your mom. That's rough. You're young."

"Not that young," she shrugs.

"How young is not that young?" I ask, and now I'm genuinely curious. I was expecting this woman to stay on my ass the entire lunch and give me hell, but it turns out I'm actually having fun. When Addie isn't screaming and trying to terrorize a man, she's damn good company.

"I'm twenty-four," she says and I have to say I'm surprised. I knew she was young and I guess twenty-four isn't that young, I'm turning thirty-two this year, but I thought she'd be older. I mean she runs her own business. It's not like her age is anything to me. If I think on it, I don't know why it should upset me that she's so young.

Okay not so young... but she's still young.

"Well, actually I will be twenty-four in a couple of months," she adds.

Motherfucker.

"How about you?" she asks and she seems interested. I shift uneasily in my chair for some reason.

"I'm not twenty-three, I'll tell you that much," I grumble. Hell, I don't think I remember twenty-three.

"Oh come on. It's not that young. How old are you?"

"I'm thirty-one," I tell her, just wanting this conversation done for some reason.

"Oh my God! You're practically ancient."

"Very funny," I mutter, taking a drink of my coffee.

"It's very commendable that you're still working at your age. It must be hard on you."

"Having fun?"

"Surprisingly, I am," she says, shocking me. "Are you?"

"Well, you haven't tried to kill me yet and I've not been stung by a killer bee, so I'm hopeful," I crack and again she surprises me by laughing.

She's got a really nice laugh...

Damn.

Chapter Eight

ADDIE

I like him.

How does that even happen?

I'd been feeling guilty and I know he has to deal with my dad a lot, so I wanted to pave things over. Instead I find myself laughing and enjoying being with the big dummy. He's funny, and sweet and those two things even manage to make me forget that he's a tall drink of water, with bedroom eyes—at least every once in a while they make me forget.

I'm only human!

We've had lunch and we're still sitting in the diner talking. I know he needs to get back to work and I really need to go too. I need to check on some applications I submitted. I need a job and I'm really hoping to put my degree to use.

"My company boring you, Princess Addie?"

I jerk my gaze back to him. My breath catches in my chest as once again I'm blown away by those beautiful eyes of his.

They really should be illegal.

"I'm sorry?"

"You keep staring at your watch, darlin'. From my experience, that's never a good thing."

"Oh! I have an appointment in Redmont—*soonish*."

"New client?"

I stumble for a second. I should just tell him the truth, but we've been having such a good time, I don't want him to know who my dad is yet. My whole life people have been nice to me because Dad's money or because of who my family was. While Black might not be interested in my money, he might treat me differently if he knew that my dad is essentially in control of his money requests and other things. Dad controls everything when it comes to the budget of the police station. Somehow, I think knowing my dad is the mayor would make Black stay away from me and I don't want that.

"I'm hoping it will be. I'm trying not to be nervous, but I hate these interviews."

"Do you usually have to interview to get hired to take care of lawns?"

"You have to interview for everything these days," I tell him, feeling horrible for not just confessing everything. Someday soon this will all blow up in my face.

I really don't want to think about that right now.

"Fair enough, but I mean what are you going to do? Hop on a lawnmower and show them how you mow?"

"You really have a hang up about women landscapers don't you?"

"No—"

"Yeah right," I mumble, looking around the table for the bill.

"Seriously, I don't," he says grabbing my hand when I would reach for the bill.

"You—"

"I just wanted to know if I should call 9-1-1. You know, just to get an ambulance on standby," he says with a smirk.

"You really are an asshole, Black."

"Words hurt, Addie," he replies and I giggle. I never giggle, but here I am—sounding like a school girl.

"Hey! What are you doing?" I ask when he grabs my phone off

the table. My heart starts beating faster. If he looks at my contacts and sees my dad's number, will he recognize it? He will if he sees my pictures. I'm in the middle of a mini-panic when he asks me for my code.

"Why?" I ask, almost whining.

"I'm going to key in my number so you can call me and let me know if you got the job."

"Why would you care?" I ask him, studying his face.

"You're full of questions, but I've yet to get your number..." he hedges and he may be mostly looking at my phone, but I get the feeling he's studying me.

It's a gamble, but I find myself telling him my code to unlock my phone.

"Thank you," he says with a smile. Men with eyes that deep shouldn't smile—especially when they have dimples and laugh lines that make a woman's insides tingle.

"De nada."

His left eyebrow quirks up and somehow that makes him even sexier.

"You speak Spanish?"

"I'm fluent with several words," I brag.

"Words?"

"I can count to three. I know the meaning of de nada and I can say one or two very explicit curse words."

"Where did you learn those?"

A picture of our maid Rosa comes to mind. She left the states not long after my mother died. I miss her too, but we keep in touch through emails. I don't really want to explain that to Black though, so I shrug.

"That's a story for another day."

"I'll hold you to that Princess. There, now you have my number. So you can call me to let me know if you got the job, or..."

"Or?"

"Or if I need to come bail you out of jail because you ran over the homeowner," he says standing up. He instantly helps me up and puts his hand at my back. He's tall, a good five inches taller than me, and he's broad. I feel tiny beside him and it's a feeling I find that I like. I can't stop myself from looking up at him.

"You'd pay my bail? It almost sounds like you like me, Black."

"I'm a cop it's my job to protect and to serve."

"To serve... me?" I ask with a smirk. "Sounds kinky."

"To protect innocent bystanders from you," he says with a wink and I roll my eyes—but I do it with a smile.

Really, I smile the whole time Black pays our bill, refusing to let me help. I smile as he walks me outside to my car and I smile as he opens my car door for me. And I *really* smile as I head out of town, looking in my rearview mirror to see Black's ass in those tight uniform khakis he's wearing. I slow down to watch as he walks toward the sheriff's office.

Any girl would really... I just happen to be the lucky one.

Chapter Nine

BLACK

"I thought you forgot about me, Princess Addie."

"Does that happen often?" Addie laughs. Even over the phone her laughter rings out and seems to grab me. It's the strangest thing. I wanted to strangle her yesterday. I sure didn't see myself enjoying her company. One lunch with her and everything turned around. I found myself disappointed when she didn't call me about her interview. I hold the phone out from my ear and check the time. It's almost eleven. I knew it was getting late, but I'm glad she called just the same.

Of course hearing her voice while I'm naked in bed might not be a good thing. I reach down and adjust my cock which is waking up with just the sound of her laughter. I guess it could also be a good thing... *better if she were in bed with me...*

"Does what happen?" I ask, bringing my mind back to our conversation and not my cock which is now starting to more than wake up—it's practically standing at attention.

"Your crisis in confidence."

"Afraid I'm not following, Princess."

"I'd wager to guess that not many women ever forget you, Black."

"There's been one or two I wish would. Does that count?" I ask her, my mind instantly shifting to my crazy ex, Linda Jones.

...annnnd just like that my cock deflates.

The bitch is still messing with my life almost a year later.

"Totally counts," Addie whispers, and I try to concentrate on her voice. It's warm and sleepy and she sounds so sweet—deceptively so, since she's given me hell like no other woman I've met—including my mother.

"How did today go?" I ask, when she doesn't say anything more.

"Good, I think. There are several others being interviewed so I can't be positive, but they told me I made their short list and would be in contact with me no later than next week."

"Damn. The world of landscaping must be pretty demanding. I had no idea."

"You'd be surprised."

"I guess so, but then I'm just a poor country boy. I usually mow my own grass. Except when I lived in Dallas, my HOA fees paid for lawn care."

"You lived in Dallas?"

"Yeah for a while. I've only been back in Mason for a little while."

"And already in the position you're in. That's pretty impressive, Black."

"If you think that's impressive, you should see my—"

"I think it'd be best if you didn't finish that sentence," she laughs. I close my eyes and it's easy to imagine her smile and those gray eyes of hers twinkling, her blonde hair draped over a pillow. It's entirely too easy to imagine that hair lying over my dick....

"What are you wearing right now?" I ask her, grinning.

"You so did not just ask me that," she laughs.

"But, I did."

"What do you want me to be wearing?" she says and she giggles.

Damn I really like it when she giggles.

My first answer is, "me". That answer is probably not what I should say since we barely know each other. Besides, I don't know her well enough yet. She could turn into another Linda and I'm not sure I can survive another crazy ex-girlfriend.

"I'm thinking those overalls. You know, the beige ones like Jason wears in all of those millions of movies he kills people in."

"You want me to be wearing blood stained overalls..."

"Well not bloodstained. There's a lot to be said for cleanliness."

"You're a freak, you know that?"

"That's my brother, Blue."

"You have a brother named Blue?"

"Yep, we're twins. Although the older we get the easier it is to tell us apart. Plus, his hair... the boy has no style."

"You have a *twin* brother?"

"Yeah. Though just between you and me, I'm much bigger in size."

"You're not talking about height are you?"

"I'll leave that to your imagination, darlin'," I joke.

"I don't know if I should be more scared that there are two of you in the world, or that I'm enjoying our conversations so much."

"Make no mistake, Princess Addie, there's only one of me."

"So I assume you two fight a lot and that's why they call you Black and Blue?"

"Fight with Blue? Nah, he's too quiet to fight with."

"Talking with you makes my head hurt," she whispers.

"You should talk to my Mom sometime," I laugh.

"I better get to sleep," she murmurs while yawning.

I want to tell her no, because I really am enjoying talking to her. I can't remember the last time that I just talked to a girl on the phone and it made me happy. That's a clear sign that Addie might mean trouble for me, but I'm not sure I care. It's been a really long time since a woman has appealed to me this much.

"Sweet dreams, Princess Addie."

"Sweet dreams, Black."

She hangs up the phone and I'm left holding mine wishing she was still on the other side.

She's definitely going to be trouble.

Chapter Ten

ADDIE

"Run over anyone today?"

I read Black's text and giggle out loud. I haven't seen him or talked to him in two days—not because I didn't want to, but I just haven't. Dad came back and I've been spending time with him.

"What's so funny, Princess?" Dad asks and I look up from my phone.

"Just a text from a friend," I answer, with a sly grin, because it's more than that, but I don't want to talk to Dad about it yet.

"Not yet, but the day is still young." I reply to Black.

"Are your friends missing you already?" Dad asks.

It would probably surprise him to know that I don't really have friends. I was so busy trying to learn and hone my craft that I had no friendships out of class. I was so tired after working that I never tried to contact the few friends I had at school anyway.

"Something like that. What are we doing today?"

"You're going to hate me, Princess..."

"Dad," I sigh, already knowing what's coming.

"It's an emergency committee dinner."

"What is an emergency committee dinner? Everyone got hungry at the same time and have to go grab Big Macs together because they're starved?" I grumble sarcastically. I shouldn't be upset, I know, but I was looking forward to spending time with him. He wasn't around a lot as a bank president, but this is kind of ridiculous. I mean, we haven't seen each other since Christmas. Maybe I'm being a giant kid, but it still hurts that he keeps shoving business in front of me.

"It's a working dinner. We're in a huge gridlock over the expenses on the proposed water plant for Mason. I need to sway the council to vote to approve the additional cost."

"And that can't wait one night so we could actually have dinner together?" I ask. Somewhere in the back of my mind, I feel like I've heard my mom ask that same question a hundred times before. Does Dad even realize that?

"How about I go to the dinner and get this done and tomorrow I leave work early and we go bowling?"

"Bowling?" I ask, and if I sound like he's grown two heads right in front of me, there's a reason. I haven't been bowling since I was seven. My parents took me to an all-night bowling alley and it was all done up with black lights and the pins and balls would glow in florescent pinks, blues, yellows and greens. It was fun... *when I was seven.* Still, he's making an effort and it seems like the only way I'm going to get to spend time with him.

"What do you say, Princess? It will be like old times," he says and I look up at him.

I love this man. He wasn't around a lot. He was and *is* definitely a workaholic, but he taught me to ride my first bike. He used to build forts made of sheets and pillows in my room and he'd read to me at night when I was sick and couldn't sleep. He's a good man and most of all, he's really the only family I have left since my mom passed. I want us to be closer. I ran away to France. It was good for my chosen career, but that wasn't why I left. I need to try and repair our relationship. It's what mom would want and it's really what I want too.

"Okay, Dad. Bowling it is," I answer giving in.

"That's my girl," he says ruffling my hair and getting up. He leans down and kisses the top of my head and takes off to his room —I guess to get ready for his meeting... Big Mac dinner... *whatever.*

I sit there for a few minutes wondering what I can do for dinner now. I don't really want to cook. Normally cooking relaxes me and I could spend hours in the kitchen, but when you're only cooking for yourself the appeal just isn't there.

My phone vibrates in my pocket and I take it back out— already smiling. I don't know what it is about Black, but he makes me happy. He's sexy, but he can also be funny and goofy and he makes me laugh easily. I don't laugh a lot, I haven't in a long time, not since mom got sick really...

"How'd you like to go out with this cop I know?"

I read his text and I'm not imagining the way my heart seems to kick inside my chest.

"Are you fixing me up?" I text back.

I expect him to text back, but within a minute my phone is ringing.

"Hi," I say softly into the phone, feeling warm all over.

"Hey, beautiful," he says back and that could sound cheesy coming from anyone else but him.

"You're so smooth," I answer—grinning.

"All over, baby. Now, about dinner."

"Are you really trying to fix me up?" I ask, wanting him to admit the dinner is with him—or at least I hope it is. If not, I'm obviously a fool and should give up on ever trying to read signals from men again.

"Something like that, but you'll like this guy. He's really hot. At least that's what all the girls say."

"Does he have big feet?"

"Feet? Uh... do you have a foot fetish, Princess Addie?"

"No, but these are things a girl likes to know. You know what they say about big feet. It means everything else is big too."

"Everything else? Damn. In that case, he has big feet. Huge, really. His shoes have to be special made and shipped to him from the Netherlands."

"The Netherlands?"

"Everyone knows, Princess, that the Netherlands are home to the tallest men in the world. They're like a land of giants and their feet are so big they can only make their shoes out of wood—nothing else will fit."

"Oh, I do remember something about wooden shoes."

"And now you know the rest of the story," Black says and I can hear his laughter in his voice and for some reason that makes me happy.

"Does he have all of his teeth?"

"His teeth?" he asks, and I stifle a giggle because I'm enjoying playing with him.

"Oral hygiene is very important in prospective dates."

"No worries there. He takes anything oral very serious."

"What about his hair?" I ask, trying not to dwell on thoughts of Black being serious about oral. I don't really succeed. I can feel my body react and I have to squirm a little on the couch while I try to control my thoughts.

"His hair? No worries there. He makes sure his hair is clean and soft enough you can run your fingers through it constantly."

"Damn it. I'm sorry, but this just won't work with your friend."

"What? Why not?"

"I only like men without hair."

"You don't like men with hair?" he asks, and he sounds like he's trying to gauge if I'm serious or not.

"Nope I like their heads to be smooth as a baby's bottom."

"So you only like bald men?"

"Yep. Something so smooth I can run my tongue over."

"Well, that does sound... interesting, but I'm afraid he likes his hair."

"Damn it. I really think this might be a deal breaker."

"I bet you're loads of fun for the guys in the old folk's home," he grumbles and I have to hold my head away from the phone as a laugh pops out that I can't hold in. "What if he *agrees* to think about shaving his hair off if the date works out?"

"I guess I could agree to that concession." I sigh out, sounding as if I'm in mourning.

"Then it's a date?"

"I suppose. What time and where?"

"My friend would prefer to come pick you up. He's old school, really likes to treat a girl right."

I almost agree, but then remember he doesn't know who I am. It'd be hard to explain that he could pick me up at the Mayor's house, because then I'd have to explain the mayor is my dad...

"I need to run out anyway," I lie. "Besides first dates can always end badly. I can just meet him..."

"You do realize that I'm the—"

"Just this once?" I plead, interrupting him. I'll tell him the truth over dinner—*if I can just get up the nerve...*

"Okay," he gives in, but he doesn't sound happy. "How about we meet at the Marina? There's a restaurant there overlooking the water."

"We?" I prompt with a grin.

"I mean of course your date and you," he backtracks.

"Sounds good. Can't wait to see you again, Black—I mean I can't wait to see my date."

"He can't wait to see if you like him enough to give him your address," he mutters.

"Bye, Black," I whisper, again chickening out before I confess who I really am.

"Bye, Addie," he says and then in a moment I hear the click of his phone. I hold my phone in my hand for a few minutes afterward—worrying.

Will he really be upset when he finds out who my father is? Should I be this worried? Is Black really the type to pull away from a woman if he finds out he kind of—but not really—works for her father?

The problem with being too chicken to confess your secrets is you're left with a bunch of questions... and not one answer.

Chapter Eleven

BLACK

I haven't been nervous about a date in... *Shit.* I've never been nervous about a date. I'm not sure what I'd call the feeling I'm having right now. Anxious might be a better word for it. I'm definitely anxious to see Addie again. So anxious that I showed up thirty minutes early.

I'm standing by my truck—like a chump. If Blue could see me now, he'd be howling in laughter. Then again, I don't think Blue dates. My family thinks he's afraid of women, nothing could be further from the truth. That's his life however. He can make his own choices. I keep hoping that someday he'll meet a woman that will make him break those harsh rules he imposes on his life. I'm beginning to wonder if he ever will.

I didn't dress up. Suddenly, I'm wondering if that will bother Addie. She doesn't seem like that kind of girl. She works hard for a living too, she's not like a spoiled rich girl—not like Linda—so I don't think she will.

Damn it, I need to snap out of this. I've been on dates, I'm in my thirties not sixteen.

I'm wearing jeans and a buttoned shirt, that's freshly pressed—thanks to my mother. I don't do laundry. When I lived in Dallas, I kept the cleaners in business, and Linda did what little laundry I had. With hindsight, that probably wasn't my wisest decision. She somehow moved in—I still think I had to be drunk when I agreed to that—and it just kind of naturally happened. I should have stuck with a housecleaner.

I have horrible taste when it comes to women. I really do. My normally good judgment when it comes to people flies out the window when I'm dealing with a woman I like. It's like the moment my dick gets involved that sixth sense I have when solving crimes runs away. Addie's probably as insane as Linda was... or she's looking for a husband. I'm definitely not husband material. I mean, I'd like to be. It seems to have worked out great for Gray and White. But my brothers just got lucky with CC and Kayla. Women like them are few and far between.

I jerk out of my thoughts when I hear a horn blow. I look up to see Addie waving from the driver's side of a hot as fuck, brand new, crimson red metallic Mustang. It has a fade in it too, like there are different shades of the same color fading in and out of each other. Christ, it's gorgeous. The type of car that would make a man's balls ache to own. It's not practical here in Texas and definitely not affordable on a cop's salary who needs to find a house and put money in his IRA.

Apparently landscaping pays damn good.

I watch as she pulls into a parking spot beside my truck and just like that my nerves are gone. She gets out of the car wearing a long dress that stops around her ankles. It's a soft yellow color that shows off her golden skin. It doesn't have sleeves and I find myself wanting to run my tongue along those thin straps. Maybe bite into that skin, marking her...

She looks beautiful, a hot dream in the flesh, but the dress doesn't look expensive either. It does look soft—though not as soft as her skin. She's probably the best looking woman I've ever seen in that simple dress and it's as far from the dresses that Linda used to wear, that easily cost over eight hundred dollars, that I can imagine. I can picture Addie walking at the farm in her dress. I begin to relax. This was a good decision; Addie is *not* my past.

She gets out of the car, closing the door and meets me as I'm walking to her. She's wearing a huge smile and the smile spreads to her eyes, which seems to light them up. Her blonde hair has been pulled up high on her head and gathered with a clip, leaving a long flowing stream of hair going down her back.

She really is the most beautiful woman I've ever seen in my life, and she looks like she's not even trying. I make a note to take her out dancing one night.

How would she look in a dress with a slit up the side I could slide my hand into...?

"Hi," she says so soft and sweet that I can't help but lean down and kiss her gently on the lips.

"You look beautiful, Addie."

Her lips taste like berries... strawberries maybe and when I pull away, I instantly want to go back and take longer, deepen the kiss and drink from those beautiful glossy lips. Unfortunately, I don't do any of that.

"Where's my date?" she asks, mischief in her eyes.

"I arrested him."

"You what? I thought he was a cop?"

"He showed up for your date drunk. I had to haul him in."

"You can arrest people for just drinking? Was he driving too?"

"No, but he was being a public nuisance, I had to arrest him, it was out of my control."

"What was he doing?" she asks, and she's not even bothering to hide her laughter.

"He was swerving back and forth," I mumble, concentrating more on the beautiful color of her eyes and how they seem to sparkle right now.

"But, you just said he wasn't driving," she responds and I can't stop myself from pulling her closer to me, and letting my hands brush along the side of her face.

"He wasn't, he was walking."

"And that was being a public nuisance?"

"Well he has large feet and was naked, so that means his *appendages* are very large too."

"I don't think I understand..."

"He had things swinging left and right," I tell her, wondering if using the word dick is a hard no on a first date. Then, I wonder why in the hell I'm worrying about these things with Addie when I never did before.

I see the moment she understands, her eyes go round and she giggles again.

Damn it! That giggle may be the death of me.

"Oh... I see. And that was making the women stop and stare and causing issues?"

"What? No. They were running in terror."

"Terror?" she asks and she snorts in laughter this time and I smile so big I think my jaw might break. I *really* do like this woman.

"It was frightening. I'm just saying, Addie, I mean I know this stuff is out of my area of expertise," I tell her, and I put my hand at her back and start walking her toward the restaurant. I try to pay attention to the conversation, but I can't help but catch the scent of her hair. It's soft and sweet just like I imagine Addie is all over. This is going to be a long date if I'm going to be hard all night long.

"But?" she asks and it takes me a minute to realize I had lost track of the conversation and didn't finish my sentence. I was too damn busy imagining what her skin tastes like all over her body, especially the soft, sensitive area around her navel and further down... "Black?" she asks, prompting me again. I manage to close my mouth because it has somehow dropped open allowing my tongue to lick my lips, while imagining licking her...

"There's such a thing as *too big*." I finally manage to get the words out without looking too much like a fool.

"There is?"

"Definitely. And too big can be *very* bad."

"Bad how?"

"Well your date was breaking windows…"

"Windows?"

"Windows on the second floor," I say in all seriousness—at least all I can manage.

"The *second* floor?"

"Exactly. There's a lot to be said about settling for medium size instead of large, Addie," I tell her as we make our way to the hostess to get a seat.

"Is this your way of confessing something, Black?"

"I guess you'll just have to investigate and see," I dare her.

She looks at me then. I don't know what she's thinking, but from the look on her face…

I think I like it.

Chapter Twelve

ADDIE

"I had a really good time tonight," I whisper as we're standing by my car.

He's holding my hand and his thumb keeps brushing back and forth over my knuckles. It feels good, sweet and completely distracting. If that wasn't enough, those bright blue eyes are hypnotizing me.

"I did too, Princess Addie."

His nickname for me makes me smile, but the heated look in his eyes makes me blush. It's heated, intense and it gives me tingles —*all over.*

"I should go..." I whisper, before I can jump up and wrap my legs around him.

"I could come with you," he suggests, wrapping a strand of my hair around his finger.

I swallow, my heartbeat so erratic that I'm sure he can feel it slamming against my chest if he tried. The insides of my thighs are wet, painted with my desire for this man and I *so* want him to come home with me. I don't think I've ever wanted anything more. It's on the tip of my tongue to tell him yes and then I remember...

He doesn't know who I am.

I could confess, but Dad's back in town. I don't think he'd like me bringing a man home and sleeping with him...

"That's probably not a good idea right now," I hedge, hating the words even as I'm saying them.

"I bet I could convince you it's a very *good* idea," he murmurs.

He tilts my head up and his eyes feel like they pierce my soul. I'll never get used to the deep, shiny blue color, or how they glitter with heat at times. Then, inch by inch—almost as if it is in slow motion—his lips come down softly against mine. I sigh into his mouth. I've wanted his kiss all night. I've longed for it with every laugh, every smile, every sweet comment he's made. My gaze has been drawn to his mouth... *wishing.*

For a second neither of us move. It's as if the simple press of our lips is enough, and then his tongue slides inside. Instantly, my knees go weak. I'm surrounded by the masculine smell of his aftershave and sex... *God.* I don't know how it's possible but with just the touch of his tongue along mine I smell sex everywhere. The good kind. The kind that leaves your bodies a sweaty mess, your limbs weak and your heart pounding even an hour later.

The kind I've never had, but have read about and dreamed of forever.

Our tongues begin dancing, sliding against each other to the tune of my heartbeat and then it changes. Black groans and I whimper in response, because he definitely becomes the aggressor now. It's as if he's declared war and my mouth is the prize he's intent on claiming. He's relentless, owning me, marking me, ruining me for any other man. I instinctively know that—maybe I always have. Black isn't a man you can forget. He's a man that will wreck you, one that will haunt you forever. He's the kind you know you should stay away from, but you just can't.

My fingernails dig into his body as I hold on for his kiss, my knees so weak that it is a miracle I remain standing. When we break apart, I can only lay my forehead against his chest and let my heart calm down. It's no longer beating—it's thundering, my breath coming out in gasps.

"Damn it, Addie," he growls, his voice hoarse and dripping with hunger. "I knew kissing you would be special. I just didn't know it would bring me to my knees."

"Black—" I stumble over saying his name, because that's exactly how I feel. I don't get the chance to tell him that, because he's tilting my head back up to look at him and I'm lost in his eyes again. A shiver runs through my body as if it has been charged with electricity. Staring back at me is a hunger so deep and intense that I should be scared...

He pulls me up close, inserting one of his legs in between mine, bunching my dress up to my thighs. His leg slides against my center and my breath stalls in my chest. I'm so wet. *Can he feel that through his jeans?* I tremble, but at the same time I can't stop myself from tightening my thighs on his leg, rocking on him. The hard fabric of his jeans rakes against my thin panties and I can't stop the moan of need that spills from my lips.

"I'd get on my knees for you, Addie. Get on my knees and beg you to give me more," he growls. His fingers bite into my thighs as he moves my body back and forth on his leg. I whimper, knowing I should call a halt to this, but it feels so good. My head goes back as I feel his teeth bite into my neck, gently but with a sting of pain that makes my hips thrust forward. He pushes his leg even harder into my pussy and I swear I can feel the fabric slide against my clit.

"Black," I moan, quickly losing control. One of his hands comes up and holds my breast, squeezing it almost in time with the way he moves me against his leg. He licks my neck until I feel his hot breath at my ear. His tongue darts out and he sucks the lobe into his mouth. It releases with a wet popping noise and my eyes close as I envision that same noise happening as his fingers slide in and out of me.

"I'd get on my knees and slide my head between your legs," he declares wickedly, teasing me as he whispers in my ear. His hand continues to knead my breast. "I'll make you feel good, Addie. If you let me," he whispers. As he's talking, his tongue slides into the shell of my ear. It darts around, and I bite my lip at the sensation his actions and words are combining to make inside of me. "I'll slide it along the inside of your thighs, tasting your skin and then further up," he adds as he rolls my nipple between his fingers.

"Oh God," I whimper, all the sensations becoming too much.

I'm riding his leg now. There's no other way to say it. I'm riding it hard and he has me wishing it was his face. I can feel it building inside of me. It wouldn't take much and I'd come for him... maybe harder than I've ever come in my life.

"I'll pull the lips of that pretty little pussy you're hiding apart and push my tongue inside of you. Would you like that, Addie?" he asks, his hands biting into my breast harder, his thumb pushing against my nipple which is so hard it's painful.

"I would," I answer. There's no point in lying. He knows the truth and I don't want to pretend with him. Besides, I'm about one minute away from shattering into a million pieces—just by riding his leg.

"Let me come home with you, Addie. Let me make you feel good. Let me eat out that pretty little pussy and make you beg for more."

Jesus. Never has a guy spoken to me like this before. I wouldn't have dreamed any of them talked like this in real life. Maybe I've just been too damn sheltered. All I know, is that I like it. I like it and I definitely want more of it.

"I'll go home with you," I tell him, deciding that I'll worry about confessing to Black tomorrow. His body goes stiff, for a second. He pulls away slightly and I want to scream no. I was right there! I just need a few more seconds and...

"Let's make it your place," he says.

"I have a roommate and they've kind of claimed the place tonight," I tell him. It's not really a lie....

"Shit. I have the same problem," he growls rubbing the back of his neck as he steps away from me.

Disappointment fills me. My pussy is throbbing, my breasts are sore and I just want to cry. I try to calm my traitorous body, but it takes everything in me not to scream for him to finish what he started. I have a small warning bell going off in my head. I ignore it

—probably because I need laid at this point—*plain and simple.* Still, he seems awfully old to still be living with roommates. I just imagined he had a home of his own.

"Then I guess tonight is off," I sigh, hoping he tells me I'm wrong. *Praying he finishes this tidal wave of need he's set off inside of me.*

"Well, we could get a hotel room, but..."

It's on the tip of my tongue to say yes, but then I think of my father and his position. Just because Black doesn't know who I am, it doesn't mean other people don't. The last thing I need is for the gossip mill to start talking about the Mayor's daughter being a slut. In his position, I'm sure he doesn't need that kind of gossip either.

"I've not been in Mason long, but even I know how things spread through small towns. That wouldn't do either one of us any good," I tell him.

"So I guess we have to say goodbye here," he grumbles and hearing how unhappy he is at least makes me feel a little better— not much. I'm going to have to dig out my vibrator when I get home. I hadn't unpacked it yet, but I'm definitely going to need it tonight.

"I guess so," I agree, sounding as miserable as he does, but I can't help it.

"I have to go out of town tomorrow to Dallas, but I'll be back the next night. How about I call you tomorrow and if you can't ditch your roommate we'll plan a night out in Carson?"

It seems weird he'd be willing to go all the way to Carson. Why go all the way to Carson? Can't he get his roommate to leave for the night? Is he just looking to get laid?

Do I care about any of it at this point?

That might be the most important question, because I want Black enough right now to bargain with the devil if it meant having him.

"Sounds good," I murmur, letting my questions and concerns fade away when Black kisses me again.

Chapter Thirteen

BLACK

"What's got you all bent out of shape?" Blue asks and I look up from the table to watch my brother. He's changed a little over the last few months. There's something going on with him and I feel guilty that I haven't taken the time to ask him. Still, I know there's something. Being twins we have this sixth sense about each other. But life has been such shit that I haven't taken the time to talk to him in months—at least not about anything substantial.

"Woman trouble," I respond, pushing my cereal bowl away. Food is the last thing on my mind.

"That crazy chick back at it?" he asks, concern on his face as he sits down across from me.

"No... at least I don't think so. It's been quiet since she succeeded in getting me fired."

"That was some shady shit there. I still say you should have fought it," Blue says taking a drink of water from the bottle he just got out of the fridge. He's got a water and a banana. That's his breakfast every morning. If I did that, I'd be eating everything that wasn't nailed down an hour later. Blue is regimented in everything he does. I've always been the complete opposite. I never regretted it until Linda. Maybe if I had been more like my brother I never would have gotten into the mess I did.

"There was no fighting it. She was sleeping with my Captain. Hell, even if I had gone to IAB or filed something against him, they would have still found a way to make my life miserable. You don't turn on one of your own, it's more than just an unspoken code," I grumble.

"I don't see it that way. Fuck, every single one of those assholes turned their backs on you."

"It's fine. It worked out fine. I just have to go back today to pick up Kong and then it will finally be done."

"Yeah, well, I think that situation is shitty too. I mean you had that dog before she was in the picture. How she can keep it away from you for over a year—"

"She claimed Kong was hers, at least the judge ruled in my favor," I grumble. I really don't like discussing this stuff. The mention of Linda tends to make my skin feel as if it's crawling.

"She's had you in limbo for two years and you had to get a court order to settle it. That shit is whacked."

"Whoa, this hell hasn't been two years, let's not go crazy," I argue, not wanting to feel like I've wasted that much of my time on this woman. It has been over a year, almost a year and a half, and that sucks more than I could even express. I don't need him adding time to it—I already feel stupid as hell for dealing with her. If not for Kong, I wouldn't fool with her at all anymore.

"Close enough," Blue grumbles, and the way he's going on you would think Linda ruined *his* life, not mine.

"Today is it. I'll go to Dallas, get Kong, along with what little of my stuff is still there, and it will be over. The court ordered Linda to be gone, so I won't even have to deal with her. A neighbor will be there as a witness. I get it and go. *That's it.*"

"You really think it will be that easy with Linda involved? We are talking about the same woman who took a baseball bat to a girl's car because she thought you were cheating—and all because you changed the woman's flat when her and her infant son were stranded beside the road," Blue grumbles still not happy about the whole situation. He knew the girl from high school and I get the feeling he was sweet on her. Not sure what happened between them, but he won't even discuss her now.

"It's been long enough. I'm sure she has another pigeon in her sites by now. Whatever happened to that girl? Shoot what was her name again... Patty? No, that's not it... hmm..."

"Meadow," Blue responds, avoiding my eyes. It's not like I don't know her name. I do. I also know that Meadow is moving back to Mason and is divorced now. I've not told Blue that yet.

"Oh yeah, Meadow. Mom would love that name."

"What name is that?" Mom enters right on cue. It's like the woman has a sixth sense or something.

"Meadow," I answer and I swear for a minute there, I can see panic in Blue's eyes.

Interesting... Very interesting.

"I do love that name! Leddie named her daughter that, bless her soul. I hate that she's so sick," Mom says, having no idea what can of worms she has opened—or hell maybe she does—this is Mom I'm talking about.

"Leddie's sick?" Blue asks, and maybe he's trying to act like he doesn't care, but I hear something in his voice and I'm sure my mom does too.

"Doctors say it's only a matter of time. She had a heart attack and it done way too much damage."

"Damn," I mumble. I hate to hear that. "Leddie is a good person, she'd give you the shirt off her back if you needed it."

"She is," Mom responds. "Hard to understand why things happen the way they do. Not that I want to question the good Lord, but I sure don't always agree with his choices," she mutters. "Anyway are we ready to roll?"

"Ready to... *What?*" I ask, fear hitting me all at once when I see the intent written all over her face.

"To head to Dallas. I'm going with you!"

"Mom, that's not necessary—"

"Nonsense. If you think I'm going to leave my son at the mercy of that she-cat."

"She-cat?" Blue asks and I pinch the bridge of my nose and hold my head down. It was already going to be a long day; I have a feeling it's about to get a lot longer.

"She-cat."

"What does that even mean, Mom?" Blue asks and I covertly flip him off, because he's just helping to get her pissed off—*and he knows it.*

"An alley cat always in heat, always wanting petted and always —*but always*—packing in fleas."

I'd like to deny her assessment, but I can't really. So, I wisely remain silent. Mom, however, is not done.

"I swear I know the good Lord gave my son's brains. They were smart until they moved out on their own and now it's like every dang one of you have mush in your head. Thank the good Lord above that CC and Kayla came along to yank Gray and White's heads out of their asses. Who knows what would have happened to Orange if Petal hadn't saved him. Poor boy might have ended up just like his daddy and that would have been a damn shame."

I shake my head at the mention of Orange—the honorary name that Mom gave Luka when he and Petal remarried. My mom is one hell of a woman, but she is definitely *special* at times.

"Fine, let's go. But try to contain yourself if you can," I mumble, suddenly anxious to get on the road and get back home.

"Why do my kids always tell me that? It would serve everyone right if I just started saying exactly what's on my mind whenever I felt like it," she complains—but, she does it walking toward the front door so I call it a win.

"You're right, Mom. I'm sorry," I tell her, thinking that's exactly what she does anyway. I'm not about to argue with her though. I try and pacify her instead, trying to make my trip easier.

"Good to hear you admit it, son. Now, while we're traveling you can tell me all about this girl you went out with last night. Blue tells me she's a good girl. Are you sure she's prepared for you?

You're not known for being sweet," Mom rattles and I hear Blue laughing in the background.

I look him dead in the eye and then I do something that I don't regret one bit.

"Hey Mom? Did I ever tell you about the time Blue and I stopped to help Meadow when her car broke down?"

"*Motherfucker*," I hear Blue mutter behind me and as I close the door it's *me* who is laughing this time.

Paybacks are a bitch brother. Paybacks are a bitch.

Chapter Fourteen

ADDIE

"And that is how you roll a gutter ball," I giggle as Dad turns around looking dejected.

"I swear this was easier when you were younger," he mutters and that makes me giggle again.

"Don't look now, Dad, but I'm whippin' your butt!" I brag and I really am—and I don't even like bowling.

"I love hearing you laugh, Princess."

"I'm having a good time, Dad. I'm glad we did this."

"Me too. How about we take a break from bowling and go get a dipped cone at the concession?"

"They have dipped cones?" I ask and I know my ass will hate me tomorrow, but I just don't care.

"They even have the cherry topping instead of the chocolate," he says, knowing just how to tempt me.

"What are we waiting for then?" I ask grinning. Dad stands up and pulls me until I'm standing too and then we walk toward the concession/restaurant area. It's actually in another room. For a small town this is a huge complex which has movies, bowling, roller skating and the restaurant all housed in it. It's always crowded too—probably because Mason is small and doesn't have a lot to choose from.

We order our cones and I can't help but look at my silent phone. I haven't heard from Black all day. I mean, after last night I thought he would at least text through the day. It's been radio silence, so to speak. I thought about texting him, but I feel weird. I mean I basically agreed to go home with him last night after one date.

Does that make me a whore?

I didn't think so, but then I also thought I'd hear from him today. Did he give up because I didn't go to a hotel with him? Has he already moved on? Shit, I'm going crazy. I'm not this person. I'm not someone who obsesses over a man and is unsure of herself—at least I never have been. Then again, I've never reacted to a man the way I do with Black.

"Oh there's Petal."

"Petal?"

"She's Luka's wife. You'll like her. She works at the local hair salon in town."

"Luka?" I ask, my heart skipping in my chest. It feels like cold water has been dashed over all of my nerve endings.

"The sheriff. Remember you told me about him on the phone the other night? How he brought some papers over?"

I hear dad, but I feel like I'm about to throw up.

Oh I know who he's talking about...

"Petal! I'd like to introduce you to my daughter," Dad calls out motioning the woman over to us.

"Hey, Mayor Harrington. It's great to see you again," the woman says and her voice is sweet—sickeningly so. It irritates the hell out of me that she sounds like someone I would like.

Damn it.

She's shorter than me, though not by a lot and she's curvy, totally feminine and the type of woman that I could see Black with. She's got golden honey hair that's pulled up high on her head and there's a cute little boy that looks like her standing beside her and she's holding a little girl... a little girl that kind of reminds me of Black.

Son of a bitch.

"You too. I wanted to introduce you to my daughter, Adelle. She's just moved here after studying abroad."

"Hi, Adelle. That sounds like such fun!" Petal says and I know I should say something here, but I can't for the life of me, so instead I give her a tight smile. At least I tried to smile, I'm not sure I truly did.

"How's Luka doing? I haven't got to check in with him since I've been back in town."

"He took today off because we haven't got a lot of time together lately."

"I told him he needed to take a vacation. He's got men to step in. It's not like Mason is the crime capital of Texas, thank God," Dad says.

"He's planning on it soon. Today though he mowed the grass and got a migraine. I figured he'd better be alone. So, the kids and I decided to meet up with CC. She has William and Violet alone tonight while Gray's traveling for business."

"Sounds like a fun evening," I whisper, just to try and appear normal. I shouldn't have bothered. I don't feel normal and I'm sure I don't act normal. All I can do is look at Petal and wonder if Black thinks it is okay to label his *wife and kids* as roommates!

"You would think that wouldn't you? But nothing is ever just simple with children," she laughs, apparently not catching onto the fact I feel sick to my stomach, I want to scream, cry, scratch her eyes out and then cut off Black's balls. I'm not even sure in what order I want to do all of it. Everything is coming at me too quick and all at once.

"Mommy! I got to piss!"

"River, I've told you a hundred times not to say that word."

"It's what Daddy says!"

"God, save me. I better get. Mayor it was great seeing you again. Adelle, you too," Petal says with a strained smile on her lips.

The little girl in her arms seems to be snuggled in and has fallen asleep. She's a beautiful child and for some reason my heart hurts.

"I'm glad to have met you," I tell Petal, which sounds weird as hell—*but, what do you say to the wife of a man you wanted to boink all night long!?!?!*

Besides, I *am* glad I met her, if not I would have slept with... *a married man.* "I hope your... husband feels better in the morning," I tell her, and I do... I want him to feel great... *right before I kill his sorry ass.*

"Uh... I'm sure he'll be right as rain tomorrow," she says, but she's looking at me very strangely at this point and so is my father...

I guess I didn't keep the anger out of my voice like I wanted.

"Goodbye, Mayor... Adelle..." Petal says, leaving with her children. She looks back over her shoulder at me and damn, I can tell she's wondering what's going on. Then... so is my father.

"Princess are you okay?"

"Sorry, Dad. I just started feeling sick to my stomach all at once."

"Maybe we should skip the dipped cone and go home?" he says just as they call our number to pick them up. I turn to look at the hard-coated, cherry confection and wish Black was here so I could dump it on his head.

"I'm sorry," I whisper and I can't figure out if I'm telling him I'm sorry for ruining our night or sorry that I ever laid eyes on Sheriff Parrish.

"It will be okay, Princess. It will be okay," he says pulling me into him.

I let him lead me out of there and I hear what he's saying, but suddenly it feels like nothing will ever be okay again.

Chapter Fifteen

BLACK

"It's a shame you moved away, man. We miss you around here," Gary tells me while opening the door to what used to be my home. I could have kicked her out—after all, Linda and I weren't married. It wasn't like she got the home in a break up. The truth was by the time I was really done with Linda, her crazy had bled over into so many aspects of my life that I just wanted away. I tried to kick her out and she kept refusing. I finally said fuck it and when I realized I was going to have to go to court to get custody of Kong, I had my attorney have the court file a paper, transferring my lease over to Linda and making her responsible for all payments. As fucked up as this has all been, I guess I'm lucky the judge didn't order me to continue making those for Linda. I'm sure it was a near miss, because I'm almost positive she was sleeping with the judge too. If my lawyer hadn't been female, I would have thought they were banging nightly too. Hell, I'm still not too sure they weren't. Shit, with the way Linda liked to spread the love—and her legs—I'm sure old Gary here has sampled her.

"I'm settled back home. I'm good there." *Really good.*

A few days ago that would have been a lie. I was getting restless. Since meeting Addie, as crazy as it sounds, I'm glad I'm back home. If I weren't, I never would have met her.

Or I would have met her while investigating a hit and run involving a lawnmower here in Dallas.

I find myself smiling and how that's happening when I'm back here, dealing with the remnants of the shit storm that was Hurricane Linda, is beyond me.

But I am.

"Interesting," I hear my Mom whisper beside me and I look up quickly and she's staring at me. She's caught my smile. Fuck, her eyes say that she's caught on to a lot more than that. I feel sweat break out on my brow. *Christ.* I know better! Mom's like a damn blood hound and when she catches scent... Shit. Shit. *Shit.*

"Well, here you go. I'm supposed to stay in the house with you while you get your stuff, but I know you, man. I can stay out here—"

"No, it's fine. I'd prefer you stay close that way you can see exactly what I do and I can't get blamed for anything I didn't do," I tell him.

"Let her try to say you did something. She thinks she can cause a firestorm? She hasn't even had a taste of me. Which is your fault, Black. If you had told me what was going on—"

"Let it go, Mom."

"I'd have rained fire on her damned head. That's all I'm saying," she mumbles and again I smile. She would have, there's no denying that. My brothers and I had to hold her back as it was, when she did find out. I smile, almost regretting not letting the wrath of Ida Sue rain down on Linda's head. Lord knows that Mom would have made her life hell.

The smile quickly disappears however, when I see what's on the couch—the same couch I paid a hell of a lot of money for. It's solid Italian leather and was in excellent shape when I left it here. Now however, it looks like shit and I swear there's duct tape acting as a band-aid and joining torn strips of the leather together. I walk to it, letting my fingers move over the tape—inspecting it. It doesn't take a rocket scientist to discern that someone has taken a knife to the leather. So much for taking the couch with me. The back has letters spelled out with duct tape. On closer inspection the word has been carved into my sofa, and repaired with the duct tape so I can see the word without guessing. B-A-S-T-A- R-D

Bastard.

Well I've been called worse. Still this is going above and beyond. Linda is nothing if not thorough.

"Jesus she really is coo-coo for Cocoa Puffs," Mom says, and I turn slightly to see her looking at the sofa. "Think of the Hamburger's that were sacrificed to make that sofa," she says adding a mournful sigh that makes me shake my head.

She can eat steak like no one's business, but the woman wants to boycott anything made of out leather.

"It's Italian leather, Mom."

I don't tell her to point out the difference in expense, I merely want her to understand I didn't buy and set on Hamburger's long lost cousin.

"Italian cows have feelings too, son. Besides my Hamburger is one quarter Italian stock," she boasts.

"He is not."

"I'll show you his pedigree when we get home," she says with a wave—as if she's tired of fooling with me. I don't respond, there's really nothing I can say. She probably does have her damn cow's DNA. It shouldn't surprise me.

I look across the room at Kong's empty bed. I don't want that, I bought him a new one. Kong is my English bulldog that I've had since he was a pup. He's three now and I've missed him so much. I didn't realize how attached I was to the big lug until I couldn't see him every day. I hope we don't have any problem bonding with each other again. I know we won't on my part, but he may think I deserted him. Pets are finicky creatures and he has no idea the hell I've gone through to get him back.

"Kong?" I yell through the apartment, more than a little worried. Even if Kong was upset with me, it's not like him to not be at the door inspecting guests. "Yo! Kong! Where you at boy? Come give Daddy lovin'!"

"Daddy? God's toes, my grand kid is a dog," Mom mumbles. "Moving to the city destroyed you, boy."

"Kong!"

"She said she'd have the dog in the bedroom. He can get destructive when she lets him run loose," Gary says. "She had to replace all of the area rugs last month before she sent him for training," he adds and Gary definitely knows way too much about Linda's business and my damn dog. He's definitely caught a ride on Linda's free train.

More power to him.

"She sent my dog to training?" I ask, thinking that's weird as fuck because Kong has had the best training around. I called in a favor from the canine handler with the P.D. here in Dallas to get that for him.

"Yeah, it made a world of difference in the little guy."

Later, when I look back, I will know that I should have listened to Gary closer. I should have paid more attention to exactly what he said and what those words implied.

I didn't.

So I wasn't prepared—and when I say that I *really* wasn't prepared.

When I open the door a small—tiny—*extremely tiny*—like fit-in-the-palm-of-my-hand tiny—dog, with his entire lower half tinted pink, comes running at me with a high pitched yap. He immediately starts biting on my ankles, but I ignore him. I'm looking desperately around the room for my Kong, my bulldog, my best friend... I barely notice that the damn Chihuahua is now busy humping my damn leg like I'm the first female he's seen in the last one-hundred years. To be fair my pants are the same color as his skin—the part that's not pink—because he has *no* hair. What kind of dog doesn't have hair on his body? At least short hair. Kong had a beautiful coat—"

"Damn he's hornier than a one-eyed sailor on leave during dollar night at the whore house," Mom mumbles.

"One eye?" Gary asks.

"That way it looks like he's got twice as many women," Mom explains, as I bend down to pick up the dog.

"I don't think it works that way," Gary whispers, clearly not having been around my mother much at all.

"Where in the hell is Kong?" I growl, holding the damn Chihuahua, who is now shivering in my hands.

"But that is Kong," Gary says and I jerk my head around to look at him.

"It fucking is not!" I yell and the dog bites my hand and I jerk it away looking at it while it growls back at me. "Shit!" For such a little mongrel, it has sharp-ass teeth.

"But it is. I hate the thing, but Linda said you insisted on getting rid of the bulldog and finding a pet that she felt safer around. Which made sense. Your bulldog hated Linda..." Gary answers.

"That's because he was smart," Mom says as I use my thumb to turn the tag on the Chihuahua's collar. Sure enough *Kong* is engraved on it.

Motherfucker.

"Things didn't go so great today, and I'm having a bad night. Sorry I didn't text sooner."

It's midnight when I get Black's message. I know because I'm lying here in bed staring up at the ceiling wondering how I could have been so wrong about him. It's stupid because I barely know him, and we've had what establishes as one date—but, I really liked him. The more I was around him, the more I liked him and I loved being around him. Plus, he was the first guy in forever that had me excited to be a woman—or just had me excited in general.

I think about not replying at all. I'm going to confront him tomorrow, I'm too damn tired tonight. Besides some things require a face to face meeting. I've never allowed any man to play me like a fool and I'm not about to start now.

"Guess you're sleeping, goodnight Princess Addie."

I read his second text and frown. To think that I actually liked that nickname before makes me sick to my stomach now.

"You could have called."

I text him, thinking of only goading him on. I mean he doesn't know that I'm aware he couldn't call me because of his wife!

"I thought you might be sleeping."
        "Heading there now. I'll see you tomorrow."
        "You promise?"

God. I hate him. I literally hate him. Asshole texts back you promise like he really misses me and is anxious to see me or something. Prick!

"Trust me, I wouldn't miss it for the world."

I make sure my text goes through and then I turn my phone off before he can respond. I can't hold onto my temper much longer and I don't want to call him out on his lies until tomorrow.

Tomorrow I'm going to take Sheriff Luka-Everyone-Calls-Me-Black-Parrish down a few notches—and I'll do it in a way to make sure his unlucky wife finds out!

I toss my phone on the nightstand, pull the covers up tight and burrow my head into the pillow. I let my anger free, I nurture it, because if I don't... I might cry and Black doesn't deserve my tears.

Chapter Seventeen

BLACK

I rub the tension at the back of my neck. It was a rough night and I slept like shit. I was hoping to hear Addie's voice—for some reason, I thought that might help. That didn't work out and I know it was just a text, but something seemed different with her. I shrug it off. After the hell of yesterday and reminder of just what kind of hell a woman can put a man through, I'm just being paranoid. Just because Linda was certifiably insane, it doesn't mean Addie is.

Addie is completely different from Linda. She's sweet, funny, and completely drama free...

"I thought I'd find you here."

I jerk my head up quick to see Addie standing at my desk and she's mad... No. *She's pissed.* Her face is even red with the emotion. That should be enough to set off alarm bells, but instead I find myself looking at the way the dress she's wearing clings to her curves. It's a summer dress in white and lilac and rather simple to be honest, but damn she makes that dress look good. I try to get my head in the conversation though, because if there's one thing I know, it's a woman who is upset is a dangerous thing to behold.

"Well, this is where I work, Princess Addie," I tell her with a grin, though I'm holding back on the charm because she looks like she wants to punch me.

"Don't you do that!"

"Do what?"

"Call me that! My name is Adelle and you can't call me that either."

"Addie, I'm not sure what's going on here—"

"I said my name is *Adelle!*"

"Well, *Adelle*, maybe you'd like to explain what's got your panties in a bunch—"

"I said you couldn't call me that!" she screeches. "And don't talk about my panties. My panties have nothing to do with you anymore! They never did!" she looks around the room—which is way too crowded for this shouting match, but there's not much I can do. At least five of the other deputies are in the office. Not to mention Luka and the Mayor are in his office. *Correction.* They *were* in Luka's office. The door just opened.

Great... just great. When will I learn that women destroy a man? The last thing I need is the new Mayor witnessing this shit. It's not going to end well. I'm sure he doesn't want a deputy on the force that causes drama like this in a public office.

"Addie maybe we could talk about this out—"

"I said, don't call me Addie! You lost that privilege! And just so *everyone* knows, he never got into my panties!"

I hold my head down and pinch the bridge of my nose, thinking I should have skipped cereal this morning and went straight for the Jack Daniels.

"Princess? What's going on?"

My head jerks up and this time I'm eyeing the Mayor. *Princess?* Motherfucker, does she have every man in the world on a string? I really know how to pick them. I'm going to move to Tibet and become a freaking monk. That has to be an easier life.

"Crap. You're here? Why are you here? You said you were going to a business meeting this morning!" She sounds flustered, and I guess I can take solace in the fact her sugar daddy has caught her fooling around on him. No wonder he keeps her on as landscaper. She's obviously trimming more than his hedges.

"I do," he responds. "With Sheriff Luka—"

"Well, you'll just have to get in line. I have some things to say to him and they can't wait."

"You do?" Luka asks.

I say nothing. At this point, I'm just being quiet, waiting for this shit-show to end.

"I do! You're such an asshole! How could you do this?" Addie asks, only this time she's not looking at Luka, she's looking at me. I start not to answer, but really I'm grieving the loss of my dog. I have Tani looking at local shelters and faxing pictures of Kong to them, but so far she's come up with nothing. Linda is deranged. She probably had Kong put down. If I didn't feel so broken, I'd want to kill her. Right now, I just want to make it my mission never to see the bitch again in my lifetime. If I do, I'm not sure I can be held responsible for what I'd do to her.

"It's been a long fucking night, *Princess*, and so far the day isn't getting much better. So maybe you could explain to me what in the fuck you think I've done to you exactly?" I literally growl the words. I stand up too, because I'm done with letting women stand over me and scream. Linda pulled that shit all the time and I let her get away with it. I'm done with that too. I don't know how much more I'm supposed to take, but I've had it with women.

Completely had it.

"Oh, you *know* what you've done!" she yells. I'll be surprised if they don't hear her across the street at the diner.

So much for trying to get out of this with a little dignity.

"No, I actually don't, so enlighten me," I invite.

"You're really going to play dumb?"

"He doesn't normally have to play too hard," Mom chimes in helpfully.

The moment I hear my mother's voice I want to leave. Nothing good—*absolutely nothing*—can come of this.

"I—" Addie stumbles on her next tirade to look at my Mom. "Who are you?"

"Black's mother," she replies and fuck she's brought that damn Chihuahua. I look at the little dog and he instantly snarls at me.

"Is that your dog?" Addie asks, momentarily sidetracked.

"No, it's Black's. Ain't he cute?" Mom asks petting it like it deserves to be praised. Damn thing curls into Mom's hand like it doesn't have a care in the world.

"That's *your* dog?" Addie asks, her eyes round.

"Do you want to tell me why you hate me? Or am I just supposed to guess?" I ask her instead, but then my head jerks back to Mom.

"Mom! Did you dye that damn dog's skin pink again? I told you to take that shit out of it!" I growl, wanting nothing to remind me of Linda at all—if I can manage it.

"What? Of course not."

"Then why is—"

"It has to wear off. Besides, I think it makes Kong look adorable."

"That damn thing is not Kong!"

"Do you always talk to your mother like that? I'm learning more and more about you and with each new thing, I dislike you more!" Addie says and I let out a sound that's a mix between exasperation, frustration and irritation all rolled into one.

"What has Black done, sweetie?"

"My name is Addie, you can call me that. *He* can't."

"Oh that's a sweet name. Do you have a middle name?"

"What? Umm... no," Addie responds and this time she looks confused. It's about time somebody is other than me.

"You should totally add one. I'll think of one for you."

"I... uh... okay."

At this point Addie looks shell shocked and everyone— including the damn Mayor—is standing around waiting to see what happens next. I just really want it over with, so I give her a nudge.

"You were telling me what I possibly could have done to piss you off into such epic proportions that you felt the need to come down to my place of employment and give me hell. Maybe you could get on with it, before we all turn gray-headed," I prompt.

My voice must have been too loud. All at once the little pink mongrel jumps out of Mom's hands and lunges at me. I catch him mostly on instinct and he bites my chest—which would have been alright because he's little, I mean, how sharp can his teeth be? The problem comes in when he bites into my damn nipple and even through my shirt the damned thing's teeth seem to penetrate. He slings his head back and forth like he's trying to kill a damn snake. I yank him hard and *Christ!*... I wouldn't be surprised if the dog didn't rip through my skin. I literally throw him down on my desk. Addie and Mom both reach for the dog at the same time. Addie seems to win the fight and takes the damn thing in her arms, holding it against her breasts. The damn thing turns and licks Addie's hand where she's petting his head and curls into her palm.

"Oh, you poor baby," Addie coos and it whimpers!

"Jesus Fu—"

"Black don't you finish that! You're not so old that I can't take lye soap to your damn mouth," Mom yells and the little pink nightmare turns at me and snarls. Addie just lets her eyes shoot daggers at me. I can hear Luka laughing in the background, but I don't look at him, because I have no inclination to see Addie's sugar daddy standing beside him.

"Even your dog hates you!" Addie declares and I just roll my eyes heavenward at this point.

"If you can't tell me why you're upset then—"

"I'll tell you why I'm upset," she huffs. I do my best to pay attention, but I'm rubbing my nipple through my shirt. I'm pretty sure it's now pierced—by a damn dog's tooth!

"Finally,"— that's said by my *mother* and even though she's echoing my thoughts, I'm worried.

"I met Petal!"

"So?" I ask, because I was lost before, but now I'm completely lost.

"I met Petal!" she yells—*again.*

"You don't like my sweet Petal? She's a good girl. Hasn't always had the best of tastes of course, but—" Ida Sue starts, while I'm just frowning.

"Ida Sue—"

"It's mom now, Orange. And you know I love you, let's not rehash dirty laundry, shall we? Especially in front of my new grand-pup!"

"Grand-pup?" Luka laughs.

"And I met your children!" Addie cries.

"What the hell?"

"Your children?!?!"

Before I can decipher who is saying what, Addie's hand comes out and slaps the hell out of me. I hold the side of my face, the skin burning from her hit. I narrow my eyes at her. I'd never hurt a woman, but the urge to pull her over my lap and smack her ass raw is there.

"I don't know what kind of woman you thought I was, but I can assure you I don't agree to sleep with a man lightly! I sure wouldn't sleep with a married man!"

"Married?" Mom asks, but my eyes are trained on Addie trying to figure out exactly what in the hell is going on.

"Thank God I didn't agree to go to a hotel with you. You have roommates! That's rich! Did you get a good laugh about that one? It's *not* roommates, you asshole, it's a wife and kids!"

"I'm not laughing about any of this shit. I still don't know what you're yammering on about!" I say through grinded teeth.

"Yammering? You know what? I feel sorry for Petal! She must be a saint to put up with your ass!"

"I—"

"I'm sorry I ever met you!"

"You didn't meet me! You almost ran over me!"

"And I should have kept going! I would have done Petal a favor!"

"What—"

"You can go to hell, Luka-Parrish-they-call-me-Black! They probably call you Black because of your black heart!" I fall back against my chair, sitting down as Addie storms out.

"She thinks you're me..." Luka says, sounding puzzled. "Why would she think you are me?"

"Why have you been trying to sleep with my daughter?" the Mayor asks, and I jerk my head up to look at him.

"*Your daughter?*" I ask before I can stop myself.

"I think we've got some problems here..." the Mayor says.

"I'll say so," Mom says, still staring out the door. "That girl just kidnapped my grand-pup."

Luka starts laughing and I just lay my head down on the desk, wondering if I can book a flight to Tibet today....

Chapter Eighteen

ADDIE

"You're such a cute little thing. I bet Black broke your heart too," I coo to the little Chihuahua. He seems to instantly understand because he whimpers and pushes his head against my face.

I pet him as I close my eyes. It's been over 5 hours since I confronted Black, and with each hour that passes, I seem to only hurt more.

There's a knock on my door and I want to bury my head and ignore it. But it might be Black—I did kind of kidnap his dog.

In my defense, I didn't mean to. I just wanted out of there and I had the dog and...

I kind of hope it is him. I want to see him; I want him to beg me to forgive him right before I tell him to go to hell. Probably won't happen, but still...

I open the door and immediately I frown. I can't see a person just a giant fur covered cat perch like thing. I've seen them in a pet store. They're tall—though this one is even taller than normal—covered in shag carpet, and it has a perch which is meant to contour to a cat's body and several little tunnel and private dens. It keeps coming at me, so I reach out my hand to grab it before it knocks me over. I take several steps back and that's when I see the woman from the police station earlier.

Black's mother.

"Uh..."

"Hi! Sorry for stopping by unannounced. I just gathered up some of Kong's stuff and wanted to bring them to you."

"Kong?"

"My grand-pup you're trying to hold there," she says. I blink and she reaches over and takes the dog from my hand. To be fair he was hanging on precariously while I tried to hold onto the monstrosity that she shoved at me to get through the door.

"Grand-pup? Listen I didn't mean to take the dog. You can have him back."

"Oh no. I can't."

"You can't?" I blink.

"Of course not, Daffodil!"

"Daffodil?"

"I'm trying out flower names for you. I thought Rose first, but honestly that flower is just too serious for you. You're all over the place, you need a name to reflect that."

"I'm all over the place?"

"Now don't get pissy about that. I wasn't criticizing you. I'm like that too. Personally, I think all good women are. But still, you need a name that reflects that. I like Daffodil, though if I know my boys —and sadly I know them down to the DNA in their bones—most of which—thank God—is mine—anyways, if I know my boys they'll start calling you Daffy and I'm pretty sure you don't want that."

"Um... no... not really."

"So, I'll keep trying. Do you have a favorite flower?"

"I... Orchids..." I tell her.

"Ohhh... I like that! They're complicated and they do best in hot houses, and again no offense honey, but you do take off with a full head of steam," she laughs.

"I don't think I understand what's going on... Ms..."

"You can call me Ida Sue. I'm just here bringing you some of Kong's things so he will feel more at home."

"At home? But he's Black's dog. He belongs with his wife and kids and—"

"Oh child! That bone-headed son of mine hasn't explained things to you at all yet, has he?"

"I... Ida Sue, I'm following about zero percent of what you're saying. To be honest, I'm trying to figure out why you brought the dog's things here and why the dog has a cat jungle gym...."

"A cat? Well damn. That explains a lot. I was wondering how they expected poor little Kong to climb way up there to get on the perch..." she says, staring at the item in question like she's just now seeing it for the first time. "Oh well, he likes the little bottom hideaway."

"I'm sure you mean well and things but, I can't have Black's dog," I tell her.

"Why on earth not? I mean, you kind of claimed him and he likes you!"

"I can't because Black hates me!"

"Oh, honey. He doesn't."

"Uh, were you not there today? He *does*. Besides, I don't care. I know he's your son, but he's a liar and a cheat and poor Petal—"

"Is his sister, Dahlia."

"I..."

"Too much?"

"I don't like that name," I answer, still blinking in shock.

"Poo. I liked it. If Cyan had been a girl, he was so getting that name," she says with a sigh like I took away her favorite toy. "I guess we'll just stick with Orchid."

"Thanks... I think... Did you say that Petal was—"

"Black's sister," she says with a nod of the head, putting the dog on the floor. He instantly goes into the small hideaway at the base of the cat thingy. Guess Ida Sue was right about that. But...

"How is she Black's sister? Dad told me himself that Petal was married to—"

"Sheriff Luka Parrish and she is. That's my son-in-law—though you should know he prefers to be called Orange Parrish."

"Orange Parrish?"

"Exactly that."

"Why on earth does he like to be called Orange?"

"Purple Lucas didn't have the same ring."

"I... Ida Sue I'm confused."

"Honey, Black isn't the sheriff, he's just a deputy."

"Then why did I—"

"Honey I don't know how you came up with that, but I figure it's because Black drove you crazy."

"I—"

"Trust me, I carried Black and his brother in my stomach at the same time, those boys could drive a saint to drink."

"He's really not married?" I ask, my heart tripping over in my chest.

"Definitely not."

"Oh no!" I cry, flopping down on the arm of a chair.

"Now why does *that* upset you? I got the feeling you were sweet on my boy?"

"I, well, I don't know him that well, but I was... kind of..."

"Then why are you so upset to find out he's single?"

"Because I stormed into his office, made a scene and slapped him!"

"Oh..."

"He has to hate me now. I need to find him and apologize."

"Well, that's one option..." Ida Sue agrees.

"Option? I don't think I have an option. I owe Black an apology Ida Sue."

"That you do, but a little bump in the road is good for my boys. It keeps them on their toes."

"So you *don't* want me to apologize to him?" I ask, not understanding—but I'm starting to think not many people do understand Ida Sue.

"Well, not right away. Besides, my boys can hold grudges when they get a bee up their ass."

"I think you mean bonnet, Ida Sue."

"Whatever."

"So, if I don't find him and apologize, what do I do?" I ask, completely lost, but figuring she knows her son better than anyone and I'm sick to my stomach thinking of what I've done.

"Absolutely nothing," she says. "Black will make the next move."

I frown. "How can you be so sure?"

"It's simple Orchid. You have his dog," she responds with a wide smile, and I have a very bad feeling about that grin on her face...

Chapter Nineteen

BLACK

"Where's the mutt?" I ask Mom. The house is way too quiet tonight. Jansen is still out of town at a convention discussing the latest techniques in raising cattle. Mary is working a double shift, and Cyan... Lord only knows what that boy is doing, but I wish I had joined him. Anything would be better than eating dinner with my mom on a Friday night, alone in the house.

If you looked up loser right now in the dictionary you would see my face.

"You mean Kong?" Mom asks, looking over at me and I really don't like that smile on her face. *I don't trust it either.*

"That mutt is not Kong."

"The mayor's daughter kept him. She took all of his stuff."

"She stole my dog?"

"Well, you didn't want him did you?"

"That's beside the point! She can't just steal my damn dog. There are laws against that kind of stuff!"

"But, you didn't want the dog, Black," Mom says calmly—too calmly. I should take note of that and proceed cautiously, but I can't. I didn't have a bit of luck tracking down Kong today. The mess with Addie is just a fucking cherry on top of the sundae. I'm so stressed and frustrated and I can't take it out on Linda. If I do that, it invites her back in my life to fuck with me. So, I'm focusing it on the other woman in my life who is destroying the peace I'm trying to build.

Adelle Harrington.

Oh I got her texts apologizing for thinking I was Luka and explaining how she took it for granted when I delivered papers and told her to tell the Mayor who they were from. I can even kind of understand it, but damn it! We spent time together, we went out on a date—we made out—all of that and she didn't even know Black was my real name—just a nickname the town gave me. Like, why would they do that? She's insane. I have a knack for attracting insane women... *insane women who like to mess with a man's dog!*

"That's not the point! She can't just take my dog. Why do women think that's okay? A man's dog is sacred! Kong was sacred!"

"And little Kong?"

"His name is *not* Kong. Shrew or Mini-Linda maybe but *not* Kong."

"Don't give the poor little guy that name. That's just animal cruelty. Now if my grand-pup was a snake... Linda might be a good name."

"Quit distracting me. I'm upset. I'm going to get the damn dog back."

"I knew you loved Kong!"

"I do not! Thanks to that mutt I now have a pierced nipple."

"Those can be fun. I've got two."

I stop talking. I'm pretty sure my life flashes before my eyes.

"Mom. I love you, so I'm going to say this only one time and then after I go and get that damn dog, I'm going to come home and drink myself into a coma and pray I never remember what was said tonight."

"What's that?"

"Never, ever tell me about your nipples. Actually—never tell me about any part of your boobs... or heck even your anatomy in general."

"Is this what we have come to Black Horn Lucas?"

I hold my head down on the table.

"You are never to call me Horn either. You know I took that name off my birth certificate as soon as I legally could."

"I know, it hurt my heart. It's a beautiful name and I have such fond memories of that night in that restored Model T with the shiny black horn. That rumble seat is the main reason you and your brother are here. Your daddy—bless his soul—had to squeeze that horn over and over to drown out the noise ..." she trails off recalling her memories before ending in a heartfelt sigh. The trip down memory lane might be nice if we weren't talking about my parents having sex—and the despised middle name I got rid of.

"Mom—"

"Fine, fine. I get the message. I'll hush. You've gotten so grouchy since you moved back from Dallas, do you realize that, Black?"

"I can't do this right now. I'm going to go get my dog."

"What are you going to do? Just march over to the Mayor's and demand the dog back?"

"That's exactly what I'm going to do and if Adelle Harrington doesn't give him back, then I'll—"

"Yes, son? What exactly will you do to the *Mayor's* only daughter?"

"I'll arrest her for theft!"

"You should do that," Mom nods, giving me approval I wasn't really expecting. I walk to the door and grab my keys off the hook on the wall. My hand is on the knob and I'm almost home free when Mom says something that stops me in my tracks. "Of course, since you don't want the dog. It seems like to me you're just looking for an excuse to put Orchid in handcuffs."

"Orchid?"

"Her new family name," Mom says and it feels like I've got

damn fish flopping in my stomach when she says that with that damn grin I'm starting to hate.

I'm falling into her plan. I know and I can't seem to stop myself. Instead I'm picturing Addie in handcuffs...

I walk out and slam the door on my Mom's laughter.

Son of a bitch.

Chapter Twenty
ADDIE

"Yeah, Dad, I'm fine. Just take your time. I'm just sitting here with Kong watching *Men In Black* for the millionth time."

"I'll be home before long. I just have to give my speech after the fundraiser dinner. I wish you had come with me," he says, and I instantly feel guilty. My hand tightens on my phone in reflex. I should have, I know. I'm just not extremely comfortable in those settings, plus I didn't want to leave Kong alone. He seems sad.

Who could blame him?

Black hasn't returned my text and I'm sad. This is his damn dog and he can't be bothered to check on him. How can anyone not care about such a cute little animal? I still can't believe he has a Chihuahua. I mean, not that there's anything wrong with that I guess. I just figured he'd have a German Shepherd, Great Dane... *something*.

"Are you there, Addie?"

"Sorry, Daddy, I was just thinking,

"About that Lucas boy," he grumbles.

"Dad—"

"Don't, daddy me, Addie-girl. I don't like that he put the moves on my baby."

"It's not like he knew you were my dad. If anything, I get the feeling that's something else to make me not appealing to him."

"Then he's a fool," Dad grumbles.

I look down at the dog and sigh, sadly.

"I can't really argue with that. Quit worrying about me. Get back to your dinner. I'm fine."

"Okay, you call me if you need me. Bye sweetheart."

"Bye, Daddy."

I hang up the phone, shaking my head. I have to snap myself out of it. I'm worrying him—and that's the last thing I want. We're just now learning each other again. That's what I should be focused on.

Not Black Lucas.

I jerk, causing Kong to complain, when I hear the doorbell. I put him down against the arm of the sofa and walk to the door. My heart pounds erratically when I look through the side glass panel of my door and see Black.

An angry looking Black.

I step back, close my eyes and prepare myself for another round with the man. I know I was an idiot and deserve a little of his wrath, but I was hoping he'd be rational. Anyone could have made the mistake I did.

"Hello," I answer, unsure of what exactly to say.

"You stole my dog," he says. That's it. There's anger on his face, but his voice is just stoic—no emotion whatsoever.

"I didn't steal him," I deny. As if on cue Kong jumps down off the couch and I hear his little feet running on the tiled floor. As he gets to me he's growling like he's going to tear Black up.

For such a little dog he sure can sound vicious.

"Then what do you call that?" Black asks, his face steeped with annoyance.

"The dog *your* mother *gave* me."

"I don't see how she could give you *my* dog. It's mine. I'm the only one that can do that."

"Whatever. Come inside and I'll get his things and you can have him back."

I walk away from the door, so frustrated I could scream. He's being such an asshole. He's not even giving me the chance to apologize and now I really don't want to. If this is the real him, I'm better getting him out of my life now.

Kong is keeping beside me, growling at Black with every breath. I feel sorry for the poor thing—he obviously hates Black too.

"This is more like it," Black says. I turn around to see him looking over the main room of Dad's house.

"What is?"

"Living in wealth. It suits you much more than being a gardener," he shrugs.

"*Landscaper,*" I correct. "And this is my *father's* house —not mine."

"Whatever, I hear you've been living overseas. You've obviously been living off of Daddy's money."

"Wow. I can see you have a high opinion of me."

"If the diamond tiara fits..." he shrugs.

"*I know what I'd like to fit up your ass.*"

I mutter the words under my breath as I turn around. There's no point in engaging the asshole. That's probably exactly what he wants.

"What did you say?" he demands, but I ignore him.

Instead, I finish getting the new dog bowl and puppy bed I bought for Kong. Then I walk into the kitchen and get the dog food I bought. I wanted to get him the healthier food that's made from real ingredients. It seemed wrong not to. I begin sacking it all up and I hear Kong whimpering. I look down and he's sitting down looking up at me with the most pitiful look I've ever seen in my life. My heart almost breaks. I bend down to scoop the little guy up, pulling him to my chest. He burrows into my neck whimpering.

"Poor little baby," I coo, helpless to know what will make this situation better.

"What's all this stuff?" Black asks, looking at the food on the counter.

I cringe. I went a little overboard. There's enough food on my counter to feed probably three dogs for a good month.

"Well—"

"There's no way my mom went out and bought all of this," Black says picking up some of the cans and reading them.

"Well, no. But, I didn't know what his tastes were. I wanted to get him some healthy food. So, I bought a variety until I figured out what he liked best," I try to explain. Really, it's hard to explain why I spent a hundred bucks on dog food for a dog that technically isn't even mine.

"This isn't a variety, it's.... *Did you buy out the whole damn pet store?*"

"What? Of course not!" I deny, ignoring the fact that I did buy all of one particular brand—or at least all that was on the shelf. I'm sure they had more in the back.

"It sure as hell looks like it."

"Whatever," I mumble—which might become my favorite word around Black...*not that I'll be around him after he gets his dog.* "You don't have to worry about it, it's not like you have to buy it."

"I will if he runs out, you've obviously got him used to this fancy crap."

"I have not!"

Maybe I have a little—but I'm not admitting that to Black at all.

"And he won't stop growling at me!" Black mumbles. "You've obviously done something to him."

Okay, so it's true that he's growled at Black the entire time. He's even growling at him now. Of course Kong's head is on my shoulder and his body is mostly hidden by my hair—but he's still growling.

"I think the problem is he just doesn't like you."

"He's my dog, why wouldn't he like me?" Black asks, still

looking at all of the food on the counter.

"Maybe because you gripe and complain every time you're around him."

"Maybe you think that because I'm always yelling at you when I'm with the dog—mostly because you drive me insane."

I frown, because he probably has a point.

"I don't know why. I've done nothing to you."

"Except bitch me out and slap me for no reason—in front of the entire department, I might add."

"You just did," I mutter.

"Just did what?"

"Add it."

"Add what?" Black asks.

"Add that I slapped you in front of the whole department. You don't say you might add, when you clearly already added the words in the first place."

He stares at me blankly for a minute and then shakes his head.

"You're clearly unbalanced. I have a knack for picking out women like you."

"Women... Listen here! You didn't *pick* me out. I don't have a thing to do with you," I yell, causing Kong to get scared and put his little body in reverse. He tries to jump down my back, his sharp little claws digging into my skin. "Ow!" I cry, because damn it, it hurts. I curl trying to get Kong, but I can't reach him and I can't help but whimper every time he grinds his nails into my skin.

"Shit," I hear Black growl. "Why do I always attract the clearly deranged women? Why can't my dick find a nice normal woman it goes crazy over?"

If I wasn't trying to bend in half to get Kong off of me, I'd probably try and kill Black at this point. Instead, I'm almost thankful when he lifts Kong off of me. I turn back around in time to see him bending down to let the dog go. Kong plants his teeth into Black's hand almost immediately.

"Fucking hell!"

Black screams the words, loud enough that dad's neighbors

next door probably hear him.

"Hush!" I reprimand. "You're scaring him."

Black ignores me, dropping the dog immediately—luckily it was just a couple feet to the ground. The minute Kong's little feet hit the floor he takes off out of the room. I watch as he runs straight under the couch.

"Damn thing broke skin. We'll have to have him tested for rabies!"

"Oh we will not. Here, let me see," I respond, reaching for Black's hand.

"How do you know?"

"For one, he has a rabies tag on his little collar, but you should know that. He is *supposed* to be your dog."

"A woman shouldn't mess with a man's dog. That's sacred," Black grumbles and his voice sounds different. He's hurt—clearly upset and I feel bad. I didn't realize he'd think I was keeping his dog away from him.

"I'm sorry. I'll help you get him and you can take him home—"

"I don't want that damn mutt," Black growls and I stand up, my back going straight.

"But he's your dog—"

"He's nothing to me. I hate him. You keep him," he mutters and he turns away from me, heading towards the door.

"But, you came all the way over here to get him. You can—"

"I *said* I don't want the damn dog. You and him just stay out of my way. I don't need your kind of crazy back in my life."

I blink. I have no idea what to say to that. So I just let him go.

Minutes after the door slams, I'm still staring at the door. Kong finally comes out from under the sofa and I bend down to get him and hold him close to me, soothing his little body which is still kind of shaking.

"Your daddy is a very strange man," I whisper. I half expect Black to walk back through the door screaming, *I'm not daddy to a damn dog.*

I refuse to admit I'm disappointed when he doesn't.

Chapter Twenty-One

BLACK

"Son of a bitch!"

"What's crawled up your ass?" Luka asks.

"I can't find Kong anywhere," I growl, raking my hand through my hair.

"You could take Wacky Linda back to court," he suggests, sitting at the desk across from me.

"I've thought about it, but fuck, dealing with that woman is poison. The more you interact with her the bigger the fucking mess."

"So you let him go. I know you don't want to hear it—"

"She could have had him put down." I finish for him. "I've already thought that, Luka and it's killing me."

"Sorry man. I wish I knew what to tell you, but I really don't."

"Nothing to say."

"About what?" Petal asks as she walks in the door. She goes straight for Luka and he opens his arms immediately, rolling his seat away from the desk. She curls into his lap and they immediately kiss. There's no hello, no exchange of words, nothing. Just instant kiss. They're like magnets drawn together and it just seems to get more intense with every day that they're together. That's what I want... or wanted, rather. After the mess with Linda and whatever the hell Addie and I started, I don't want anything now but peace. It's clear I don't have a brain in my head when it comes to women.

There are worse things than being alone.

"I missed you," Petal whispers with a happy sigh. I watch as my sister clings to her husband and lays her head on his shoulder.

"You too Lo," he murmurs into her ear. "Love you baby," Luka adds in a low voice right before they kiss again. It's enough to make a grown man sick.

"I think I'll go out on patrol for a bit," I mutter, feeling like a third wheel at my own damn desk.

"Not until you tell me what's wrong with you, big brother."

"There's nothing wrong with me," I answer, wincing as I say it because I sound damn defensive.

"Black's having women problems," Luka replies helpfully.

"Linda?" Petal asks.

"I still can't find my damn dog. I've torn up half of Texas looking for a clue to what she's done with him and I'm coming up with nothing."

"Did you ask Meadow?"

"Meadow?" Luka asks, before I get the chance.

"Leddie's daughter. She's moved back and taken over the Mason County Animal Shelter."

"I doubt Linda was nice enough to put Kong in the local shelter, Pet."

"Gee, Black. I know that. Smartass. I just meant, she lived in Dallas and volunteered at several shelters there. She also was a foster home too. She may have connections."

"What kind of connections could she have? Sounds hopeless to me," I grumble.

"You got any better ideas?" Petal asks and I get up from my chair with an exasperated breath, because she's right.

I have absolutely no other ideas.

"Fine. I'll go talk to Meadow," I tell her putting my hat on my head.

"Oh! You should totally take Blue!"

"Why would I take Blue?" I ask, and even depressed I can't help but grin. I wonder if Blue realizes the whole damn family knows he has a weak spot for Leddie's girl?

"Why wouldn't you?" she asks.

"You're entirely too much like our mother lately."

"Black! What a horrible thing to say!" she says, but she's laughing as she says it.

"Good luck, Luka," I say with a smirk at my kid sister and walk out to the sound of both of them laughing.

Chapter Twenty-Two

ADDIE

"Can't I go anywhere without running into you? Are you following me? There are laws against that, you know."

My head jerks back the minute I hear his voice. I close my eyes, cursing my own bad luck. Then I curse him, because really... *How full of himself can he be?*

"What are you *screaming* about now?"

"You're following me!" he yells.

I briefly wonder how much time I'd get for hitting him over the top of the head with something heavy—maybe a baseball bat. I figure whatever time I get it would be worth it. *Too bad I don't have a bat.*

"Will you stop being absurd. I'm in a public park and can I just point out that *I* was here *first*. So technically, you are probably the one following me."

"You'd like that wouldn't you?" he asks and I look up at the sky —maybe the man upstairs could grant me some patience.

"Only if I can duct tape your mouth shut."

"I—"

"Save it, Black. I'll tell you what I'm going to do, just so this is easier for both of us..."

"What?"

"I'm going to leave you alone with your pissy attitude for company and move over to the other side of the park. Will that be far enough away for you?"

He looks me over for a couple of minutes and then he surprises me.

"I guess I am being a jerk," he admits. I almost can't believe my own ears. In my experiences guys never admit to that kind of thing, and I sure didn't expect Black Lucas to.

"A big one," I agree, not completely willing to let it go.

"Listen, I've been going through some crap and I took it out on you, and I probably shouldn't have."

"Probably?"

"I'm trying to apologize here."

"You're doing a bad job of it," I grumble. I really liked Black and he's been an ass. I don't want to admit it, but it hurt.

"Do you always have to bust a man's balls if he's trying to be nice to you?"

"Were you trying?" I ask him, and now I find myself trying to hide my smile.

"I was," he says. "Although right now I can't for the life of me figure out why."

For some reason that makes me laugh. I don't even try to hold it back and when I look back up at Black's face, he's smiling and I like that even more.

"You want to sit down?" I ask him, sliding down the bench to make room.

"That depends. Are you going to keep raking me over the coals?"

"That depends," I respond, mocking him. "Are you going to keep being a bastard?"

"Probably," he says with a sigh, but he sits down. "Where's your dog?"

"I left him at the groomers. I'm just waiting around here until it's time to pick him up."

"The groomers? The damn thing doesn't even have any hair," Black complains.

"You know, for a man who used to own this dog, you're being kind of an ass. Even hairless dogs get shampooed and a conditioner applied to keep their skin from getting too dry."

"They do?" he asks, sounding like he doesn't quite believe me.

"They do. Didn't you ever do that for him? He seemed well cared for..."

"He's not really my dog," Black says and I frown.

"Kong? But you... your mom..."

"He's not Kong either," he responds, and he seems agitated. He rubs the back of his neck and dodges my gaze. Then eventually he looks up and he looks almost... miserable. "Listen before I moved back to Mason, I lived in Dallas. I was a detective there."

"And you didn't like living in Dallas?"

"I loved it. I loved being a detective," he says and I frown. I can sense there's a lot to the story, but for some reason he's having trouble telling me.

"Then why move back to Mason?"

"There was a woman," he says and I frown. I get this weird feeling in the pit of my stomach. I don't know why. I mean, we've shared a kiss... but, it's not like we were dating heavily and even if we were, there were bound to be women in his life before I met him. It's weird and stupid, but just hearing Black talk about another woman bothers me.

"I see..." I say like a dummy, because clearly I don't.

"She was insane, and I don't just mean that as in it was a bad break-up—which it totally was. I mean this woman would probably boil my rabbits."

"You have rabbits?" I ask, blinking trying to picture that.

"No. I meant if I did. You know, like that old movie?"

"Uh... no..."

"No?"

"I have no idea what you're talking about," I tell him, and I really, *really* don't.

"Where the guy had the affair and the woman was off her rocker and when he broke it off she boiled his little kid's rabbit," he explains. "I mean I didn't watch it closely. Linda wanted to watch it so I did—which with hindsight should have warned me she was unstable. "

"When did this movie come out?" I ask and Black frowns.

"I don't know, why? Eighties I guess."

"I wasn't born in the eighties. How old are you again?"

"Don't you have cable?" he asks, obviously not going to answer the question, which again—makes me want to grin. When Black isn't making me want to kill him, he's making me laugh.

"Not for movies where innocent rabbits are boiled!" I grumble.

"Didn't you go overseas? People eat rabbits you know."

Guilt immediately hits me.

"I know. I cook them, but they aren't my pets."

"You cook rabbit? Is that because you're a gardener?"

"What?"

"You know, you catch rabbits eating gardens so you trap and kill them and then..."

"You literally are insane. That's not a *landscaper's* job. But, I guess I should confess I'm not, nor have I ever been a landscaper."

"I kind of figured, since your dad owns banks."

"I don't live off my father," I complain.

"You live at home with him."

"So? You live with your mother. Does she pay your bills?"

"Of course not."

"Then why do you assume my father pays mine?"

"Well you're—"

"If you say because I'm a woman, so help me God, Black Lucas..."

"We're making progress, I guess."

"What does that mean?"

"At least you know my real name now," he laughs. "And I know you're the mayor's daughter, not his *landscaper,* that likes to cook rabbits on the side," he jokes.

"I'm not a landscaper," I whisper. "I'm a chef."

"Looks like we have a lot more to learn about each other," he says.

"Looks like we do, but I have to go pick up Kong..."

"How about," he says, standing up and then reaching down for my hand, "I walk with you and tell you about my dog—my real dog."

I don't know what that means exactly, but Black is holding my hand and wanting to spend time with me and I've missed him. So I do what any sane woman would do who has any trace of hormones at all in her body.... I agree.

Honestly, I'd go wherever Black leads me for a chance to have him hold my hand and look into those eyes.

Chapter Twenty-Three

BLACK

"Your ex is a bitch," Addie says, her voice a mix of anger and shock.

"Trust me, I know."

"And you can't find your dog anywhere?"

"We're still looking, but so far no," I answer, hating the worry and pain that rolls in my stomach at the words. I don't know why I felt the need to tell Addie everything that's been going on, but I did. It felt better actually sharing it with her. Christ, everything feels better just being around her. I've been fooling myself. I'm more than just attracted to Addie. There's something about her that just calls to me and I definitely want more of it—more of her. It's as if, when I get around her, extra electricity fires through my body, making me feel more alive.

"I'm sorry, Black," Addie says and she stops walking. I turn to look at her and she reaches up, sliding her hand along the side of my neck. She goes up on the tips of her toes and I lean down as she pulls me to her lips. She kisses me, it's a brief kiss probably meant to bring comfort, but it's been so long since I've had a taste of her that I don't let her get away. I deepen the kiss, taking it over, owning her mouth and letting her know that I'm still hungry for her. She melts against me and I groan as I feel the weight of her body against mine. Her tongue tangles with mine, just as hungry—just as full of need.

When it's over I keep her against me, closing my eyes and listening to her breathing as she buries her head against my chest. Nothing much has felt right in my life lately—nothing except Addie. We've fought more than we've kissed, but damn it I like that too. I like everything about her. I'm going down. I've watched it with Gray, White and I saw it up close and personal with Luka and Petal last year. I know the signs and I'm there. I just hope Addie is in this with me. With a kiss like that, all signs point to yes, but you just never know.

Especially with a woman...

"Go to dinner with me, Addie," I whisper to the top of her head. I hadn't meant to say it, but I don't want to let her go.

"Just dinner?" she asks, her eyes dark with what I hope is desire.

"For now," I respond, waiting.

"I'd like that, Black."

"Shit!"

"I don't have to—" she says startled.

"It's not that. I forgot I was supposed to go by the farm and pick up my brother. He's going to drive out to the animal shelter with me."

"You think Kong might be this close?"

"No, but I was hoping Meadow—the woman who runs the shelter—might have connections with other shelters..."

"Then I'm coming too," she says. Panic immediately hits me. I don't think I'm ready to have Addie at the farm with my family. Hell, my mother will probably start giving her things to make sure my little swimmers don't have to swim upstream. I'm not ready to be a father yet.... "What?" she asks, clearly reading me easily and prompting me to get my brain on the conversation and not on getting Addie pregnant—which for some reason was exactly what I was doing.

"We'll have that mutt and I'm not sure he and I can travel in the same vehicle," I invent.

"Kong? Oh, crap! I'm going to have to rename him... Can you even rename a dog that's used to his name already?"

"I don't know, but there's no point. It only bothered me when I had to see the damn dog every day."

Addie doesn't like my answer, I can tell. I don't quite get it until she steps out of my arms.

"You just kissed me."

"I remember," I smile. She's got that look on her face that says she's going to give me hell, but I don't care.

I like it.

"You can't kiss me and not expect to see me or my dog at least once or twice a week on the regular, Black."

"On the regular?"

"Exactly."

"So you're upset because I told you that you didn't have to rename the dog?"

"No!"

"Then I think you've lost me again, Princess."

"I told you to stop calling me that!"

"You're kind of acting like a princess at the moment," I tell her and I really shouldn't be smiling. I know women and smiling when you're pissing them off might get you de-balled. But, again, I can't seem to stop myself.

"I'm *upset* because you just kissed me like you meant it and—"

"Let's make this clear right now," I respond, letting my fingers move to thread through her hair. I might even give it a slight tug—I can't help myself. "I *did* mean it."

"Well you can't kiss a woman like that and then announce you aren't planning on seeing her that often."

"I don't remember saying that," I respond casually. I want to keep up with this conversation, but I just noticed the red dress she's wearing has a deep cut along the neck that shows cleavage and when she moves there's this cute little beauty mark that flashes...

I want to lick that mark...

"You implied it when you said I didn't need to rename the dog."

"You know what I like about you, Addie?"

"What?" She sighs to indicate that she's exasperated with me and that shouldn't make me want to laugh—but it does.

"You're direct. Something bothers you, you don't hold back and you immediately let me know—you say it like it is."

She studies my face and some of the anger seems to leave and her stance becomes less rigid.

"It'd be nice if you liked my personality or heck my boobs or my ass... not my mouth," she grumbles.

"I need you to trust me when I tell you, Addie, that I like everything about you."

"I—"

"From your feisty attitude, to the curve of your neck," I tell her, letting my fingers slide along her neck to accentuate my words.

"Well, then...."

"To that sexy ass of yours that I alternate from wanting to spank because of your attitude and wanting to spank for the pure pleasure of it."

"Black—"

"And you don't need to worry, Addie, because I love your breasts too."

"You do?" she asks, swallowing.

"I want to bury my face in them," I confirm.

"That sounds romantic," she laughs, but her nipples are pushing against her shirt, so I think I'm getting my message through.

"And just recently I've noticed this sexy little mark on your chest that I really want to play with," I tell her and then I lean down to press my lips against the mark.

Addie's hands come up and her fingers dive into my hair as I place a kiss there and I know that I'm not imagining the way her body shudders against mine when I do it.

"Black..."

"In fact, I want to play with your whole body and that's going to take a lot of time, Princess. *A lot of it.*"

"Then I guess we'll have to rename the dog."

"I guess so," I smile, against her skin, placing one more kiss before stepping back. My cock is hard, pushing against my pants and it's painful, but I resist the urge to adjust myself.

"And I'm still going with you to the shelter," she adds, letting me know that my tactics didn't divert her at all.

I sigh, but I don't disagree. Looks like I'm taking Addie home...

I guess it would be foolish to pray my mom behaves herself—but I send up a small one anyway.

Chapter Twenty-Four

ADDIE

"Black?"

"Yeah?"

"Is that a... *cow?*"

It's a silly question. I clearly see that it's a cow. I can also clearly see that he's lying on his stomach in the yard letting two little boys rub his belly...

"That's a cow... but he's more like a pet cow...."

"A pet cow?"

"Yeah, he uh..." Black hesitates, putting his hand on his neck and massaging there, his face full of more than a little apprehension. "He thinks he's a dog."

"Oh... well that makes sense," I mumble.

"It does?"

"Not really, but he *is* acting like a dog," I respond, because he is... his tail is even wagging.

"Uncle Black!"

Two boys come running up to Black. One has blond hair and looks kind of familiar. The other has darker hair, but they still look a lot alike. One thing is clear... *they adore their uncle.*

"Hey guys. What are my favorite monkeys up to?"

"We're not monkeys!" one of them denies, and the look on his face makes me grin. The way Black rubs his fingers over their heads, ruffling their hair and the clear look of love on his face makes me do more than smile. I'm pretty sure every female part inside of me melts.

"I want you two to meet someone. This is Addie. Addie these two bandits here are Terry and River," Black says pointing to each child as he says their name.

"Very nice to meet you both," I grin. They're beautiful kids and full of energy.

"What are you two doing here? Wasn't there school today?"

"We got sent home," River says.

"What did you do?" Black asks.

"Aw shucks, Uncle Black, it wasn't nothing," Terry chimes in.

"What kind of nothing?"

"River was trying to make Mr. Cradeson's hair look good. He was doing him a favor, man!"

"That's right I was!"

"What did you do?" Black asks again.

"I thought I told you two mongrels to go clean out Hamburger's doghouse?" Black's mom asks.

Doghouse?

Black's arm moves over my shoulders and gives me a squeeze.

"Aw Gramma! It smells!" River complains.

"Yeah man. Hamburger shits a lot!" Terry adds.

"Terry, what did I tell you about that mouth? You two quit your whining and get back to shoveling, before I tell your mama's what you did to Mr. Cradeson's hair," Ida Sue warns them.

"Oh crap! Let's go, Terry," River yells over his shoulder as he runs to the... there's a giant doghouse painted white with a red top that is about seven foot tall. I'd think it was a small barn or even a one horse stall, but it has an oval shaped opening with a slanted sign tacked above that says Hamburger. It looks like the Snoopy doghouse... on steroids.

"Orchid! What a pleasant surprise. I hope this means my son has got his head out of his ass."

"I—"

"Mom, try to be on your best behavior and not scare Addie off."

"Black try not to annoy your mother," Ida Sue responds and then she takes my hand and pulls me away from Black. "I've been meaning to call you. I was wondering how my little puppy is getting on?"

"He's good. Black and I left him at the groomers. I'll have to pick him up a little later—along with my car."

"I can't believe you didn't bring my little grand-dog with you."

"He and Black don't exactly get along..."

"Now there's an understatement. Well, come on in and you can tell me about that fancy restaurant you got a second interview for."

"How did... How did you know about that?"

"Why your daddy told me at the town council meeting yesterday."

"Since when do you go to town council meetings, Mom?" Black asks.

"I've been thinking of getting more involved in our community," Ida Sue shrugs.

"God help the community," Black mutters.

"Black Horn Lucas you are treading on some mighty thin water. Orchid honey, when you have kids make sure you teach them to respect you. I failed somehow in that endeavor," Ida Sue says, shaking her head as we reach the front door.

"Okay..." I answer quietly, looking back at Black. "Horn?" I mouth to him. He shakes his head and I'm quickly distracted by Ida Sue's next question to see what he does next.

"How do you feel about having children, Orchid?"

"I... well maybe someday..."

"You can't ever start too soon. Children need a sense of family and it's best you do that when you're younger."

"You're probably right, but there's things I want to achieve in my career first..."

"Careers are good too. In today's world you can totally do both. Don't you agree?"

"I... Yeah I suppose so," I answer, suddenly not sure what we're talking about.

"Mom—"

"Now, Black—"

"Just let it go. Tell me what my nephews did to Cradeson's hair piece."

"Oh that. Do you remember how Terry has always had a fondness for nature?" Ida Sue asks as we go through a back door and find ourselves in a huge kitchen with an even bigger farm table right in the center. It's so big it nearly swallows the room—though I guess with as many kids as Ida Sue has that you need a table that big for family gatherings. Black pulls out a chair at the table for me and I grin up at him and sit down. He looks nervous, so I squeeze his hand and he winks at me—but, he still looks tense.

"Yeah?"

"Well Terry was convinced old Cradeson would look better if his rug was painted up like that pet he brought back from the woods at the back of Magnolia's place."

Black laughs, but I'm not sure I understand.

"So, they painted the toupee?"

"They sure did. I got to admit it did look better. Old Cradeson's rug was a bright red and about four shades brighter than his real hair. He puts that thing on and I swear it looks like the top of his head is a massive head wound that's just bleeding profusely."

"Yikes."

"Sweetheart," Ida Sue says over the sound of a blender, because as soon as we got here, she began making something. "You don't know the half of it. It's something you really have to see to believe."

"Well what did they paint it? Brown like a rabbit?"

"Close. Black and white."

"Black and white? But... the only animal with those colors is a skunk... *Terry had a pet skunk!?!?*"

"He did until poor Magnolia managed to get him out of the house. They had to move. The landlord was none too happy. I hear he had to completely tear out Terry's room and remodel it."

"Oh my..."

"Needless to say Magnolia lost her security deposit."

"Uh... yeah. I can see why the boys were sent home."

"Oh that wasn't why," Ida Sue says, shaking her head.

"It wasn't?" Black asks.

"No. They got sent home after the boys started arguing because Terry thought River painted it wrong."

"Painted it wrong?"

"Yep and you know how Terry is when he wants to prove someone wrong."

"What did they do?" Black asks.

"Terry met River at recess and showed him how to trap a skunk."

"And they got one? That easy?"

"Well yes and no."

"Huh?" I ask, getting more confused by the moment.

"They'd been at it for a few days. They agreed to hide the toupee until they could compare the color schemes—so to speak. Cradeson thought he had just misplaced his hair, so he used his spare. The trap worked last night apparently, but not exactly how the boys planned."

"How did it work?" Black asks his mom.

"They caught a mama opossum in the box and carried it into the school so they could compare it up close."

"Oh no," I whisper giggling, because I finally understand.

Ida Sue comes over to me and puts an orange colored shake in front of me, and sits down grinning.

"I see you're getting the picture. The mama had twelve babies on its back and when it took off running down the hall and into the gym room the principal was not happy."

"I'm surprised they didn't get expelled from the school," Black laughs.

"Well, baby boy, they might have except for one small thing."

"What was that?" I ask still giggling. I take a drink of the shake. It's not bad—kind of tangy. I definitely taste peaches...I love peaches so I take another one.

"The principal was in the gym room knocking boots with his secretary. His very *married* secretary."

"Uh oh. My guess is the secretary's husband wouldn't like that," I murmur.

"Neither would the principal's wife," Black laughs.

"Exactly," Ida Sue agrees. "So, in exchange for discretion from our family and promises that the boys would keep the secret to themselves..." she shrugs. "They just get a couple of days off."

"This is really good Ida Sue. You're going to have to give me the recipe."

"Will do darlin'. The secret is to get the peaches as fresh as possible."

"Peaches! Mom! Damn it!"

"Black Horn!"

Black goes to grab my shake, but I keep it from him.

"What's going on?" I ask.

"Peaches are good for you," Ida Sue grumbles. "You just drink up honey. My boy has just lost his marbles."

"That's the same crap you gave Kayla to try and help get her knocked up," Black growls.

"To help her *what?*" I ask.

"Oh that's just foolish talk. Peaches just help with the blood flow."

"Then shouldn't he be drinking it?" I ask.

"Addie!"

"What? It was a simple question, *Black Horn*," I defend, hiding my smile behind the glass as I take another drink. "I mean I didn't go through medical school, but I think blood flow effects your dangly bits."

"You're so going to fit right in, Orchid," Ida Sue claims and I don't know why that makes me so happy, but it does. "It actually might. To be safe we could have him drink it too. But mainly it's just to help you be more receptive to his advances."

"Receptive?" I ask looking at Black and then at the straw and glass.

"You'll get turned on quicker so Black doesn't have to stay *up* for the party quite as long."

It's all I can do to keep from laughing—especially when Black starts cursing under his breath.

"I didn't know you had issues *lasting* for the party," I sigh.

"I don't!" he growls.

"That's a shame," I moan, purposely making my voice sound horribly sad.

"Damn it! I don't have a problem keeping it up! Jesus. I knew this was a bad idea. Just give me the drink and stop encouraging my mother!"

"Ida Sue?"

"Yeah, Orchid?"

"Drinking this drink is all healthy right?"

"Yep. It will just help make Black's workout a little easier. He's getting some years on him now, you know."

"He is a lot older," I answer with a sigh.

"Son of a bitch, Addie, don't encourage her."

I grin at Black and take a sip of the shake.

"*Christ,*" he groans. "Make me one too, Mom."

My eyes go round as Ida Sue gets up clapping her hands and practically giddy.

"Black—"

"You want to play, Princess? I'll show you just how *hard* I like to play," he says with a sly grin.

Oh boy.

Chapter Twenty-Five

BLACK

"I'm not sure it was a good idea to leave Addie alone with Mom," I grumble. I didn't want to leave her, Mom insisted and then Petal and Kayla came over followed by CC. I was overruled by women. Addie promised she was fine, but I don't think it was my imagination that she looked panicked.

"It wasn't," Blue mutters, rubbing the back of his neck.

"Asshole! You're the one that told me she'd be fine!"

"I lied. You can't be that stupid. You know leaving a woman —*any* woman alone with our mother is a bad idea, but you left her alone with the whole clan."

"Shit," I say with a sigh, knowing he's right.

"You're fucked," Blue adds helpfully.

"I hate you," I growl, because he's enjoying this way too much.

"If I were you, I'd hate me too. You left the womb first and obviously I stayed and got not only the good looks, but the brains too."

"You wish. Shit. I should go back and get Addie."

"Nah, it's too late," Blue says as he pulls into a parking spot outside the local shelter. It's not enough the asshole is busting my balls, he had to insist on driving too.

"Too late for what?"

"We're here. Besides, by the time you get back they'll be picking out wedding dresses."

"You're just being stupid now. Addie and I have only had one date."

"Have you seen how it works in our family? We get a look at the right woman and bam—there's no dating."

"Didn't work that way for Green."

"Green didn't get the right woman. He got a bad case of herpes."

I snort, because he's not exactly wrong. Green's ex is a class A bitch.

"What about you?" I ask my brother, interested on how he will answer since we're getting out of the car and getting ready to go in and see Meadow.

"Some of us aren't meant to have that one woman," he says not looking at me, his face stoic.

I let the matter drop, starting to think there's more to Blue's attraction to Meadow and their story than I'm aware of. I open the door to the shop and a bell above my head jingles.

"Just a minute!" I hear Meadow call from the back—her voice is somewhat muffled with barking dogs.

The front office smells amazingly clean. I would have thought it being a shelter it wouldn't. It looks sparkling though. Meadow has to clean constantly to get it looking this way I bet. There's a candle burning on the counter of the reception desk and the scent reminds me a little of Addie. Then again, everything reminds me of Addie these days.

I stand there waiting, Blue comes up to my side. I look at him through the corner of my eye and notice he looks... *angry*. His face is almost rigid, and he's staring straight ahead. There's so much tension in him, it makes me nervous. I elbow him.

"What?" he barks, his voice quiet, but rough and angry.

"Try and put a smile on your face, you'll scare Meadow to death. What's wrong with you?" I chastise.

He lets out a large troubled breath and looks down at the ground, rubbing the back of his neck again in agitation. "Old demons, I guess," he mumbles, not bothering to look up until Meadow comes in.

"Sorry about that. One of the new pups got out and—" Meadow comes bustling out of the back wiping her hands on a paper towel, looking pretty but frazzled. She's got long burnished copper colored hair that is a wave of tight small curls that reminds me of Julia Roberts in her younger days. Odd, but I remember Blue used to watch that damn movie about college kids trying to kill themselves to see if there was life after death all the time. I forget what it's called, but he never missed it. He always had a thing for Julia when we were younger.

Seems my brother has a type.

Meadow stops talking when she sees me and Blue standing there. Her dark brown eyes go round with shock. She is a pretty little thing. She probably doesn't stand about 5'4" barefooted, we tower over her, but I don't think that's what she is reacting to. Her gaze is centered on Blue. Her mouth falls open and she says nothing else for a moment, she just stares. I clear my throat trying to get her attention, because it seems her and Blue might be in a staring contest and neither one makes any moves to talk. Normally, I'd just watch and observe but I need to get back to Addie and see what her and the rest of the women are doing. It wouldn't surprise me if they're fitting Addie for a wedding dress. That bothers me, I won't lie—but, you would think it would panic me more than it is.

Maybe Blue is right....

"Black, Blue how... uh... nice to see you both."

"Is it?" Blue asks.

"What?" she asks, startled.

"Is it nice to see us?"

"I... Of course. What can I help you with?" she asks, avoiding his stare and I can't say as I blame her.

My brother is intense. There's more emotion behind his attraction to Meadow than I ever realized. I file that knowledge away for future reference.

"Nothing," Blue says, putting both his hands on the counter and leaning in towards Meadow. This time I jerk around to watch him too. "There's nothing you can help me with, Doe. It's my brother that's here to see you."

Doe? The nickname is interesting, but not quite as interesting as the way Meadow reacts to the name. She literally jumps. That's when I see anger flare in her eyes. You'd have to be blind to miss it. She immediately dismisses him, I can see it in the way she tightens her body and turns away from him. Blue's hands tighten into fists as he watches her. Oh there's definitely a big story here. I'm going to have to get my brother to open up... *somehow*.... Or get mom after him...

"What can I help you with Black?" she asks me, her voice still tight, but at least there's a smile on her face.

"I've lost my dog," I answer, trying to get my mind off my brother—who is currently gripping the side of the bar so tight it may break—and back on the reason I'm here.

"Oh no. When? We haven't had any new strays come in lately. Suzy Marlowe brought in six puppies that their dog had. She keeps doing that. I've given her coupons to get her dog fixed several times, but she never has. I just can't understand people. We're a no kill shelter, but we're running at capacity. I'm having trouble finding forever homes for the dogs we have. People just don't understand what an epidemic pet neglect is getting to be. We got over twenty cats alone brought in last week. It's sad..." she says, her voice soft and melodic—sweet even, but full of sadness. You can tell she really believes in her job and is bothered by the way things are. It's admirable. Then again, Meadow was always standing up for what she believed in. That's how she got involved with her ex-husband. She stayed way too sheltered. Everyone knew her ex was bad news, but she had no idea. There's lines on her face and maybe a few scars that makes me think maybe she does now.

"It is. This wouldn't be a stray and I really doubt he would have been brought in here. Honestly, he could have been brought to any shelter in Texas."

"Oh my..."

"Yeah. I'm hoping you can help me locate him. Like maybe there's a shelter pipeline you can send his picture through? Anything?"

"That's a lot of shelters, Black," she warns me. "You need to prepare yourself...."

"I have but Meadow, I have to try. My ex-girlfriend got rid of Kong, and I've got to at least try and find him."

She puts her hand over mine, as if to comfort me. Blue growls and she jumps, immediately taking her hand away.

"I'll do my best," she says, still not looking at Blue. "Do you have a picture of Kong? And anything that might help us locate him? I assume you didn't have a chip implanted, that would have made things so much easier.

"A chip?"

"Microchip. They're implanted rather easily in the pet and helps you to find them and several other uses," she says taking the picture I have of Kong.

"No... I guess I never thought about it. I never thought I'd need it. Kong was always with me..."

I feel so stupid. Hearing Meadow talk brings home just how hopeless this whole thing might be. I need to realize that I most likely will never see Kong again. The knowledge burns in my gut. I'm not a violent man but I could choke Linda cheerfully.

She's put me through hell. Am I really ready to trust Addie? Do I have a choice?

I don't think I do... the pull is just too strong.

Chapter Twenty-Six

ADDIE

"You're awful quiet," Black says as we're driving back to my car.

It's been a full day with his family. I enjoyed meeting them all. Petal even drove me to pick up Kong earlier. I was going to get my car and just go home from there, but Ida Sue said no. I've learned when Ida Sue says no... you go with it. I smile as I think of the mini-fit she threw just because I was going to go home. She demanded I not get my car—stating Black would take me to it later. Then, she demanded I get Kong and bring him to her. She said something about she needed time to bond with her grand-dog. His mom is a trip, but I love her. She made me stay for dinner even after Black got back. It was fun and exhausting. His family is hard to describe. They're like a tornado and hurricane of crazy all rolled into one big huge bundle.

"I'm just tired."

"Did my family..." he trails off like he doesn't know exactly what to say.

"What?"

"Freak you out?" he finally asks and I giggle.

"Well when your mother offered to take me wedding dress shopping, I was a little worried."

"Damn it. I knew she'd try something like that!" he growls and I bust out laughing.

"I was kidding! She didn't, I promise."

"Well there's a miracle," he says with a sigh.

"We've only just met, Black," I tell him shaking my head.

"I'm not sure that matters, Addie."

"To your mom? Of course it matters. I could be a horrible person."

"I think you're perfect," he responds and I feel all warm and flushed inside.

"You haven't seen me in a bad mood yet," I joke, feeling embarrassed.

"I don't know, the day you came in the office and slapped me, I think you were pretty pissed off."

"Well yeah, I thought you lied to me... No, I thought you were married," I correct myself.

"And you didn't like it," he says, taking his eyes off the road to glance at me briefly.

"I hated it," I admit with a stark honesty that makes me feel uncomfortable, but somehow I even find the courage to add, "I like you."

"I like you too, Addie."

"What are you going to do about it?" I ask, and maybe I'm playing with fire. I find I don't really care. I do like Black. I like everything about him and I even found myself loving his crazy family full of names like crayons for the boys and flowers for the girls. I even loved his mother. For all of Ida Sue's crazy flower child, down-home nonsense, she's loving, sweet, and she would do anything for her children. She made me feel part of a family—and I haven't felt that in a long time. So, I don't want to play games with Black. I don't want to beat around the bush.

I just want him.

"I could follow you home," he suggests and my heart speeds up.

"My father... he's not supposed to be home, but there's a chance he could show up early." I warn him, wishing things could just be simple. Especially when Black's face goes tight and I start to think this is where the evening ends.

"It's kind of dark," he says. I blink at the sharp turn of conversation.

"Yeah," I answer, puzzled.

"We're blocked by the groomers and your car really," he says and he gets a sneaky grin on his face that causes my body to tingle.

"I... you mean *here?* In the car?" I ask him.

"I need you, Addie. There's only so much a man can take," he says. I take a breath and then unlatch my seatbelt. He reaches down and hits the button pushing his seat back. Then, he lifts the fold down console between us. I swallow nervously and he grins. "I ever tell you I love the dresses you wear?" he asks.

"I don't think so," I tell him.

"Hold onto my shoulders," he orders. I do and I duck my head in close to his as he all but lifts me on his lap—scooting out so there's room for my knee against the door. Once I'm sitting in his lap, he wraps his hand around the back of my neck and pulls my mouth to his and kisses me deeply.

His tongue plays with my mouth, slowly teasing it and I get so lost in the things that he's doing that I don't even realize when he has the front of my dress unbuttoned.

"Are you sure about this?" I whisper, looking around, not wanting to be seen—but not wanting this to end either.

"We don't have to go all the way, Princess," he promises, as he slides my dress off my shoulders. He doesn't take it off my arms, he slides it down, until I can't actually move my arms much at all. When I try to move them down further, he doesn't let me.

"I like that you're at my mercy," he whispers, his eyes bright with a light that feels dirty and exciting—all at the same time. He unlatches my bra, letting my breasts free. "Damn, Addie," he rumbles. Bringing his hands up to cup underneath each breast, squeezing them in unison. He pulls on my nipples, stretching them and the sensation sweeps through me, causing me to grind against his lap.

He bends down to run his tongue around the darker skin surrounding my nipple. I moan as he gets so close to it, but never quite touching the nipple itself.

"You even taste like strawberries," he whispers against my skin, his hot breath adding another layer of torture.

"Suck on me," I gasp, shameless but needing his mouth; definitely needing more than he's giving me.

"Like this, Addie?" he groans and then he sucks my nipple hard in his mouth—so hard it's almost painful. His tongue helps press it to the roof of his mouth at the same time his hand slides inside my dress and pushes my panties to the side.

He releases my tit with a wet "plopping" noise. When he looks up at me, his face is so full of hunger and need, I'm almost afraid.

I don't want to disappoint him.

Then, all rational thought flees from my head.

His fingers tease against the bare lips of my pussy. I lean back as much as I can, sliding so he has better movement, giving him as much access as I can.

"I want to make you come for me, with nothing more than my hand. Can I do that, Addie?"

"What about you?" I ask, wanting to taste him, wanting his cock buried deep inside of me.

"Don't worry about me, my beautiful girl. You can tend to me later... on your knees," he promises. The images he awakes, cause a wave of moisture to slide out between the lips of my pussy. I know he can feel it—there's no way he couldn't. When I see his lips move into a wicked smile, he just confirms it. "Oh you like that don't you, Addie? You want to suck my cock, dirty girl?" he asks, and my hips thrust back and forth, needing that more than I can put voice to. "Fuck you're hot for me," he growls and then his fingers push between the lips of my pussy and I cry out, because I've needed this since our first date when he started a fire inside of me that's never stopped burning. "You need me to fuck you don't you, Addie?" he growls, as his finger dances around my throbbing clit, without actually touching it.

"Yes," I groan, trying to move my body so I can get his hand on my clit—but, he doesn't let me.

"Tell me the words, Addie. Tell me exactly what you want from me and then I'll let you come."

"Black," I whimper. "Stop torturing me."

"The words," he warns again and I let go of the last shield I had against him. I lay myself bare.

"I need you to make me come. Please, Black. I need you to make me come."

As if by magic his fingers graze against my clit, petting it and then pushing against it. Over and over he does those movements. My hips begin pushing up, craving even more. I can feel my climax. I know it's there, but I need more.

"That's my girl. Just feel it," Black urges and then his fingers thrust deep inside of me. I cry out at the invasion. It's been so long and two of his fingers are so tight inside of me, it's almost painful —even as wet as I am. "You like that?" he asks, bending down to suck on my breast again.

"Yes," I whimper, wishing I could tangle my hands in his hair. "I need more," I tell him.

At my words his fingers begin moving back and forth inside of me. I can hear the wet sound of my pussy sucking against his fingers. I tighten and clench on them, needing to come and riding his fingers shamelessly to get there.

"Can you feel it, Addie? Can you feel it?" he asks and I think I nod my head, but I can't be sure, I'm too far gone. "Your pussy is so slick and wet, and swollen in need. I want my dick in there, baby. I want to be buried deep inside of you and feel you taking every inch," he moans.

"I want that too," I gasp. Needing it more than I could ever tell him.

It's then he does something I wasn't expecting, something I didn't know *could* happen. He shifts his fingers somehow, so that they rake against my walls. Then he pulls them apart inside of me putting so much pressure and stretching me so much that I quake.

That's when he speeds up, fucking me harder, his fingers tunneling through me and out, only to thrust back in. Faster and harder. My body is moving thoughtlessly to his command now and I know when I shatter it will be beyond anything I've ever felt in my life. I'm right at the edge, waiting to go over and this time when his fingers thrust deeper, his thumb comes against my clit, raking it and pulling on it and I'm lost.

"Black!" I scream out his name as I come—shaking from the strength of my orgasm.

It takes a while for me to even realize where I am. I have to come back down to earth, because he definitely had me flying in the heavens. When I do, Black's kissing along the side of my face —not to excite me again, but helping me to calm. It's tender... sweet... *loving*.

"That's my girl. You're okay," he whispers and I smile.

"I'm better than okay," I tell him, my voice sounding so hoarse that I have to wonder just how loud I did scream out his name.

His lips move up to kiss my lips and I lean my whole body into him.

"Let's just stay here the rest of the night," I tell him, not wanting to leave him for a second.

"I got a better idea," he says. "How about I follow you home and you show me just how magical that mouth of yours can be?"

I look at him—really look at him.

But even after taking him all in—and there's a lot of yummy goodness to take in there—it's those crystal blue eyes and those firm lips, the way he stares down at me that captures my attention and makes me feel alive.

"I want you to. Remember, there's a chance..."

"If your Dad's home we're going to find that hotel room." My insides quiver at his announcement and the intensity in his stare. "You got any problems with that Addie, you need to tell me now. I wanted you before, but after what just happened between us baby, I have to have you. I'm dying here."

I think about Dad's house that is empty and *should* be empty until tomorrow evening. I think about spending the entire night alone with Black and that quiver turns into an all over body tremble, exciting me all over again.

"I don't have a problem with it," I whisper, my body still trembling.

Black leans down and kisses me on the lips. A soft kiss that leaves me leaning towards him when we pull apart.

"Thank God," he whispers. He slowly helps me get dressed and when I'm done he helps me out of the car and walks me to mine. Once there he unlocks my door and then leans down and kisses my eyelids.

"Soon, Princess Addie," he promises and I can feel his voice vibrate deep in my body.

Oh boy....

Chapter Twenty-Seven

BLACK

She's my downfall. I knew it, I saw it coming and I just didn't give a damn. She's the one. I'm falling just like Gray, White and Luka. I'd worry—it's not like my taste in women can be trusted—but, even my family loves Addie. I can't ignore the pull I feel towards her, I can't fight what she does to me and after the taste I just had, I don't even want to try. I'm claiming her and I'll worry about the rest later.

I'm following her car and I can literally taste her. My cock is throbbing imagining sliding inside of her. I'm as anxious as a young kid about to get laid for the first time. I'm tightening my fingers tighter and tighter on the steering wheel, each mile that goes by my anticipation amps up.

I spend the entire ride, praying her father didn't come home early. I need him to be gone. I have to have more of her. What we just shared was just a small taste and I want to get drunk on her.

When we turn up the street where Addie's father lives. That's when I hear the sirens. Then all at once cars are coming around me. I reach for my phone to call Tani and see what in the hell is going on, but it rings almost at the same time. I briefly look at the caller ID before I accept the call.

Luka.

"Luka why is the entire Mason Police Department swarming by me on Cotton Street?"

"Is Addie with you?"

"Shit, man there's a firetruck. What's going on?"

"Black! Is Addie with you?"

"What? No—"

"Son of a bitch!" Luka yells. Every cop instinct I have tells me something bad is going on.

"She's in the car in front of me. She's safe, now tell me what in the hell is going on?"

"The Mayor's house is on fire man. Call came in about five minutes ago."

"Christ," I swear.

"I'll be there in ten. I'm just dropping Petal and the kids off."

"Got it," I tell him hanging up even before I finish talking. I immediately try to call Addie.

"Hey, is someone impatient? I'm driving as fast as I can."

"Addie, honey. I need you to pull over."

"Black, we're almost at the house and I'd much rather we continue this in the privacy of my bedroom, not in a car on a street. A busy street. Did you see all the cops and fire trucks? I wonder what's going on? I see smoke up over the hill and I can smell—"

"Addie, pull over."

"Black—"

"Addie just do it!" I order, but it's too late.

As we start up the hill to her place the glow of the emergency vehicle lights shine like a beacon. Addie doesn't stop, instead she goes faster. She slams on her breaks when she gets to the road across from the house. She gets out of the car just as I pull up to a stop behind her car. I jump out and grab her barely in time to stop her from charging straight into a war zone.

"Oh my God! *What happened?!?!?*" she cries, fighting me to get away. I hold her tighter, bringing the side of her body against my front.

"Addie, baby. You can't go there. It's not safe. We have to wait until they get the blaze under control."

"Daddy's house," she says her voice miserable and full of anguish.

"I know, baby. I know," I tell her, holding her close.

"What could have happened?" she asks and I don't know what to say. "All my stuff was in there, Black."

"I know, baby. I know," I repeat, not knowing what else to say.

"Daddy's stuff was in there," she says tears falling down her face. She stops fighting me and leans into my body, letting me hold her and take her weight. She's not sobbing. I think it might be better if she was. Instead, it's just these tears falling from her eyes and her voice so sad and full of pain it hurts to hear.

"It will be okay, Addie."

"Pictures of my mother were in there, Black. I'll never get those back."

"Addie—"

"It won't be okay. The pictures are gone. My keepsakes of her are gone... it's not okay," she whispers so quietly that I can barely hear her over all the noise.

"It will be," I argue, trying to reassure her.

"It won't," she says and I give up trying to tell her it will. She's right. She's lost things she'll never get back.

"I'm losing my mother all over again, Black," she whimpers and that's when the sobs begin to tear through her. I pull her down onto the ground, sitting her in my lap and I just hold her, pulling her head close to my chest as she cries. I look out over the top of her head at the Mayor's mansion and the total devastation of the house is astounding.

"I've got you, Addie. I'm here with you. It will be okay."

I don't know if she hears me. She's crying too hard.

Chapter Twenty-Eight

ADDIE

"Are you okay, Dad?"

I wince as I ask. I know that I've asked the same question a million times. I can't seem to stop myself. He seems so despondent. He made it back from the next county over almost behind me and Black. I held his hand—while Black stood behind me, his hand on my shoulder. We watched the home disappear into the flames, we watched the firemen do their jobs and go above and beyond. We did all that together, in silence. But, in the end there was nothing but rubble. The house was a complete loss. I don't think I'd ever seen a home go that quickly.

Afterwards, Black tried to get me—and Dad—to go back to the Lucas farm to stay. I wanted to. I wanted to even after Dad turned him down, and there's a part of me that felt really guilty for that. In the end, Dad drove us to a hotel outside of Mason and we're here. We're here in a huge suite that seems to echo when we move and we're not really talking. I've had a shower. Dad's had a shower. He ordered room service but neither of us ate much. I wanted to change clothes, but then I remembered...

I don't have any.

I cried for a little while over that, alone in my room of the hotel, then I put on a robe and sent my clothes down to the laundry. Dad had a suitcase with him, so he's in casual clothes that are clean. Still, for some weird reason, I can smell the smoke. I can smell it in this clean room. It's as if it's haunting me. My eyes are itchy and dry from the smoke and the crying and just whatever else. I don't know anymore. I don't even know why I'm being so emotional. That house wasn't my house. It wasn't the house of my memories and it didn't mean much to me. Losing my mom's pictures and the keepsakes, that's what's killing me inside. I don't know about Dad. He lost those things and his new home—the home he chose to start over in. Maybe that's why the sadness is killing me inside. I may have resented him moving without telling me. I may have felt left out and hurt by him for the way he handled matters—but, I wanted him to be happy again. I wanted him to have his fresh start.

"I'm okay, Princess," he says, sounding distracted.

"Can I get you something? You didn't eat much. Maybe I can—"

"I'm fine, Addie-girl. It was just a house. I just hate that most of your Mom's pictures and things were in there."

"Most?" I ask, a small beacon of hope beginning to form inside of me.

"There's still more in storage. I haven't had time to move everything. What was in the house were some of my favorites, but not all."

"That's wonderful!" I almost squeal.

"It is. We'll be okay, sweetheart. I just need to regroup. I'll call the insurance company tomorrow and a realtor. We're going to need a new place to live and soon."

I flop down on the sofa across from the table where Dad is. It's probably a horrible time to bring it up, but I might as well—if I don't, I'll lose my nerve.

"Dad... I've been thinking... I kind of want to get my own place."

"In Houston or Dallas? I know you got a second interview with that restaurant."

"Oh," I kind of blush. I haven't talked with Black about my interview. Though, to be fair until earlier today he and I weren't exactly talking. If things had played out right, we'd have done a lot more than talk by now. I'm still nursing that disappointment too. "I was thinking here in Mason. I like this place..."

"You like that Lucas boy," he says shaking his head, though I think he smiles a little.

"I don't think you can call Black a boy at this point."

"He's younger than me and he's trying to get in my daughter's pants. I can call him boy."

"Fair enough," I mutter, avoiding my dad's eyes. I mean, what can I say to that? I can't really admit that his daughter wants Black to get in her pants.

Even if I do.

"You can't move into the apartments on North street," he says adamantly.

"Dad—"

"I mean it. There's a drug problem there that we're trying to clean up. I won't have my daughter living there."

"Well until I get a job, that may be all I can afford."

"We have money, Addie—"

"*You* have money. I'm living off what I squirreled away working in France."

"Addie—"

"You're not going to change my mind, Dad. This is something I need to do and I'm way too old to be still living off of my old man."

He looks at me for a minute and it's clear he's unhappy. The urge to give in is there, but I don't. He finally shakes his head.

"You're stubborn just like your mother. Determined to do everything on your own," he grumbles.

"I am, but if you wanted to buy me some clothes as a house-warming gift, *that* I wouldn't turn down," I try and joke.

I've just reminded him of our losses and the fire and I see it the minute his face changes. He pulls me into his arms and he holds me tight. I burrow my head down on his chest and hug him back. There's nothing quite like a hug from your dad, even when you're a grown woman.

"I'm so glad you weren't in that house, Addie. I could have lost you tonight. I was so scared when they called that you were there. I couldn't have gone on without you," he says, his voice shuddering with emotion and anguish.

"I'm okay, Dad."

"I love you, Princess," he whispers, kissing the top of my head.

"I love you, too."

I close my eyes and let him hold me. It wasn't how I imagined ending my evening, but I feel like I've somehow reconnected with my father and that was needed even more than I realized.

Chapter Twenty-Nine

BLACK

"Now this is a surprise! As long as you didn't come to slap me," I joke as Addie comes walking into the Sheriff's office.

It has been a week since the fire. Addie is slowly recovering, from the fire. The sadness left her eyes when she found some pictures of her mother in a storage container her dad had. She didn't really have an attachment to the house, which has made it easier. She's been living in a hotel with her father, while looking for an apartment—something I have also been doing. In fact, I have an appointment tomorrow to look at a place close to my cousin Faith's house.

I'd be lying if I didn't admit that I think about getting a place and asking Addie to crash there. I'm not talking anything permanent, at least not yet. That would probably be crazy. We've only had a few dates and a lot of kissing—kisses that are slowly turning my balls blue... and the memory that keeps haunting me of the one time I've made her come. The one time that's etched in my memory and replayed over and over in my head. My hand is getting to know my dick way too much—which is another reason to find that apartment sooner rather than later.

"Funny, you're so funny," Addie laughs. "Actually, I thought I might see if you're free for dinner. I have reason to celebrate."

"Well, I don't know, it's pretty hoppin' around this place," I joke. I'm on evening duty, and there's not another soul in here except for Georgia, the night dispatch. Normally, the office would be closed by now, but Luka implemented this new experimental program. One deputy will remain on duty through the night for emergencies. No one was really looking forward to it, but I volunteered. I don't have a family at home and so far Addie and I see each other through the day. We've not seen each other after the sun goes down since the night of the fire. That's bugging me. If it weren't for the kisses and the occasional second base she's letting me hit, I'd be worried she's about to put me in the friend zone.

"I can tell that you're real busy," she laughs. "What do you say, Black Horn?"

"Jesus, Addie."

She doesn't respond with words, but she giggles like a school girl. The sound makes me hard and makes me laugh at the same time.

"Explain to me how you can take a name I hate and make it sound sexy?"

"It's a gift. So, what about it? Are you down for dinner?"

"Down?" I shake my head, but she just rolls her eyes at me.

"I'd like dinner," I tell her pulling her into my arms. "But, I'd really love dessert."

"Me too," she says with a sigh that is full of regret. "I've been looking everywhere for a place of my own that I can afford, but that might be a non-issue soon."

"How so?"

"I aced my second interview! I've got a final callback next week. It's down between me and one other chef. They're going to have us cook an item off their menu and then choose which they like best in a blind taste test."

"Is this really how these places do these things? That seems more like a reality TV show to me."

"When you're paying what they're offering with hella' benefits, you can do anything you want. Especially since these kinds of positions are few and far between," Addie says, making me grin.

"Hella? You kids with your modern slang."

"I don't think that's modern slang, grandpa. So are you taking me to dinner?"

"Hey Georgia? I'm going to take my two-way with me and beeper. If you need me, I'm going to go out and grab a bite with Addie."

"Sounds good, Black. Hey Addie!"

"Hey Georgia," Addie responds with a wave.

I reluctantly let go of her, but still keep hold of her hand and we walk out.

"Where do you want to eat?"

"I was thinking the best place would be the diner. That way you're close to work if you're needed. I'm supposed to meet Petal in an hour anyway and it's close to her shop."

"Petal? What for?"

"Worried she's going to spill family secrets?" Addie asks as we cross the road to the diner.

"Let's just say that she might owe me one."

"Why? What did you do?"

"She's still bent out of shape because I picked out a dress for her to wear on a date."

"You picked out a dress..."

"It was a damn fine dress. Hell, I'd even say that they have Rain because of that dress."

"Whoa. It really must have been some dress."

"The kind men pay money to see a woman wear," I tell her as we walk into the diner. I don't bother to add that it was a hooker's dress. I doubt Addie would appreciate that fact.

"Maybe I should take you on my shopping spree."

"You're going shopping?"

"I have three outfits, Black. Don't tell me that you haven't noticed."

"I haven't really, every time I see you it's like seeing you for the first time," I croon, as I help her into her chair and then sit in the seat across from her.

"Oh that was just too much cheese on an empty stomach," she says shaking her head.

"Ouch," I laugh. "How did your apartment looking go today?"

"Not great. I know Dad doesn't want me to take a place on North—"

"Stop right there. Do you know how many times a day one of us gets called out there? There's no way you're living on North Street, Addie. That's final."

"Gee, Black, I don't remember asking for your permission," she snipes and boy have I pissed her off. I don't really care. She can get mad or she can get glad. There's no way she's going to live on North Street.

"I'm just stating a fact. I won't let it happen," I tell her plainly.

"I don't see how you can stop me."

"Try me, Princess. You'll be surprised what I am willing to do when it comes to you."

"Well, you can't do anything to me if one of us doesn't get our own place. I'd rather not make a habit of doing it in a car. That's not really who I am."

"You shouldn't knock it. I bet I could make you like it, Addie."

"You probably could, but the last thing I need is for my father to catch his little girl naked in the back of a cop car."

"What if I'm the naked one? You could wear another dress," I answer with a sly grin.

"Maybe we should change the subject since I need to go to Petal's soon and all this talk about what you would do to me is only adding to the frustration levels that I already have on high alert."

"Glad I'm not the only one," I mumble.

"Then you see the need for an apartment. I should talk to the landlord—"

"Absolutely not," I growl, putting my foot down.

"What are you two arguing about?" Addie's father asks coming up behind us. He looks at me skeptically. I see the annoyance in his face. He doesn't like me putting the moves on his little girl. I can respect that. When Addie and I have a daughter, I'll probably be the same way....

Holy shit. What did I just... Whoa.... Christ...

"Black was just telling me how he *forbids* me to get an apartment on North Street."

"Well look at that. Something Black Horn and I can agree on," the Mayor answers and I wince.

"Shit. Does everyone know that damn name now?"

Addie looks down at her lap guiltily, while her father laughs loudly, slapping me—a little too hard—on the shoulder.

"My daughter and I don't have secrets," he says, helping himself to the empty chair beside me.

"Have a seat," I grumble, seeing right quick that I'm not about to get a romantic dinner with Addie tonight.

"Nice of you to offer, Long Horn," the Mayor says flagging down a waitress.

"It's *Black* Horn," I correct him, while Addie is doing her best to not laugh. I look at her, my eyes telegraphing a promise of retribution later. The damn woman has the nerve to pucker her lips and pretend to kiss me.

I need to smack her ass... Damn, do I want to smack her ass...

I close my eyes and try thinking about Linda. That's the quickest way to make my dick go down and the last thing I need to do is adjust myself when I'm sitting beside Addie's father. He might try to unman me and I'm kind of partial to my balls—and the rest of me.

It's going to be a long night.

Chapter Thirty

ADDIE

"Addie I'll be back. I just want to run to the little girl's room and call Luka and make sure the kids haven't killed him yet," Petal says.

"Are you sure you're okay? We can stop—"

"Hush your mouth! I love shopping! I'm so glad you asked me to go with you. Luka helped make those kids, he can survive one evening with them."

"If you're sure," I laugh. I really like Petal. I like all of Black's family honestly, but Petal and I have hit it off somehow. She's like that BFF I always wanted in school and never had.

"Positive. When I get back I'm dragging your ass back to the lingerie."

"Petal—"

"No arguing! We're going to find something to knock my brother on his ass!"

"We'll talk about it when you come back," I tell her, laughing, but nervous too. I watch as she walks away and then I turn to look at the dresses.

Petal's bound and determined, but I'm nervous. I can't seem to help it. Every time I go out with Black, I have so much fun. We connect somehow and in a way I've never had before. But it's free and easy, joking, laughter... *friendship*. Since the fire, we've had a few intense moments, that never really panned out and we kiss... we kiss a lot... but it never seems to go past a boob grab. It has me frustrated, but it's also got me wondering. I mean, I know Black and I don't have our own places right now, so that is a drawback, but if he truly wanted me wouldn't he have made it happen before now? There's hotels, there's blankets under the stars, for Christ's sake. Instead, he volunteered to take a job that put him working nights.

What kind of man does that if he is interested in a woman?

Maybe I'm pushing myself where I'm not really wanted. Maybe Black only sees me as a friend, a girl to spend time with. The longer it goes the more worries I have.

"Oh that's a gorgeous dress!"

I look around to see a woman standing beside me. She's pretty, a little older than me, not by much—she might be Black's age. She's got jet black hair that falls into an asymmetrical bob around her face. She's got almost black eyes and a pale complexion that looks so delicate and girly that I'm jealous. My skin is golden tan and it takes a ton of lotion to even be passably soft. That's probably something else Black won't like...

"This?" I ask, finally looking down at the black velvet sheath dress I'm holding.

"I love it! If that's not made to drive a man insane, I don't know what is!"

"I guess so," I say, absently smiling. "It's velvet though, that makes it kind of thick and it will be hot in this Texas sun."

"Oh honey! That's not meant to wear in the sun. That's meant to wear to a man's house and tease him until he rips it off of you."

I wish.

"If only..." I mumble.

"You got man problems?"

"What? Oh... no. I don't think so. I'm not even sure I have a man," I laugh, though it's not a joyful laugh. I'm overrun by worries and I know the real cause. Tonight at dinner with Black he kissed me on the forehead before he left me alone. I mean, I know my dad was there, but if a man wants you surely they would do more than that? That got me thinking about how things have gone since I've known Black…

"Girl, if you don't know then chances are you don't."

"Well, I mean we just started dating."

"Oh that's different!" she says. "I'm Lynn by the way.

"Hi, I'm Addie."

"Nice to meet you Addie. Sorry if I'm bothering you. I just moved into the area and I don't know anyone. I guess all the alone time has me harassing people in the stores," she laughs.

"I'm always up to meeting new friends. I'm kind of new to the area myself."

"Well then! It must be fate we met!"

"Must be," I say with a smile.

"And you already found a man!"

"Yeah, I wasn't really looking for one…"

"Oh that's the best kind! I envy you. The beginning of a relationship is the best. It's all intense and heated. You can't keep your hands off each other. I miss that…" she says with a sigh.

"You do?"

"Yeah. I've been with my man forever. Sometimes we hate each other, but we always find our way back. He's the reason I moved here. He got a job here and like a crazy woman in love I agreed to follow him." she laughs.

"Wow. That must be love."

"It is. "How about you and your new man?"

"I'm not sure… I thought we were good, but now I'm wondering if he's still attracted to me." I feel like an idiot telling her that, but it's weighing heavily on my mind and it just slips out

"Ouch. Well, if you want my advice buy that dress. There's not a man alive that can see a woman he likes in that dress and not jump on it… *if you get what I'm saying.*"

"I think I do," I laugh.

I stare down at the dress, still unsure.

"Addie! Look who I found!"

My head jerks around to see Petal and her sister-in-law CC walking towards me.

"CC! What a great surprise, I thought you said you couldn't come when I mentioned it the other day!"

"No, if you remember that horn dog of a husband of mine said I couldn't, because we had the house to ourselves. But, I felt the need for a little girl time."

"How did you get away?"

"Hey you. I lied and told Gray there was a family emergency."

"Why didn't he come with you?"

"I ran to the bathroom and grabbed some tampons. He asked no questions after that," she says with a wink.

"What are you holding?" Petal asks.

"Oh. My new friend Lynn said it was the kind of dress a man would tear off..."

"Lynn?" her and CC ask in unison.

"Yeah, I—" I turn around but Lynn is gone. "Shoot, she's gone. I didn't mean to ignore her..."

"She probably just decided to finish her shopping," CC replies.

"Probably," I agree, still hating I forgot she was there for a minute.

"Whatever, that dress is a big fat no," Petal says yanking it out of my hand.

"What? Why?"

"Black is allergic to velvet," she says.

"Allergic? Like how?"

"It makes him break out in hives. No joke. His prom date wore a velvet dress once. It was bad."

"Didn't end well?" I ask.

"Girl, let's just say while most men were getting into panties, Black was getting admitted into the hospital."

"Oh shit."

"I have pictures, remind me to show you. His eyes swelled shut and they looked like two giant tomatoes on his head."

"Yikes."

"Exactly, so no velvet. Now you leave it to me and CC and we'll find you an outfit to make Black beg for mercy."

"I'm not sure that's possible. "Things have kind of cooled down lately," I tell them and boy is that an understatement.

"Oh, trust me it is," Petal giggles.

"Maybe not with me," I mutter.

They both look at me and I blush. I feel the heat rise on my face.

"You mean he's not been trying to hit it?" CC asks, disbelief clear on her face and I blush even more.

"When we had dinner together tonight... I mean my dad came by, but Black left early and when he did..."

"What?" they ask and I suddenly wish the floor would swallow me up.

"He kissed me on the forehead..."

"Oh snap," CC says and I know immediately she sees it as a bad sign too.

"Oh you two, just stop! Her dad was there for Christ's sake. Of course he's going to be reserved," Petal defends.

I like that she doesn't see it as a bad sign, but I find myself wanting her to know more so she can tell me it's all in my head too.

"He took a night shift job, Petal," I whisper, the one thing that has me worried the most.

"Honey that's just work, I mean—"

"He volunteered. He asked for night shift."

"Shit."

"Then, I'm right. Black doesn't want me. He sees me as someone to spend time with... a buddy."

"Bullshit. I've seen the way he looks at you," CC argues.

"Then why?" I ask.

"Who knows. Men get weird. If I had to guess, I'd say he's still gun shy from the breakup and fall out with Linda and he's resisting jumping into a relationship," Petal says.

"Maybe I should just move on. I don't want to have my heart broken over a man who is still hung up on his ex."

"He's not hung up on her. He hates her. She was toxic."

"I—"

"She was really toxic, Addie. So bad that she bled over into his work life and cost him a job he loved," Petal says quietly.

"A job he worked his ass off for," CC huffs.

"Exactly and if a man tangles with a woman and gets that burned, he has to be gun shy," Petal adds.

"So, what do I do?" I ask, feeling completely lost.

"You let us take control of your shopping, because we know Black's weaknesses."

"And we will use them against him," CC agrees.

"I don't know..."

"For his own good, Addie. He'll thank us for it," Petal adds, patting my hand. Maybe she's right, but I don't want to manipulate, Black.

"Thank us? Hell, he'll beg Addie for more," CC says with a wink.

I look at the two women in front of me. I take a deep breath and then I let it out.

"Addie it comes down to one thing," Petal tells me.

"What's that?"

"Do you want my brother or not?"

It's a simple question and one word literally screams inside my head.

"Yes..." I whisper.

"Then, we shop."

"We shop," I agree, and Petal and CC grin at me.

I hope I made the right decision.

Chapter Thirty-One

BLACK

"What do you mean, you rented out the place to someone else?" I growl into the phone. I loved the home close to Faith and Titan's. It was perfect and the rent was pretty reasonable, though to be honest I need to get out on my own. It's time I get my life back on track from the hurricane five destruction—also known as Linda.

"Don't you raise your voice to me, Black Lucas. I mean exactly what I said. I rented the place to a nice older couple who are moving here from Atlanta," Mrs. Hill announces.

"But why? When we spoke yesterday after the walk through you all but promised me the place," I ask, upset and frustrated. I was hoping to have a quiet dinner with Addie. We need to talk —*and hopefully a lot more than that.*

"I said if your references all panned out."

"What? Are you saying they didn't?"

"Like you didn't know," Mrs. Hill says making a clucking noise with her mouth that annoys me to no end.

"That's just it, I don't know. So why don't you explain it to me. I don't see how you couldn't rent it to me. You've known me my whole life, Mrs. Hill. I'm a cop for Christ's sake. It's not like I'm going to bring drugs and parties into the house every night."

"I realize we know each other and honestly I thought you were one of the good brothers of that clan."

"Hold up, one of the good brothers?"

"Yeah. Lord knows the devil is going to come calling one day for that brother, Cyan, of yours and I'm not too sure about Gray, though he seems to have calmed down since he met that woman."

"Are you telling me I didn't get the place because of what you think about my family?" I ask, pissed as hell.

"Of course not. I'm not that type of person. You didn't get the place because your last landlord said you left the place so bad he couldn't rent it out. He's in the middle of having to pay contractors to come fix it all."

"My last landlord..."

I got a sick feeling in my gut. I hold my head down, and close my eyes.

"He was a very nice gentleman too. I can't believe you left the place in such a mess."

"Mrs. Hill I haven't lived there in a year. My ex has. I was just there a few weeks ago and the place was fine."

"Well, it's not now. He sent me pictures. There's holes in the wall, stains on the carpet and it looked like you let the bathtub overflow and water stand on the floor for days. Poor man has to replace all of it. I don't know what kind of crazy parties you throw, but I refuse to let you do that to my home."

"*I haven't been there to throw a damn party!*" I growl.

"I will not have you talking to me like this!" she gasps.

"I—"

I stop because a dial tone rings in my ear.

My hand chokes up on the phone in anger and frustration.

"I don't want your damn place anyway, you old biddy!" I growl to no one, hitting the button to turn the phone off and tossing it on the bed.

"What's got your tits all twisted?"

I look up to see my mother standing in the doorway.

"I had the door closed for a reason, Mom."

"My house, I can open any door I want."

"Well, if I could manage to find another place to live that wouldn't be an issue."

"You really are Mr. Grumpy Drawers today aren't you?"

"Linda's at it again. Apparently she demolished my old apartment and because she was only sub-leasing and the original lease was in my name, I'm getting the fallout."

"That woman needs a come to Jesus moment...or the broad side of a 2x4 to knock some sense into her head."

"I think that's a hopeless cause," I mutter, falling back on the bed. I've barely been asleep and now I can feel a headache steadily building.

"Probably so. That gal was always one acorn short of a squirrel's mouthful."

"I don't understand why I didn't see it. I can't understand why my tastes are so far off when it comes to women," I moan—more to myself than my mother. I'm just disgusted with everything, the apartment, Linda, not being able to find Kong... but mostly myself. It's clear that I can't be trusted when it comes to women.

Mom sits down on the bed beside me, her hand on my leg and I sit back up. I almost feel like a kid again, but at least right now it's not in a bad way. Mom brings comfort and I might be a grown man, but right now comfort is appreciated.

"It's not your judgment that's off, son."

"Can't prove that by Linda. She was clearly a bad choice."

"Pfft... you didn't even like Linda, your willy did."

"Oh God, Mom."

"Well, it's true and you might as well own up to it. Men let their willies do the thinking way too often. Linda was what I like to call a cotton candy vacuum."

"A what?"

"She opens her legs and sucks a man inside—"

"Christ, I can't—"

"Don't go getting shy on me. It's true. She sucks a man inside and it's all sweet and light, so good a man thinks he found heaven."

"I may be an idiot, but I don't think I ever thought I found heaven with Linda."

"Well you might not have but the part that was in charge at the time did. There had to be a reason you kept her around, so are you going to be stupid enough now to deny it?"

"I guess not," I answer feeling dejected.

"But you know what happens to cotton candy when you take it out and try to keep it."

"I'm afraid to ask..."

"It dissolves into a shriveled mess that ants and other disgusting creatures infest."

"Jesus..."

"Speaking of which, did you ever get your willy checked after your break-up with that she-wolf?"

"I was never with Linda without protection, Mom."

"Some of that shit can eat through whatever it is you cover your crayon with boy."

"I got checked too, after I found out she was screwing my captain. My *crayon* is fine... just inherently stupid."

"Good to know—"

Before she can go off on another of her tangents the phone rings.

"Saved by the bell," I joke.

"Smart ass. I never spanked you enough as a kid."

"Hello," I answer, laughing at Mom.

"Hey Black," Addie says into the phone. My heart kicks against my chest. God I love her voice. She makes my palms sweaty and my heart race like I was a young kid. Right now, however, I feel panic. The conversation with Mom and Mrs. Hill comes back to me all at once and it feels like my skin is itching everywhere. What if I'm just letting my dick think for me again? I've got so much trouble coming at me from Linda, I really can't afford to be wrong with Addie...

"Hey, Addie. How are you?"

"I'm good. I was wondering if we're still on for tonight?"

Shit. I was hoping to take Addie to my new apartment. That's clearly not going to happen, but now I'm worried. I need to think about this before I make another mistake...

"I'm sorry Addie, I was just about to call you," I lie. "I got called into work tonight."

"What? I thought Luka gave you the night—"

"He was going to, but Daniel got sick and couldn't fill in. So I'm going to be busy."

"Oh... Well maybe I could meet you for dinner again?" she asks.

Guilt hits me, as well as indecision. My mother is standing now, looking down at me with a disgusted look on her face.

"I probably shouldn't tonight. I have a lot of paperwork to get through and things."

"Oh... Okay then," she says, sounding unsure.

Inside my head is screaming at me to stop pulling away, to stop sending Addie mixed signals and just admit what's going through my head.

"I'll call you tomorrow, Addie I promise," I tell her. If I take today to get my head straight, then I'll know what to do about Addie... I just need another day to think.

"Only if you want to. Goodbye, Black," she says and that sounds way too final. Panic of another sort hits me.

"Addie—" It's too late because she's disconnected.

"I swear I think you have shit for brains, Black Horn," Mom tells me as I put the phone down.

"I just—"

"You're just fucking up. I swear I thought I raised smarter boys but each one of you just seems to get dumber and dumber when it comes to women. Lord only knows the hell I'm going to face by the time Blue pulls his head out of his ass when it comes to Meadow. I thought you might have at least been a little smarter by this time. Do you care for Orchid or not?"

"Her name is Addie."

"Don't get smart with me, Black Horn. It might take some work, but I could manage to spank that ass of yours raw and not in the kinky way your brother seems to enjoy while thinking I don't know a thing about it."

"Uh—"

"I didn't stutter. Do you like my Orchid or not?"

"Well yeah, but what if—"

"There's no what if, son. If you like her, you have only one decision."

"What's that?" I ask.

"You are going to have to shit or get off the pot," she says matter-of-factly.

We stare at each other for a few minutes. I rub the back of my neck at the tension I feel there. Mom finally shakes her head at me, clearly disgusted and walks out of the room.

I fall back on the bed, feeling just as disgusted.

Mom's right in her oh so eloquent way. I'm either going to have to go all in, or walk away...

Chapter Thirty-Two

ADDIE

"I'm telling you, if you're going to get my son's head out of his ass, you're going to have to bring out the big guns," Ida Sue says and I throw my head back against the seat of my car and close my eyes. She's been calling me for days.

Days!

And that's because Black hasn't. I haven't heard from Black in a week. I gave him a week and I'm tired of waiting. I don't feel like I need to chase after Black. He's made his decision. I know he had the night off. Petal and Luka both told me.

He lied.

I don't have a lot of experience with men, but I know enough to know that if they lie to you to get out of a date, then you're not wanted. Which is fine. It really is. It hurt like hell the last week, but I think I'm getting better. The last thing I want to do is listen to Ida Sue and Petal on how to make Black jealous.

"I love you, Ida Sue, I truly do. But, I'm not going to try and get Black's attention and I'm definitely not going to try and make him jealous."

"You're not?" she asks, and her voice is strange, almost as if she's studying me. It makes me uncomfortable for a minute before I shrug it off as my imagination.

"Absolutely not. Besides he's the one that pushed me away, I doubt very seriously I could make him jealous."

"I see..."

"What do you see?" I ask, just as I see the realtor pull up.

"You're afraid. I can understand that, Orchid. I just thought you were made of stronger stuff."

"Now you're just being crazy! I'm not scared. I just refuse to throw myself at someone who doesn't want me!"

"I see," she says again and those two words are really beginning to piss me off.

"I don't think you do and just so you know I don't think your son deserves me. I'm a good person and a good woman! I don't need someone to make me feel like I'm not worth his time!"

"You should tell him that," she says helpfully, sounding cheerful.

"I might, but I doubt I will ever talk to him again. Now if you excuse me I need to go. The Realtor is standing out by the building waiting for me."

"You found a place?"

"Yeah over on North Street."

"Oh that's—"

"Don't bother telling me I shouldn't live there. There's not a lot of places in Mason, at least in my budget and I've heard it all from my own father. If I didn't listen to him, I don't see me listening to you."

"I wasn't going to say that dear."

"You weren't?" I asked and I'm surprised to say the least.

"No, of course not. Actually, I think it's good you're not willing to play games to get Black's attention. To be honest I'm not sure you two are well matched," she says and I should be glad she's given up, but instead I feel sick to my stomach.

"You don't?" I ask, and I really wish my voice would have come out stronger.

"No. You're obviously two very different people. Anyway! Happy apartment looking. I hope you find one you love!"

"I really don't care at this point. It will just be nice not to live in a hotel—especially since my dad has decided to build a new house."

"I understand that! Well bye, Orchid! I have some things I need to do."

Just like that she's gone. I stare at my phone in shock. Ida Sue has been calling me every day for almost a week and not just once a day, but sometimes as many as three times a day. When she's not calling, Petal or CC is. Heck even Luka and Gray called once. Then, almost as if by magic, Ida Sue just hangs up and gives up.

I don't get it.

It doesn't matter. She's finally realized what I have come to realize this week. There is no possible relationship between me and Black. It's time I move on.

And that starts with getting my own place.

Chapter Thirty-Three

ADDIE

"Damn it!"

"Is something wrong?"

I look around to see who asked the question, putting my hand on my forehead and using it as a visor over my eyes, because the sun is blinding me. I had forgotten how bright and *hot* the Texas sun is. I hear footsteps and finally a woman comes into view. It takes me a minute to place her—but, I finally recognize her as the woman I spoke to about the velvet dress.

"Oh! Hi," I say, flustered.

"Hi! Can't believe I ran into you again. It's a small world!"

"Well Mason is kind of small... Lynn right?"

"Yep and you're Addie, right?"

"Right," I laugh.

Lynn looks down at my car and immediately sees why I'm having such a bad day.

"Oh no. What happened?"

"I don't know. My tire was fine when I went into the store, but I came out and it's flat as a pancake. I called the garage, but it's early and they don't open for another hour. I hate to call Dad, but

I guess I'll have to. I just bought groceries and they'll ruin if I don't get them out of the heat."

"You don't have a spare?" Lynn asks and this is the part that makes me feel more like a dummy.

"Don't think less of me, but I doubt I could change a flat if my life depended on it. So much for being an adult and trying to stand on my own two feet. I mean I could try, but I think it might be safer to call the garage."

"Don't feel bad. I can't change them either. What about that guy you said you met? Couldn't he come help a damsel in distress out?"

"We're no longer dating," I announce, hating how the words make me feel. I see the surprise on her face. Why wouldn't she be? It wasn't that long ago I was shopping for clothes to impress the asshole.

"I'm sorry. Well, I tell you what. I can't help with the tire, but I can give you a ride to your house to put your groceries up and then to the garage if you want?"

I look at her. It's a kind offer. I don't really know her. I could and probably should call Petal or Ida Sue, but I don't trust them not to call Black. I don't want his help. I don't need him in my life —especially since he doesn't want to be there.

"I'm safe I promise, I can give you my name and you can google it. No outstanding warrants, no charges for kidnapping and torturing, or even murder," she jokes and I feel bad that she could see the indecision on my face.

"I'd really like a ride, Lynn."

"Great! I don't have any friends here yet and the apartment I thought I had rented was leased out from under me. I'm staying in a hotel and thinking about moving on down the road. I'm not sure Mason is for me."

"There's an apartment in my complex for rent. I just moved in actually. Of course, it's not in the best of neighborhoods. The rent is dirt cheap though."

"Dirt cheap—you said the magic words!" she laughs. "Here I'll help you get your groceries loaded in my car. I'm in the black Maxima over there."

"I'm so glad you came by when you did," I tell her, grabbing a couple of the bags with her and walking to her car.

"I like moving around early. It's the best part of the day," Lynn answers.

"I'm the same way," I laugh.

"See? We're meant to be friends!"

I smile at Lynn's words. They're more than welcomed. I need a friend...one away from Black, especially since he seems to be all I can think about.

Chapter Thirty-Four

BLACK

"Well you look like a sad sack of shit," Luka says coming in. It's barely eight in the morning and about the only thing stirring is the local store which is open practically 24/7 and me... and now Luka. Mason's streets don't usually get popping until nine or ten. Everything moves at a slower pace out here. It's completely different than Dallas... or hell anywhere else that I've been.

"No sleep will do that to you. You here to stay? If so I'll load my crap up and get out of here."

God. I'm sounding as grumpy as Luka used to before Petal came back into his life. I've got to snap out of it, the problem is I don't think I can. I haven't heard from Addie in a week. I've picked up the phone a million times to call her and every time I do a vision of Linda floats through my head and I lose my nerve. Luka is right. I am a sad sack of shit.

"I'm in for the day. I had to drop River off early at school for a field trip today."

"How is school and—"

"The principal is transferring. Word is your sister will be taking over the position."

"I bet that makes the secretary sad," I joke.

"She's gone. The board fired her last week—probably because the principal's wife was on the board."

"Probably. That wasn't his smartest move. I wonder where the horny bastard is transferring too?"

"Word is his wife kicked him out of the house so if I had to guess... I'd say out of the Mason district."

"Awe love. Fucked up as ever," I sigh. "I'm out of here."

"That's not love Black. What you had with Linda wasn't either," Luka says just as I'm about to open the door to leave.

"I didn't mean it was," I mumble, not turning around. I didn't really think that either. I'm fucked up, but I know I was never in love with Linda. "I know what I had with her and it was nowhere in that ballpark, Luka."

"What you had with Addie could have been," he cautions.

"Addie is better off without me, Luka."

"That's bullshit."

"Is it? My credit is ruined thanks to Linda and I can't even manage to rent a damn house. Here I am in my thirties and I'm living with my mother. Trust me, she can find better."

"You're rebuilding your credit. Maybe you need to look more long term than rentals."

"What are you saying?"

"There's a nice house for sale up above Petal and I. I know the owner and I'm sure Graves over at the bank would give you a loan. I know for a fact you have money squirreled away."

"I don't..."

"You don't know if you want to come back to Mason to stay."

"I'm not sure," I admit. "There's days... I miss being a detective."

"Then make up your mind and pursue that dream. But you need to make a move soon."

"Why?"

"Because life doesn't wait, brother. It just passes you by," Luka says pouring some coffee in a mug.

"I'll think on it," I tell him, opening the door and walking out into the sun. Damn, how did it get so bright so early. Today is going to be a scorcher.

"Hey, Black?"

"Yeah?"

"I had that chance to go to the FBI remember?"

"Yeah, I remember. Surprised the hell out of me you didn't go —if only for you and Petal to start over somewhere new with a clean slate."

"Family is important. Petal, River, Rain… they're happy here. Hell, I'm happy here and I like being in bed with my wife every night."

"Yeah well, my bed is empty so I'm not sure where this conversation is going."

"You do, you're just being stubborn."

"I told you whatever I started with Addie is over."

"Guess you don't care that she's over at the garage with Hank putting the moves on her then."

"Don't care a bit," I lie.

"That's good. Hank's got a way with the ladies, and I heard him asking her if she was single…"

"She is," I tell him, but I turn around, not wanting him to see my face. The words burn inside of me, too.

I walk out, but like a fool instead of going to my truck, I find my feet walking down the street toward CC's new garage… the one Hank Raymond manages.

Damn it.

Chapter Thirty-Five

ADDIE

I hold Kong in my lap as we wait in the small room at the back of the Mason Garage. I may need to talk to a vet about Kong. He shook in my lap and burrowed in my arms the entire ride over. He seems better now, but he's definitely acting peculiar.

Hank towed my car in, because he said the tire was beyond fixing, so I had Lynn drop me off here at the garage. I'm sure glad Lynn showed up when she did. She was going to stay, but she's got an interview on a job and I didn't want to hold her up. I don't know what I hit, but it made a long slit into the rubber—which means I'm getting two tires put on the back because Hank says it's bad to run a vehicle on mismatched tires. That's a hit to my already tight budget, but it can't be helped. Kong burrows his head in my hand and I grin down at the silly dog. It's hard to believe I'm already attached to him like I am. Probably because we are both cast offs from Black Lucas. *So much in common.*

"How you doin' darlin'?" Hank asks, sticking his head through the door. He's such a flirt. He's been flirting with me almost nonstop since I got here. It's been nice actually. It's good to know some men find me attractive, even if Black didn't.

I silently curse myself. I need to stop thinking so much about Black.

I need to stop dreaming about him too...

"I'm good. Are you almost finished?" I ask, hoping the answer is a resounding yes.

"Almost, come on out here, I want to show you something," he says.

I get up a little nervous. As much as he's been flirting, I'm a little worried at what he plans on showing me.

Kong whimpers in my arms and I hush him quietly. I don't want to let him run free in the garage—even on his leash. I just had him groomed and thanks to getting a couple of tires, I sure can't afford another one this quick.

"What is it?" I ask as we walk around my car.

"I think someone broke into your car."

"Why is that?" I ask.

"Well the doughnut tire in your trunk looks like it has a jagged slit torn into it."

"Could that have happened on the road too?" I ask, completely green about these things.

"Well, maybe. You're really not supposed to reuse these. Have you had to drive on the doughnut before?"

"Why do they call it a doughnut?" I ask, unable to stop myself. I want to giggle at the image of me driving a car with doughnuts for tires. I'd never go anywhere. I'd try to eat the tires.

"You're cute," Hank says, dismissing my question and I figure it's because he doesn't really know the answer, so I let it slide.

"It could have been driven like that. To be honest, Hank, I'm not sure. I bought the car used when I moved back from overseas."

"Just be careful. Your trunk lock has some scratches on it—like someone has picked it, or at least tried."

"I have no idea why they would have done that. Maybe that was from before I bought it," I tell him, frowning.

I've never noticed those tiny scratches before. I have to admit I never took the time to notice either though. So, it could be from before. Still, it seems weird that both my spare and my back tire would have similar slashes.

"Hey don't get that look, darlin'. It's probably nothing, but I wanted you to know, just in case. Luka told me you just moved into a rough part of the neighborhood."

"Jesus does everyone know what a person does around here?" I ask, frustrated.

"It's a small town and a girl as pretty as you? Let's just say everyone notices."

"Whatever. You're a born flirt, Hank," I laugh.

"Well when a woman looks like you do, that comes easy," he says with a wink. I watch as he continues tightening the lug nuts on my tire.

"If you'd quit flirting and actually work, the lady's car would have probably already been done."

My head jerks around to the garage bay door and I see Black. My body tightens with tension in reaction to seeing him. I increase my hold on Kong in response, and the puppy whimpers, reminding me he's there. I rub my chin on his head in apology and loosen my grip, but I don't take my eyes off of Black.

I'm not sure I can.

He looks good.... *Damn him.*

He's got stubble, that wasn't there before. I got to say that I liked him clean shaven but something about that scruffy look on him looks dangerous—and makes my insides heat. His hair is rumpled too and he's in his uniform—which is never a bad thing. His eyes are alight with anger and I can't really tell if it's directed at Hank or at me. I suspect a mixture of both of us.

"Black. Sheriff told me you'd probably be in," Hank says, making me blink.

"Luka's an asshole. What's wrong with her car?" he asks Hank, ignoring me.

"You could ask me, since you know... *It's my car,*" I respond, my voice having a bite to it. I'd like to take a bite out of Black, I'm just not sure if it would be completely out of anger.

"You're not the mechanic, are you?"

"I'm the owner, and since we're on the subject, why is it any business of yours?"

"I'm a law officer in this town."

"Is it a violation of some county ordinance to be broke down?" I ask, crossing my arms at my chest and narrowing my eyes.

"I was simply worried about a citizen of the county. That's all," he says, never quite looking at me.

"You forgot one thing."

"What's that?"

"I'm not a citizen of the county. I'm just visiting."

"I thought you were talking about staying here and being closer to your father?" he asks, and for a brief moment surprise replaces his stoic expression.

"I'm rethinking that decision. Some of the people in this town aren't *quite* what I thought they were."

"It's none of my business," he mutters.

"That's right and *neither* is my car."

"It's finished now if either of you are wondering. It might not be a bad thing for Black here to be aware, honey. Those tires just looked weird."

"They've just been sitting too long. I've not been home to drive my car much," I correct. "I had it in storage."

"Her name is Adelle!" Black says over top of my words and I sigh and roll my eyes heavenward.

Kong growls at Black then, trying to jump out of my hands to get to Black. Black takes one look at the dog and his eyes glow with anger.

"That damn dog needs a muzzle!"

"So do some people!" I growl back.

I have to get out of here.

I take my keys from Hank, luckily I paid him earlier when he told me I'd have to have two new tires at the least. I almost decided to put on four, but money is tight enough. My savings are going to run out pretty quick at this rate.

"Thanks Hank. I appreciate your help," I tell him, opening my car door now that he has lowered it from the jack.

"Anytime gorgeous."

I laugh as he winks at me. Then, I turn to look at Black. In my heart I'm begging him to apologize, take those few steps over here and tell me he's an asshole, or even kiss me...

I miss his kisses.

He does neither of those and I've got to quit wishing he would.

"Goodbye, Black," I tell him before getting into my car. I put Kong on the passenger side, making a mental note to get one of those totes you can buckle in for him to ride safely. Kong immediately goes to the window, his tiny feet slap up against the window and he snarls at Black as if he was tonight's meal. It's cute and well deserved so I give Kong a pat on his little head in thanks.

"I'll see you around, Addie," Black says and I'd like to think he sounds sad when he says it, but I'm probably just fooling myself.

"Not if I see you first," I mutter and slam the door. I don't bother looking at him as I back out of the garage.

Chapter Thirty-Six

BLACK

"Don't you need to get your butt out of bed before the sun goes down?" Mom asks, standing at my bedroom door and looking really pissed. In truth, she's been looking like that for the last two weeks.

"I just got in bed an hour ago," I mumble pulling a pillow over my head, to hide from the light she turned on, and from her. If I had my way, I'd hide from the world at this point.

"That's not my fault. You need to get your ass up and shave that chia pet off your face before you go into work."

"What's your problem?" I grumble sitting up.

"Did you really just ask me that?" Mom huffs and in hindsight that might not have been the best come back. I really need to learn to hold my mouth around my mom—at least until I move out.

"Mom—"

"Don't you Mom me. I don't think you're my blood. They switched you at the hospital. It's the only explanation."

"That's kind of hard to believe since Blue and I were born at the same time."

"Then it's clear Blue got the brains."

"Okay, Mom just come out with it."

"I'm ashamed to call you my son, Black Horn."

"Mom—"

"Don't you mom me, boy. You're dragging your dick in the dirt here and it's hurting my poor Orchid."

"I'd really rather you didn't talk about my dick. I don't see how I'm hurting Addie... *Addie,* that's her name by the way."

"*Orchid* is hurting, even if you're too dumb to realize it."

"How is it hurting her? We were just dating. It didn't get serious."

"Serious for a boy and serious for a girl are two different things my boy. Just because you didn't slam home base, doesn't mean it wasn't serious. A girl like Addie wouldn't let you even get past first base if she didn't care."

"What's with all the baseball talk?"

"Green called and we've been discussing his team. But that's not your business. Quit trying to change the subject," she says sitting down on the bed. "Don't you care about her?"

"I do," I admit and that nervous, almost painful feeling, hits me as I finally speak the words out loud. "I really do. Probably more than I have for any woman, including Linda but..."

"But, what?" Mom says, surprisingly somber.

"This mess with Linda hurt, Mom. It hurt my bank account, my life in general, it completely left me on my ass and moving back home. I'm too old for that, but here I am. And it hurt..."

"If you say your heart I swear I'm going to grab Green's bat and knock you up-side of the head."

So much for somber Mom...

"Hell no. I didn't have my heart involved... at least not deeply, but it was good enough that I would have stayed in it."

"Then you do have shit for brains."

"Not really. I never realized that there was more to relationships, at least not until I saw what Gray found with CC or White with Kayla. I saw how much that shit hurt both Petal and Luka and I never wanted that. Linda was..." I trail off because the words that come to mind sound as lame as I'm starting to feel.

"Out with it," Mom demands, never one to let me hide—let anyone hide, really.

"She was good enough... safe..."

"Because you didn't really have anything invested."

"Pretty much."

"Is that really all you want out of life? It took me years to find my Jansen. That means I'm not going to get to enjoy that love as long as I want. You need to stop being an idiot and claim your girl now. I know you boys don't think I know much, but I know one thing, Black," she says getting up.

"What's that?"

"If you don't try to fix this with that girl you'll regret it the rest of your life."

I just sit there and look at her. I think about what she says, but there's one fact that she's not understanding.

"Mom the last thing Addie needs saddled with is a man whose past includes a psycho ex, destroyed credit and who, at thirty-one, is living with his mother and can't even get an old battle axe to rent to him. Not to mention the landlord will probably sue me because Linda was sub-leasing under me, even if the court did make that arrangement. You take in the fact that I went from being a detective on a major police—"

"You can come up with excuses until the cows come home, boy. Not going to change the most important thing."

"What's that?" I ask, as Mom gets up off the bed. She walks toward the door, saying nothing. "Mom?"

She reaches down on my dresser to a paper I hadn't noticed before. Mom must have put it there while I was sleeping.

"Mr. Graves has given the okay for you to buy a house. All you have to do is find one."

"Mom I don't know—"

"It can be here or in Dallas, Black. You just need to get off your ass and decide what you want."

"Mom…"

"And if it's Orchid you might need to get a move on and get her out of that damn apartment she's living in."

"Apartment?"

"On North Street, dear. Which you would know if you had your head out of your ass," she says as she leaves.

Fuck!

Chapter Thirty-Seven

ADDIE

"I'm fine Dad. My doors are locked and I'm in for the rest of the night."

"I don't like you living there, Addie-girl."

"I believe you've mentioned that, Dad. But, I told you I'm fine here and I've got my doors locked and the chain latched too. I'm fine."

"Stubborn. You're just like your mother," he mutters.

"I'll take that as a compliment," I laugh.

"Goodnight, Princess."

"Night, Daddy."

I hang up the phone and sigh. The apartment is lonely tonight. Ida Sue came by earlier today and asked if she could keep Kong. She's really grown attached to the dog. I should probably just give him to her, but we've kind of bonded too. If I move to Houston or Dallas though, most apartment rentals there frown on pets and even if they don't... With my budget, I doubt I'd get lucky enough to live by a park where he could enjoy the day. I'd have to drive to it and my schedule will be grueling if I get the job.

I frown thinking about it. When I first came back from France

I was sure of what I wanted to do with the rest of my life. Coming to Mason... I thought I had found a home again, but now it's all weird. If Black and I aren't dating I feel weird hanging out with his family. Which pisses me off, because I liked his family. I'd like them even if I didn't like Black. The past couple of days I've wished I never met Black. That way I could have met Petal and the others naturally and...

And not feel empty because Black doesn't want to see me anymore.

"Open up, Addie!"

Speak of the devil...

My heartrate accelerates. I can feel it. I hate that excitement is the first thing I feel when I hear Black's voice. I think about ignoring him. I really should. It's been two weeks really since I've talked to him. I sit there in the chair and wait. Suits him right. He thinks he can just come over here on Friday night and think I'm home! He thinks he can ignore me then come over here and demand I answer the door!

Asshole! Black Horn Lucas is an asshole!

"I know you're in there, Addie! I see your car. Now open up the door!"

"I could be on a date, asshole!" I yell, before I even think about it. It's just the fact that he infuriates me so much!

"Well if you are, then you wouldn't be yelling at me!"

"You'd make a saint yell at you even during a holy communion with God!"

"What the hell does that mean?"

"I don't know! You've got me upset!"

"Open this damn door before I break it in!"

I stomp to the door. The big-face jerk probably would! He doesn't care that it would ruin my security deposit! Of course he doesn't! He doesn't care about anyone but his big fat self, with the pretty blue eyes and the heart of steel! No... steel is too nice and shiny it's more like lead or rusty iron!

"What do you want?" I complain, as I yank the door open.

"You need to pack your bags," he says, anger still locked on his face. It's those damn eyes that grab my attention though. I hate those eyes. They've been haunting me at night.

"I'm not packing! Asshole. It'd serve you right if I stabbed out your eyes with a fork!"

"My eyes...."

"A rusty fork! A rusty fork to match your rusty, full of iron heart!"

"Have you been drinking?"

"Not yet! But if I have to deal with you much longer, I probably will!"

"Addie, I have to get into work, just pack your damn bags and let's get out of here," he says, like he's trying to be reasonable—*like I'm the one being completely unreasonable.*

"I'm not packing my bags! Why should I pack my bags? What are you even doing here?" As I talk to him—more like yell—I'm stabbing him in the chest with my finger. I advance step by step, making him back up. When he gets off my door step and is finally on the grass of the small—miniscule really—yard, he refuses to move. That's a shame, I would have liked to have marched him all the way back to his mother's house.

"I told you not to move to these apartments," he says putting his hands on his hips and staring down at me.

"You..." I stop because, for a minute I don't quite connect. It takes me a minute before I realize what he's saying. *"You told me not to move to these apartments?!?!"*

"Exactly," he says calmly—way too calmly.

"You told me not to move into these apartments!" I scream... I think. I'm so mad that I'm not sure how loud I'm talking. Right now the only thing I'm sure of is that I want to kill him.

"Stop screaming at me like a banshee!" he orders, his voice louder but still cold, stoic and *unfeeling.*

In hindsight that is probably what breaks me. I have so many emotions where Black is concerned, but he can just stand there and be calm and cold and look at me with those eyes—eyes that are only saved because I don't have a fork in my hand—and it's like he doesn't have any emotional involvement.

"I hate you!"

"I'm getting that, but if you don't quiet down I'm going to have to run you in for causing a disturbance."

"A disturbance?"

"You're attracting your neighbors and disturbing their evening."

I don't look. Realistically, I know they're probably looking if they are home because the apartments are tiny and not exactly soundproof. The place is a dump really, but the nerve of Black!

I take a deep breath and try to wrap my head around what he's thinking.

"Why are you here?"

"I don't like you being here. These apartments are too dangerous. Your father should have never allowed you to move here, but since he failed to keep you under control, I'm here. Now pack your bags."

"You don't like me living here..." I whisper the words, mostly talking to myself. *"Failed to keep me under control..."*

"Addie—"

"Don't you dare," I warn him and this time my voice is quiet. *Deathly quiet.*

"What?" he asks and for a second I think I see a trace of emotion on his face. I don't know what it is, but it *better* be fear.

"Don't you dare come to my place and tell me that I need to pack up my shit... Shit, by the way, that I'm still *unpacking* because *you* don't think this place is safe for me. Don't you dare!"

"Princess, I just did. Now get your shit—"

"You're insane! You're completely insane. You're nobody to me, Black *Horn*! Nobody! Don't you get that?"

"I—"

"We dated—if you can even call it that and now we don't. Now it's over."

"We dated, Addie. We were a couple!" he growls, and finally —*finally* I'm getting emotion out of him. The problem is that now I just want to hit him—hit him until all the anger and hurt I feel towards him is gone.

"I don't think you can call it that, since you couldn't close the deal, buddy!"

That's when I hear the people around us. They're laughing now, not that I care. I'm about to go to jail—probably for the rest of my life—for killing a cop!

"Check it out brother!" I hear someone laughing. "Po-po couldn't get it up with the Chiquita!"

Black growls at the man, but his attention remains on me.

"I didn't *seal the deal* because there was never—"

"That's right! Never a place. Well now I have a place!"

"It's a shit place!" Black yells back.

"Well at least it's a place and I don't still live at home with my parents!" I scream back.

"Oh dude! That's cold. Copper still lives at home with his mamá!"

"Fuck!" Black barks. "Get your fucking clothes Princess or you won't like how I retaliate."

Then, before I even realize what I'm doing, I'm slamming my hands on his chest, slapping him, hard. I even try to bring my knee up and kick him, but he somehow blocks that.

"You asshole! You just kicked me to the curb without warning! You go weeks without talking to me and then you think you can just show up and order me out of my own apartment? You're crazy! You're an egotistical, self-centered, cold-hearted bastard!" I scream and with each insult I can think of I hit him. Black lets me hit him, he doesn't move. "You're a prick!" I scream.

"That does it," he growls. He lifts me up, kicking limbs and all and hefts me over his shoulder.

"What are you doing? You put me down this instant!"

Black walks to my door. It only takes him three strides, but each step bounces his powerful shoulder into my stomach. I thought he was taking me inside my apartment, but that doesn't happen he slams the door shut, and then he's walking to his car.

"What are you doing? I'm not going anywhere with you."

"You don't have a choice," he growls.

"This is America! Land of choices!" I argue. "And I choose for you to put me down and then *you* leave."

"That's not happening," he says opening the back door of his squad car.

"You can't just force me to go with you!" I argue. "That's kidnapping! You're breaking the law! You try it and I'll make a citizen's arrest and force Luka to book you!"

"It's not kidnapping," he says all but tossing me in the car. It takes me a minute to get up off my back and sit. When I do Black is completely blocking me, leaning down on the car door with his hand on the top of the car. He looks bigger somehow—and he was already huge. His face isn't stoic anymore either—it's full of anger. "I'm arresting you, Princess," he announces and he slams the door shut. I immediately scramble from the seat trying to open the door back up, but there's literally nothing to open the door with.... There's no handle... *there's nothing.* I look up as he gets into the front and there's a huge metal cage like thing blocking the front seats from the back. I shudder a little at the reason the car is made the way it is.

Who has been in here before me? What kind of person needs to be subdued in a car with doors that only open from the outside and essentially a cage between them and the law?

"Don't do this, Black! You can't arrest me! I've done nothing wrong!" I yell, a little bit of panic mixed in with the anger now. I'm claustrophobic and this small back seat with no way out is bringing that to the forefront.

"You assaulted a police officer, Princess," he says, starting the car. "That's against the law and it's my job to uphold it."

"You're insane," I whisper. "You're totally insane!"

Black ignores me and puts the car in drive, backing out of his parking spot.

I really am going to kill him!

Chapter Thirty-Eight

BLACK

She's driving me insane, that's the only excuse I have. Her dad will probably have me fired, but at least tonight she'll be safe... *even if it is locked up in the small holding cell at the department.*

I wince at the thought, then I remind myself that she drove me to it. This could have gone much easier if she had just cooperated the least little bit.

I make it to the department in record time. My head is roaring from the music I kept blasting to stop from hearing Addie rant at me. When I get out, I have every intention of allowing her to walk inside of her own freewill. I should have known Addie wouldn't be reasonable—even now.

"Get out," I tell her opening the door.

She looks at me and she's mad enough to spit nails. I'm lucky she doesn't have a weapon because if she did, I'm pretty sure I'd be a dead man.

She narrows her eyes—to the point she's squinting at me. Anger and hate are rolling off of her and I don't like it. The problem is, I don't have much of a say in it. I know I did this. I have no idea how to fix it. One thing my talk with mom and fighting with Addie has shown me.

I need her.

I feel more energized and alive right now than I've felt at any point in the last two weeks. I thought I was doing what was best for all parties involved, clearly that wasn't true. Addie has so much anger right now, that has to mean that she felt things for me... before I let my head get lost in the past.

I've let Linda fuck with so much. That needs to end now. *Jesus.* Mom was right.

Addie huffs...or maybe it was a snarl. But she gets out of the car, her gaze locked on my face and never leaving. Once she's standing, she puts her hands on her hips and looks at me as if she dares me to make a move. My dick is pushing against my pants. She wouldn't look so sure of herself if she knew how much I was dying to make a move... *and not just any move.* I want her. I want inside of her. I want her screaming out my name not in anger, but in passion. I want... Fuck, I want her. That's it in a nutshell.

I just want her.

"Oh look!" she says and an evil smile stretches those plump, juicy lips of hers. "My father is walking over here," she announces with delight. "He'll have your job for this."

She looks so satisfied and happy that I can't resist turning to look in the direction of the street. When I do, I don't see anything, I search but the streets are pretty empty. Mason isn't known for its nightlife. If there are people milling about they're usually at the bowling alley. It houses a movie theater, roller rink, arcade and several other stores all under one roof.

By the time I turn around, Addie is running out of the parking lot.

"You can't run from me, Addie," I warn her, fighting a grin. Then, she turns around, bends down and scoops up the dirt and gravel that cover the parking area and hurls it at me.

"Bastard!" she yells and then takes off running again.

The smile disappears and in its place is a burning desire to make Addie submit. I take off after her, it's not that hard, my strides are definitely bigger than hers. I wrap my arms around her, locking her body against mine.

"Got you," I tell her, my chin on her shoulder, my voice—full of victory—close to her ear.

That was probably a mistake. Addie rears her leg back connecting with my shin. Then her fingernails dig into my arm trying to loosen my hold. Her body squirms against my hard cock as she tries to break free. I was hard before, but damn it if she doesn't stop my cock is going to rip through my pants.

"Let me go, you pig!"

"You shouldn't call me that," I warn her, my anger starting to take over.

"You're right! It's an insult to pigs everywhere!" she yells and she brings her head back and tries to head-butt me. It wouldn't have worked, but I'm crouched over trying to talk in her ear—hoping to talk sense into her. The back of her head connects with the side of my face and damn if the woman doesn't have a hard head in more ways than one.

"Okay, that's it. I tried to be nice here," I growl.

"Nice!?!?! You arrested me for being in my own home!" she yells. I ignore her and use a little more force to hold her, turning her around and throwing her back over my shoulder. "You let me down right now Black!" she orders. I continue to ignore her. "I hate you. I'm going to have your job for this. When I'm done you won't ever—Ow!!" she cries out when I smack her on the ass. It does make her go still though. "You hit me! I can't believe you just—"

"Spanked your ass. Something your father obviously never did enough," I grumble.

"Oh my God! Help! Help!" she cries as I open the door to the department. "Help!"

"Black?" Tani gasps. She's filling in for the night dispatch because she had to be off today to take her daughter to the dentist. It's just as well. Tani is easier to contain.

"You have the night off, Tani."

"Black I don't think... *What are you doing?*"

"He's molesting me!" Addie cries and I roll my eyes heavenward.

"Oh for God's sake! Addie shut up," I growl.

"Black you do know... I mean that is the *mayor's* daughter..."

"That's right I am! Tani? Is that your name? Listen, you seem reasonable," Addie cries. "Call my father. Call the state police! Call the mental facility closest to Mason. I don't care who you call, just call *someone!*"

"Tani, go home. I have this handled," I instruct, as I walk to the hall, intent on getting to the back of the station, where the small holding cell is.

"If you're sure..." she says nervously.

"*If you're sure?!?!?*" Addie screeches. "What in the hell is wrong with you? Have you not heard of the sister code? You're helping him molest—"

"Damn it, look up the meaning of molest, this is not it!" I growl, tired of hearing that word.

"You spanked me!"

"To molest you I'd have to touch you sexually and I haven't—not yet, but if you don't quit screaming at me, Addie, so help me..." I warn her.

I slam the door, praying Tani takes my advice and leaves. The mayor probably will have my job, she doesn't need to get caught in the crossfire. I make it to the back room, slamming the door and let Addie down.

"You'll what," she dares me, pushing her hair out of her face and adjusting her clothes.

"I'll put something in your mouth so you can't scream."

"I'd like to see you try!"

"Really?" I ask her.

"Really!" she turns around looking around the room. I know immediately when she spots the holding cell. It's the exact moment I undo my pants....

Chapter Thirty-Nine

ADDIE

"What are you doing?" I screech the words. Good Lord the man is turning me into a banshee.

My eyes widen as I watch him undo the zipper on his pants—the belt already open.

"Finding something to stuff your mouth full," he growls. The words are coarse, his voice angry and my body reacts.

It just doesn't react in the way it should.

My nipples instantly grow taut. It's like someone dipped them in ice water. My body feels like electricity is pulsating through it, my breath seizes in my chest and it takes effort to exhale. I feel the insides of my thighs grow wet. If I knew I was going to deal with Black, I definitely would have put panties on under my yoga pants.

Maybe the sexy ones Petal and CC made me buy.

"Black you can't do this," I tell him, my voice quivering—much like the rest of me.

"Sure I can. Isn't that what you said? That I didn't *seal the deal?*"

I back away from him—more afraid of myself than him. Afraid I'll... *attack him.*

"Black..." I stumble back through the open door of the cell. Normally that would freak me out but I'm more worried about making a huge mistake with Black. It hurt when he pulled away before. If I do this—if I have sex with him—it will kill me when he leaves me alone again...

"Don't worry, Addie. I just plan on sealing the deal," he says and he begins following me.

He takes one step and kicks his shoe off, then the other. He takes another step and pulls his shirt off. I need to say something, *do something*. Instead, I stand there like an idiot with my mouth open. He's got a stark white t-shirt on and that comes off next. I watch as he uses his feet to pull on his socks and then step out of them. Somehow he even makes that look sexy—in a funny kind of way.

"Black, you need to think about this," I tell him, stalling for time as he stands at the door of the cell. He's blocking me from running away, but I don't really want to leave. In my head, I know I should, but my body isn't exactly listening. "You broke up with me," I remind him.

"Are you telling me you don't want me?" he asks and I know that this is it.

The moment of truth.

I might have stood a chance if he hadn't pushed his pants down. He reaches down and pulls them off. I try not to look... *there*... I also fail.

He's huge. Well, in my very limited experience he is... and broad...

Oh my, is he broad.

"Wow..." I whisper. I don't know if he hears me say it, but I can't stop myself. Sometimes you just have to appreciate greatness.

"You didn't answer, Addie. If you don't want me, you need to tell me now."

"I don't like you," I tell him, and he doesn't need to know I'm lying.

"Maybe. I probably deserve that. I know I've been an asshole. But, sweetheart, you're standing there licking your lips," he says as he reaches down. His hand wraps around his cock and I watch as he gives himself one long, slow stroke. I choke down the whimper that wants to escape.

"If I give in, Black, it doesn't have to mean anything."

"It will mean something, Addie."

"It doesn't have to," I repeat, not sure why I'm holding onto that... Maybe to give him an out... *Maybe to give myself one.*

"Take off your shirt," he orders.

"You don't play fair," I complain, but I lift my shirt over my head and toss it toward him. He catches it easily and throws it on the floor.

"No bra. I should spank your ass for running around like that," he says, his voice rumbling so deeply I can almost physically feel it.

"I'd like to point out I was in my home, relaxing... *alone.*"

"Ditch the smart mouth and give me those pants, Addie."

"How did I not know you were so bossy?" I mutter.

"You like it. I can tell by the way your nipples are swollen and hard."

"It's cold in here." I push my pants down, quickly fighting being embarrassed. Normally I wouldn't have the nerve to do this, but it helps that he keeps being a sarcastic ass.

"No panties either..."

"You like it. I can tell by the way your dick is swollen and hard," I tell him and throw them so they land on his face. He grabs them, pulls them away from his face and his eyes lock on me as he brings them back to his nose slowly and then inhales.

"That I do," he says with a sexy smirk on his face.

"You're such an asshole," I grumble.

"That mouth of yours needs something to keep it busy..." he says as he walks into the cell with me.

I tremble... but not from fear... I'm so turned on it's almost painful and damn it if I'm not licking my lips again.

Chapter Forty

BLACK

Fuck. To think I almost lost her because I was such an ass who was living in my past—or at least the harsh lessons from it. Everything about Addie is different, even when she's pissed she makes me want to laugh.

I'm an idiot.

But no more.

"I'm done dragging my dick in the dirt."

Addie looks up at me, one eyebrow going up in surprise that somehow is sexy as hell.

"You're impressive, Black, but I don't think that's possible... unless maybe you were crawling. Come to think of it, I think I'd like to see that."

"Maybe another time," I tell her, laughing—finally feeling my body ease. I didn't realize I said those words out loud, but whatever. All I can think right now, is that it's not too late. This is *not* a mistake. I feel that all the way to the soles of my feet.

Addie is not a mistake.

I walk over to her, it's just a few steps but it's steps that make me feel like I'm closer to... *my future.*

She talks a good game, but I can see the nervousness in her face she's trying to hide. I can also see the small trace of fear in her eyes. I put that there being stupid, and I have to be the one to erase it.

I put my hands on her shoulders lightly. She jumps, but her gaze stays trained on me.

"You're beautiful," I tell her, letting my hands slide slowly down her arms until they rest on her sides. My fingers play with the indentation of her ribs. You can't see them but the tips of my fingers can feel them. She's delicate, smaller, but she's trusting me, and that makes me feel even more possessive than I already was. She's a drug going straight to my head.

"You don't have to give me sweet talk, Black. I'm standing naked in a jail cell with you. I'm thinking I'm pretty much a sure thing," she jokes, those plump lips smiling at herself. I can't resist touching mine to them—just briefly, if I kiss her like I want, I will get distracted.

"I think it's pretty clear what an idiot I am, Addie. It's not sweet talk, darlin', it's the straight-up, God's honest truth."

"Oh... well, in that case," she smiles, a rose colored blush stealing over her face.

I let my hands move slowly to her hips, the soft skin there gives under my hold and I groan at the heat between us. This is unlike anything I've ever felt with a woman, but then, this is Addie and one thing is very clear to me.

She's special.

"So beautiful," I whisper again, my hands moving up to tease the soft skin on her neck, then out to let her hair slide though my fingers. "So fucking beautiful you haunt my dreams."

"Black..." she gasps as I run the pad of my finger against the wet, glossy lips that have my attention.

"I've lived with the memory of you coming with my fingers buried inside of you for what seems like forever now, Princess."

"Me too," she admits her warm breath like a caress on my finger.

"You don't understand, Addie, but I can make it clear to you," I tell her, my finger following an imaginary line down her chin and then under it to follow the gentle slope of her neck. She leans her head backwards, giving me access—so receptive to my wants and needs.

Perfection.

"You can?" she breathes.

"I've been remembering it every night while I'm lying in bed," I confess. I watch a shudder go through her body and I lean in to taste her throat, the salty skin exactly how I remember it. My hand moves to her breast, her nipple so hard it stabs against my palm. "I squeeze my cock and dream it's your mouth, Princess. Your mouth sliding down my shaft, your mouth making inch by inch of me disappear."

"Yes..." she whimpers, her body shuddering. I lean down and suck her nipple in my mouth. Her fingers tangle in my hair, trying to hold me to her body. I capture the hard little nub between my teeth and flick it with my tongue, increasing pressure so that there's more than a little pain—*but just enough.* "Black," she cries brokenly.

"I need your mouth, Addie. I've come so many times by my hand while memories of you crying out in climax haunt me. You owe me that sweet little mouth, Princess."

"Yes," she gasps.

I let go of her breast. And pull the chair from the small table around so it faces her and sit down. I spread my legs apart, allowing room for her body... *and wait.*

Maybe I'm a bastard. I should give her sweetness. I should be making love to her at home in a bed with flowers and candles and all of the shit women think of in their minds—but I can't. Not now. I've been waiting too long. I'm going to take her mouth in this jail cell and make her swallow my cock and then while my cock is still wet from her damn mouth I'm going to fuck her hard and raw.

It won't be romantic, but it will be real. It will be honest and I'll make sure it's exactly what she needs... *what we both need.*

"On your knees, Addie. Get on your knees for me and give me that mouth," I order, unable to hold back the hunger inside of me.

Chapter Forty-One
ADDIE

"On your knees, Addie. Get on your knees and give me that mouth."

My body feels alive with his harshly ordered words. Maybe I'm stupid, maybe I'm a million different other things to give into Black after everything between us.

I don't know.

All I know is that I want him... *I want this.*

I close the small distance between us, sliding down on my knees in front of him. He's beautiful like this. A man in control, holding power, his cock standing at attention, demanding more. My gaze stays on his face, on those expressive blue eyes as I curl my hand around his hardened shaft. He's so big and thick. My fingers meet, but not easily. I want to feel him inside of me, but I want this even more. As much as Black says he's been dreaming of it... so have I.

He's supposed to be the one in power here, the one demanding and in complete control, but as I flatten my tongue out and press against his balls, letting my hand carefully stroke his cock slowly... I feel powerful. Especially when his head falls back with a groan that is a mixture of satisfaction and need.

"Addie," he growls, as my tongue moves up and I lick my way up his shaft, following a hungry, pulsating vein that's throbbing in his cock. "Fuck, baby," he hisses, as our eyes meet. I curl my tongue against the head of his cock and now I groan as some of his pre-cum hits the tip of my tongue and I taste him for the first time.

Salty... Earthy... Man. *My man.* I'm determined to mark Black somehow, make it so he can't ever forget how good we are together. I need that, because I know in my heart I'll never be able to forget him... but then.... *I knew that from the beginning.*

"You taste good," I whisper and then I suck the head of his cock in my mouth, all while twisting my hand and giving him a half stroke, causing more pre-cum to trickle out.

"Jesus," he moans. "Stop toying with me, Addie. Take all of me in that mouth. Make my cock nice and wet so I can fuck you hard," he orders, his voice so hungry and dark my pussy spasms and I feel wetness against the insides of my thighs.

I'm getting as hungry as he is.

I pull his cock closer as I slide my mouth down his cock, sucking him inside. He fills my mouth completely, stretching me to make room for him. There's no way I'll be able to suck all of him.

He's just too big.

I use my hand at the base of his cock as a stopping place and I slide his cock in half-way and then slide back off. I do it a few times to get used to his length and girth.

"That's it baby," he growls. "Take my cock," he says and this time his voice is commanding.

I can feel his thigh push against my bare breasts, teasing my nipples. I'm so wet and needy that I'm pretty sure one touch from Black could send me over the edge. I started this to make him come, but I'm starting to think I can come just from sucking him off.

His hand wraps in my hair, pulling it tight and taking control. Maybe I should hate it but I'm trembling with hunger.

With him in control I take more of him. He hits the back of my throat and I fight to keep my gag reflex in check. A small sound escapes though and Black instantly begins pulling me off of him, knowing I hit my limit.

I brace myself on his leg with my free hand, letting him use me... *and loving every minute of it.* He slides me up and down his cock, and I suck him as hard as I can, letting my tongue paint his shaft, drinking in his essence as I go.

It feels as if he's getting harder. I don't know how that's possible—but it does seem like it. I know he can't be far off from coming and I want it. I want him to fill my mouth.

"That's it. You got my cock so wet, Princess," he praises and before I realize what he's doing he lifts me off his cock. I slide back, sitting on the floor, looking up at him in confusion. I bite my lips, desperate for the taste of him again.

"Why," I whine, so far gone, and desperate for him.

He stands up, his cock so wet and hard it looks dangerous. He leans down and picks me up, carrying me to the cot in the room. I lay back on it, horizontally. My feet still on the ground, legs spread apart in invitation.

"I can't come in that sweet mouth this time, Addie. I've got to get inside you. I'm so fucking tired of waiting. You're mine and before we're done here, you're going to know it."

"Please," I whimper, beyond trying to be cautious. The chance for that ended the minute clothes started flying off.

"I'm going to make you *feel* it. Every time you fucking walk, Princess. I want you to miss having me between your legs," he says, his voice hoarse.

He pulls my legs up to his hips and drags my body beyond the edge of the cot, so my ass is hanging off of it. My hands flail out to grab hold of the mattress to keep from falling. I don't need to worry because Black is holding me.

He's in complete control.

I feel his fingers, slide past the swollen lips of my pussy and my eyes close in thanks. If he just hits my clit, I know I will explode. He doesn't give me that, however. His fingers glide through my wetness, teasing my entrance, instead.

"You're so fucking wet for me, Addie. You're about ready to come just from sucking me off, aren't you Princess?"

"I would come," I huff. "If you'd quit torturing me."

He takes his fingers out of my pussy and my eyes open and I whimper, frustrated so much I could scream.

"Look at me, Addie," he barks and I do. What I see, nearly steals my breath. He's holding his fingers up—fingers slick with my juices. His gaze is locked on me as he licks them clean.

"Black..."

"Tastes like ... mine," he murmurs... and those words seem to have the power to mark my soul.

Then, so quickly it makes my head spin, he pulls back and I feel his cock at my entrance. The next second, he's pushing into me. I cry out as he tunnels inside, stretching me... *owning me.*

"Fuck... you're so tight, even now," he growls. I buck against him and he brings a hand down and smacks the top of my pussy. I shudder, my pussy clenching against his cock.

I wrap my legs tight around him, as he moves his hands to my ass, squeezing it and pulling me in deeper. He fucks me hard and I know he's about to come. I'm right there with him. I just need...

"Play with your tits, Addie. Pinch those nipples and pull on them. I want to watch you while I fill you with come," he orders.

Our gazes lock and I do exactly as he tells me. Our bodies work together, and in this moment it feels like we've merged together—so in sync are our movements.

"Black," I whisper because this feels bigger... bigger than just sex...

Bigger than anything I've ever experienced in my life.

"Watch me, Addie. Watch me as I come inside of you, sweetheart. Watch me."

I watch the minute his orgasm takes over. I see it all right there on his face and through it all we never break eye contact. And his climax triggers my own.

We come together and it feels...more.

More than I could ever describe.

It feels like... love.

Chapter Forty-Two
ADDIE

"You're beautiful, Addie. So damn beautiful," he groans in my ear.

My heartrate has barely slowed. My breathing is still ragged and my body feels so tired I'm not sure I ever want to move again. Sweat seems to be glistening on Black and me. He's holding me close, as if I'm something precious and I know in my heart it's a feeling I could get used to. Although, I'm still a little gun-shy wondering if Black is going to pull away again.

"You were worth the wait," I whisper into his chest, kissing his salty skin and closing my eyes wanting this to last a little longer.

We're lying on the cot together now. Our bodies exhausted. I can feel his fingers tangle into my hair as he holds me tight.

"This does change things," he whispers.

I don't really know how to respond. My head is a mess. So I murmur a, "Mmm..."

"Addie are you on the pill?" he asks and I fight back the urge to yell at him to stop. I want to enjoy this moment with him. I don't want reality to intrude.

If it does... I'll remember all the reasons this was probably a bad idea. I'll worry over the amount of emotions I feel for this man.

I'm not ready to face that.

"I'm protected and clean," I tell him, trying to be an adult, because it's too late not to.

"I am too, Addie, I swear."

I nod against his skin. Not wanting to ask any of the questions that bubble up in my mind. I close my eyes wanting to get lost in his touch again.

"I've been an idiot, Princess. But, I need you to know that I never meant to hurt you," he says and it sounds like those words were hard for him to say. Hearing him does help smooth over some of my fears and the hurt I had inside. *Some of it.*

"You did," I tell him with an honesty that is almost painful, but after what we just shared I need him to know that I don't want to play games.

"But you're going to give me a second chance," he says and just like that the sweetness in the moment is broke by him being an arrogant ass.

"And how can you be so sure?" I grumble, pushing him away and sliding off of the cot, needing some distance because I feel way too vulnerable. I concentrate on the anger he's arousing. That emotion seems safer around Black.

"Because of what we just shared," he says straightening his body and pulling the pillow under his head. He's staring at me... *leering really.* Suddenly, I feel entirely too naked.

"Sex? Lots of people have sex," I mumble, leaving the cell to find clothes. I start to put on my clothes, but that will take too long and I need to be shielded from him right now. I grab his shirt he threw down earlier, choosing it over the white t-shirt because it's longer. I button it up, his shirt hits me about mid-thigh and I feel better now that my body is covered.

"What we just had Addie, was not sex."

"It was and pretty good sex too," I joke.

"Addie, it wasn't just sex. I've had *'just sex'* and this was not that."

"Black—"

"Having sex with someone fucked my life up and nearly cost me you. That's not going to happen anymore. If you can't tell the difference between what we shared and just sex then I'll show you."

"I—"

"Come here, Addie."

"Black..." I'm turned on, but I'm scared. He's made a hundred and eighty degree turn and I'm scared to trust it. His face, his voice, his command, they're all completely serious. I want to trust it...

If I do will I regret it?

"Addie, I know you're scared. I know that's my fault. I know me going hot and cold has you gun shy, but I need you to believe in me here. I need you to believe in us."

"If you're playing with me Black, I swear I'll turn you from a stallion to a gelding," I warn him.

"Christ, you're starting to sound like my mother."

"She would have been more... *colorful*."

"Probably. Are you going to come here or what?"

"You really don't think we'll be bothered the rest of the night?"

"Tani would have locked up. The phone hasn't rung once. We're safe. Now come here. I have the urge to taste my woman."

"Taste?" I whisper, experiencing a whole body shiver.

"Come climb up on my face and let me taste you, Addie."

I'm holding onto the cell door, my heart telling me to jump, while my head is telling me to be cautious. I study his face and something inside of me melts. If it's a mistake, then at least I'll have the memories, because I know in my heart that this is a man I could love.

I take one step, still holding onto the door and I see him smile.

"That's my girl," he says and I like that. I like it a lot.

I want to be his girl.

I throw caution to the wind and walk toward him.

"Addie! Don't!" I jump when he yells, unexpectedly. "Close the door," he sighs.

I frown and look at him and then at the cell door that swung closed behind me.

"What?" I ask, but I turn, to open the door, just in case something is wrong.

"It locks when you shut it," Black moans, flopping back on the bed.

"Well open it, you have a key," I ask not understanding why he sounds so upset.

"Sure. Just get them out of my pants pocket," he says.

I look around the room and there's no clothes there, and that's when I get this sick feeling in the pit of my stomach.

"They're over by the desk..." I answer.

"Yeah," he answers, not sounding happy at all.

"That means..."

"We're locked in here until someone comes in."

"Until someone comes in...." I reply... "But, Black! I'm naked!"

"No, Addie. You have my shirt on, I'm naked."

"Oh crap," I whimper. I'm so deep into my misery I don't hear Black get up until he's behind me. He pulls my back against his chest and wraps his arms around me.

"I guess I'll just have to wear you," he says with his swiftly hardening cock pushing against my ass...

Chapter Forty-Three

BLACK

"Oh my God! How can you be horny at a time like this?" Addie cries and I have to laugh.

I kiss her shoulder and make my way up to her neck. Slowly, my hands move up her hips, dragging my shirt out of the way as I go. I want her naked again. Addie's body is perfection. She shouldn't have clothes on to hide it from me.

"You're here," I respond, because the answer is that simple. Sliding inside of Addie and watching her eyes as I took her settled something inside of me that I didn't even know was there. I finally understand what Gray and White meant when they said the world changes when you find the right woman.

Addie is the right woman.

"Last week, or heck even the week before that, you didn't care if I was around or not. I'm not sure I trust this change in you," she mutters and I hate it. I hate that I put this doubt in her head.

I hate that I haven't managed to fuck it out of her—but, I'll damn sure keep trying.

"I cared," I respond. "You just didn't see it. Now I'm trying to *show* you."

"Can you show me after you find a way to break us out of here."

"Addie, sweetheart, my skill is locking men up in jail—not getting them out."

She turns around to look at me, annoyance sparkling in those pretty eyes of hers. I wonder if I dropped to my knees and licked her sweet little pussy if hunger would show in them...

"Are you saying you can't pick the lock?"

"It's doubtful. It's just a holding cell, but it *is* for a jail. Still, it might be possible," I shrug.

"Oh thank God! What are you waiting for!?!?! Try it!" she urges, nearly jumping up and down with glee at the thought. It almost —*almost* makes me sad that I'm about to burst her bubble.

"Sure, Princess, just pass me something to pick the lock with," I joke, taking a step back.

"Sure, I... what can we use?" she asks, looking frantically around.

"My guess is nothing," I tell her, picking her up. She wraps her legs around me—my guess is because she's afraid she will fall. Then she uses her hands to slap my shoulders.

"What are you doing? We have to find something to pick the lock with!"

"Addie, there's nothing in here to pick a lock with," I assure her, walking her over to the small table. I put her down on it, and then pull up a chair to sit in front of her.

"You don't know that! How can you be sure?"

"Think for a minute, Addie."

"I can't think! Any minute now someone is going to come in here and find us together. They're going to take one look at me in your shirt and you...with your dick bouncing around like a giant neon kangaroo and—"

"Neon kangaroo? Have you seen many of those?"

"Oh stop! You know what I mean! They're going to know what we've been doing! In a jail cell!"

"We're probably not the first, if it makes you feel better," I tell her calmly, while taking her feet and placing each one on the arm of a chair.

"Of course it doesn't make me feel—Wait... *What do you mean we're not the first?*"

"I caught Luka buttoning his pants one morning with Petal coming out of the cell."

"I... do they do that often?" she asks, as I let my hand move up her legs, carefully.

"I have no idea."

"You don't?" she asks and her voice breaks off into a surprised moan as my fingers trace the lips from her pussy.

"I don't exactly keep up with when and where Luka puts his dick in my sister, Princess."

"I... Oh... I guess that makes sense," she mumbles, her body jerking as my fingers slide into her wet pussy.

"What are you doing?" she whimpers her body shuddering as I hold her open and expose her clit to the cool air.

"Being locked in the slammer makes me hungry."

"It does?"

"Hell yes, it does," I tell her, kissing the inside of her thigh. I let my teeth drag against her skin, teasing the tender area, so close to where I plan on burying my face but far enough away to tease her.

"I don't think we're supposed to be doing this, Black," she moans, but her fingers tangle into my hair, and she tries to pull my face deeper between her legs. I kiss all the way up, letting my tongue follow the path my teeth make, soothing her. I stop only when I get to the lips of her pussy. At first I don't touch her there. I just let her have my breath for a minute, knowing how hot it will feel against her skin.

"Don't think, Princess. Just feel..." I whisper, as I flatten my tongue and begin licking the lips of her pussy. She practically yanks my hair. I know what she wants, but I'm not ready to give it to her yet.

"Black... Stop toying with me!" she mumbles, her body trembling. She leans back, opening herself up to me.

"But, Addie, you're my favorite toy," I murmur, kissing her clit gently.

"Don't stop," she gasps.

"You don't have to worry about that," I murmur, sucking her clit into my mouth. I tease her like that, sucking, teasing it with my tongue, licking... anything I can do to make her wetter... to make her lose control.

"Promise," she orders doing her best to grind that sweet little cunt into my face.

This time when I suck on her clit and pull it into my mouth, I slide two fingers deep inside of her. She cries out and her hunger just feeds mine. "Make me come, Black. Please make me come," she orders, yelling out the words as she greedily rides my face trying to take over. I don't let her, but I'll make sure she comes... more than once.

I'll make sure she comes so hard that she never doubts that she's mine.

Chapter Forty-Four

ADDIE

"Hey Black you back here? The front office was empty." I hear a voice calling from the other room, but sounding ridiculously close to this one. He's coming back here—*whoever he is*... I don't think I've heard the voice before.

"Black! Wake up! Someone is coming!" I whisper-scream. I jump off of him, in a near panic.

I may have fallen asleep lying on top of him. It may have been the best night's sleep ever. *Whatever.*

I find his shirt and pull it on, trying to button the buttons furiously.

"Seriously Black! Wake up!"

This wasn't a whisper. This was a full-fledged panic yell. It works though, he's grumbling and jerks up, looking at me.

"Someone is coming!" I hiss.

I'm still trying to button up the shirt. I realize straight away that I might have missed a button or two because the end is all wonky, but I don't have time to go back and figure it out. Why can't my boyfriend wear t-shirts with cool band names on them or something?

Boyfriend....

"Looks like someone already came..." this deep voice behind me says and I close my eyes.

Shit. I'm going to have to turn around and I really don't want to. I haven't brushed my hair and I know I have some serious sex hair going on, because Black was none too gentle last night while feeding me his cock. That thought makes me shudder all over, but I try to tamp down the memories which spring to mind.

This is not the time to get excited and needy. Besides, after last night you would think I'd be good for at least a week—maybe even a month.

"Fuck," Black growls getting out of bed. I hold my head down as he stands up in his birthday suit. There's really no way to hide what we've been doing. At least Black grabs the pillow and hides his dick behind it. He walks over to me and kisses me briefly on the lips and despite the gravity of the situation, I lose myself for a minute and definitely kiss him back. When he pulls away my eyes slowly open. "Morning, beautiful," he whispers so quietly and solemnly that I feel the words in my soul, and despite standing in a jail cell with my hair frizzed up to the heavens in and a shirt I don't even have buttoned right and nothing else, and even despite doing a total I'm in hell version of the walk of shame, I *feel* beautiful. I feel cared for and for some reason that makes the panic leave me. Why feel shame about being with someone like Black? It wasn't sleazy or something I hope we don't repeat again—or a lot of agains.

"Morning," I whisper, smiling up at him. He stares at my face for a minute and slowly he smiles too. He's never looked sexier than he does right now. Tattoos everywhere, ruffled hair, sleepy blue eyes and a smile that is a mixture of humor and sex.

I love him.

I hide those words away in my brain. I'll think about them after we get out of here and I have a shower.

"What are you doing here?" Black grumbles, walking around me to stand between me and the man. I turn around, but with Black blocking my way, I can't really see.

"I just got in early this morning and I couldn't sleep. Mom sent me over to check on you."

"I'm fine," Black mutters. I'm distracted from the conversation, because I'm looking at Black's ass. I didn't fully appreciate it last night. I know one of his brother's is here. I've met Gray and Blue and Cyan. I wonder which one this is, but not enough to look away from Black's ass. Mostly I'm wondering if I can get away with touching his ass without his brother noticing.

I'm a slut. Who knew?

I almost want to giggle at the freedom I feel this morning and all because of a simple kiss by Black.

"She wanted me to ask you if you've pulled your head out of your ass yet, but from the looks of things, I can already tell the answer."

"You can kiss my ass," Black grumbles. It's funny that when he talks the muscles in his ass actually flex. I wonder if everyone's does that. I've never really noticed before.

"No thanks. Not on an empty stomach. Besides, it looks like someone else is already enjoying your ass. Hey there, little lady," Black's brother says, in a thick down home accent that is cute and sexy and if I wasn't obsessed with Black, could make a girl tingle.

I peek around Black's shoulder; I'm sure my face is blazing red, having been caught staring at Black's ass. When I look up my breath catches in my chest.

"Oh my God!" I screech. Black jerks, half turning around to look at me.

"What in the hell?" Black complains, but I'm busy ignoring him now. Fan girl mode has clearly stepped in.

"You're Green Lucas!" I yell, practically jumping up and down.

"That's me," he says, looking a little surprised, but grinning at me. A grin I'm all too familiar with because I've watched every game the man has been in and swooned with every postgame interview.

"You're Green Lucas!" I yell again, because I really can't believe it.

"Addie, what in the hell is going on with you?" Black demands, sounding really pissed.

I drag my eyes away from a laughing Green Lucas, to stare at Black like he's insane.

"That's Green Lucas!"

"Addie—"

"You didn't tell me Green Lucas was your brother, Black!"

"I sure as hell did."

I stop and think for a second. Hmm... "Okay! Well you did, but you didn't tell me that your Green Lucas was actually *the* Green Lucas, major league star and current record holder for the fastest pitch ever!"

"Christ, you like baseball?"

"Like it? Oh my God, Black, you don't *like* baseball. Baseball is part of life. You're American, you like baseball. That's it."

"Amen," Green laughs, while Black just sounds like an animal who has had his dinner disturbed.

"You broke Chapman's world record. That's the fastest pitch I've ever seen in my life!"

"You were there?" Green asked surprised.

"Sadly no. I was in France, but I saw it on the sporting reports, it made news even there. It was one-hundred and six miles per hour. Crazy!"

"Damn, I think I like you, Addie."

"I can't believe I'm talking to you!"

"You won't be much longer," Black growls. "Don't you have some place to be?" Black grumbles.

"Not really, Mom's doting on Allen, I'm free. I thought I might take you out to breakfast," Green says and then he turns around and winks at me. "And of course you too, Addie."

"I'd love—"

"We're busy!" Black yells over me and I look at him like he's crazy.

Because he is.

"No we're not," I argue.

"Yes we are," he growls back.

"How are we busy?"

"I'm taking you to the flea bag you rented and helping you pack up your shit."

"Why?"

"Because you're moving," Black says and he lets his pillow drop while he crosses his arms at his chest.

"I most certainly am not! And could you stop waving your dick around like— Oh hell, I don't know whatever waves!"

"You wave a kite," Green says helpfully and I turn around and try to clear the irritation off my face—because he is *Green Lucas.*

"Thank you," I smile.

"You're welcome, Addie." Green says, with a playful wink.

"Eyes on me, Addie," Black growls. "Green if you wink at my woman again, your baseball career will be over because I'll make sure you're not able to wink again," he adds and I gasp.

If you asked me why the fact that Black being jealous makes me quiver, when Green's wink didn't, I'd refuse to answer. But, I like that Black is jealous. I'll enjoy it... after I stop being pissed at him and make it very clear that I'm not moving.

"Jealousy... interesting, but I'm with Addie, you need to cover up your dick, bro."

"Give me my pants over there and I will," Black says. "Addie, you're moving."

"Black, I'm not," I argue back.

"You are," he growls yanking the pants that Green feeds through the bars and putting them on. He has to all but stuff his dick to the side to zip them up, because for some unknown reason he is hard again. I don't know how that's possible, but I'm guessing since his brother is a world record holder for the fastest pitch that Black could be the world's record holder for fastest erection.

Which sadly, even I admit, is more impressive.

"I'm not."

"Damn it, Addie those apartments aren't safe," Black says stubbornly, finally getting his pants zipped—although the outline of his cock pressing against them is *crystal* clear.

"Damn it, Black, I've been living in those apartments for two weeks while you ignored me and I'm fine!"

"You ignored her?" Green asks.

"He told me last night that he'd been dragging his dick in the dirt," I supply helpfully.

"*He* said that?" Green laughs.

"Several times," I confirm. "It's not the greatest thing to say to a woman when you want in her pants," I sigh.

"I can imagine," Green replies and he laughs harder this time. It's a good laugh. Inside I'm more than a little gleeful that I made Green Lucas laugh! I'm so posting that on all my social media when I get home. I don't care if that makes me a dork.

"You weren't complaining last night. In fact, you were begging for my dick and you weren't wearing pants."

"Oh my God!" I cry. "I can't believe you just said that!"

"Why not, it's the truth," he mumbles, having retrieved his keys from his pants pocket and opening the door, albeit having a little trouble because he's on the wrong side of the bars.

"We're not alone! You can't hold it over my head what we did last night, especially in front of your brother, who just happens to be *the* Green Lucas!"

"I can, especially when you seem to have forgotten about what we did last night and need to be reminded. And so help me God, Addie, if you refer to my brother as this god or rock star again, I'll—"

"But he is! He's the world record holder for—"

"That's it," Black yells. "I'm going to kill him," Black announces.

"Hey now, I prefer love not war. These hands, after all, are a national treasure," Green says and even with death threats he's still grinning. Of course, I don't think Black would actually kill Green. Still, he is kind of scary when he's being all surly.

"They are," I tell him. "You should be very careful with them."

Black lets out a growl that I'm pretty sure is what a grizzly bear does when he attacks.

"Will you stop that. I refuse to let you hurt Green. It's not his fault you're unreasonable."

"I'm not being unreasonable. I happen to care about you and I don't like you living in those apartments."

"Do you still live with your Mom?" I ask, deciding another train of logic might help me out here, because Black seems to have missed the train that says I'm a grown woman who makes my own decisions.

"Oh that's cold," Green says, pulling up a chair.

"It's true though," I shrug and Green nods.

"It is kind of sad," Green agrees.

"You still live at home too, asshole! And you're older than me!"

"I'm on the road all the time. It made more sense to invest in an RV so Allen always has the same surroundings. I want him to feel like he is at home—wherever we are."

"Oh that's very smart," I tell him, and it is. Plus, it shows he cares about his son. I mean, I always saw in the magazine articles on Green and the pieces in the sporting news that Green was proud of Allen and always put him first. Still, hearing this makes me respect him even more.

"I try," Green answers with a shrug, right before Black throws a pillow at him and hits him in the face.

"Will you keep your attention on *your* man. If you even remember I'm here, for Christ's sake."

"I remember you're here, you've yet to answer the question," I tell him, but inside I'm only hearing two words over and over and my heart is running away with me.

Your man... Your man... Your-freaking-man...

If I wasn't trying to prove a point here, I'm be squealing in joy.

"I do live at mom's, but for not much longer. I've got some things lined up," he says and I almost feel guilty for throwing that in his face because it's clear it upsets him.

"I liked being with you last night," I tell him. He doesn't

respond, but he does look a little confused, so I decide to clear it up for him. "I *really* liked it."

"Well, I could kind of tell," he says, but some of the anger leaves his face.

"Oh Lord, Addie, don't feed his ego," Green complains. Black's gaze never leaves my face but he flips Green off.

"I can't help it. It has to be said, Green. Your brother is *really* good between the sheets... or just a plain mattress I guess..."

"I really didn't want to know that, Addie, but thanks for telling me."

"You're welcome," I grin with him.

"Addie," Black says warningly.

I sigh out, exasperated. The man really is testing my patience.

"I was merely pointing out that I liked it so much that I want more of it—more of you."

"About damn time you figured that out," Black grumbles.

"Of course, I think I'd prefer you with duct tape on your mouth," I respond, sighing mournfully, because every time he opens his mouth this morning he's managing to piss me off.

"If I had duct tape on my mouth," he says and now he's grinning and his grin isn't like Green's. His grin is sexy and dirty and God how I love it. "I wouldn't be able to eat out that hot little snat—"

"Black!" I scream, taking the one step to him quickly and capping my hand over his mouth. "You can't say that word! Especially in front of your brother!"

Green and Black both laugh—although Black's laugh is more than a little muffled. He grabs my wrist carefully and pulls it away from his mouth.

"I'm pretty sure that Green's heard that word before, Addie."

"I have, even used it once or twice," Green agrees.

I roll my eyes at both of them.

"You can't use it in front of me, especially when it's *about* me."

"Why?"

"Because it's a horrible, disgusting word," I tell him.

"It is?" he asks, clearly shocked.

"It is," I confirm.

"You didn't mind it last night. In fact, I got the distinct impression that it turned you on."

"No it didn't," I kind of lie.

"Really? Because the way your pussy got so wet it ran down on my face, might call you a liar, sweetheart."

I hold my head down in mortification as Green laughs yet again. I liked his laugh, now I want to throw something at it. I've also decided I'm definitely not posting that I made Green laugh on my social media accounts.

"Okay, well *that* word is hot when your face is buried between my legs," I mutter, blushing as Green's laugh gets louder. "It's not hot when it's broad daylight and your brother is here."

"I'll make note," he says and he's grinning again and those damn eyes are shining too. I'm in over my head with Black Lucas.

"Anyways," I mutter, trying my best not to get distracted again, "we can't do that at your Mom's, and we're not trying it in a parking lot again."

"Parking lot?" Green asks, but I ignore him.

"And hopefully not a jail cell again."

"Holding cell," Black corrects me.

"Whatever. So, I'm keeping my apartment until something better comes along," I tell him, and I'm deadly serious.

"Then I'm moving in."

"I... *What?*"

"If you're going to insist on living there, I'm moving in."

"Black you can't just announce you're moving in with a girl, that's not the way this works," I argue, even if inside I want to go home and make room for him in my closet.

"It does, because I just did," he says, grabbing his white t-shirt and pulling it on.

"Black—"

I don't finish because he picks me up and cradles me against his chest. I wrap my arm around the back of his neck, afraid to fall even though his arm is at my back and another is under my legs. His fingers on my thigh feel as if they're branding me.

"Tell Green goodbye, Addie."

"I—"

"Green you're on duty until Luka comes in," Black yells back already leaving the room.

"I'm not a cop," Green argues.

"I hereby deputize you," Black says, not stopping.

"Bye, Green. Hope I get to see you again," I tell him, settling against Black, because I suddenly really don't want to fight anymore.

"Oh, I'm sure you will, Addie. Welcome to the family," he says and it feels like my entire body flushes. I don't respond, because I don't really know what to say to that, but I feel hope inside of me that he's right.

I lay my head down against Black's shoulder and sigh wistfully. I look up into Black's face and he's staring at me and that gaze is so heated it makes my toes curl. It erases every thought from my brain but one.

I love Black Lucas...

Chapter Forty-Five
ADDIE

"Is it bad that I don't want you to go," I mumble, still holding onto Black.

It's two deliciously wicked nights after being locked up with him at the police department. Black has pretty much moved in here and it's perfect, all but one small detail...

"I don't think Little Kong has that issue," Black sighs, looking over at the puppy who is currently sitting on the sofa, snarling–which is what he does most of the time when Black gets around me.

"He'll come around, you just need to pet him more," I giggle.

"The last time I pet him I almost lost a finger," Black grumbles and it makes me giggle more.

"He just doesn't like anyone else getting close to me," I try and defend.

"He's going to have to get used to it," Black murmurs, diving back in for another kiss.

Our lips softly slide against each other and I'm the first to sneak my tongue into his mouth, tasting him. That's nothing new, where Black is concerned I'm always greedy for more, and pushing the issue. Black on the other hand likes to tease and torture me, which is evident by the way he takes over the kiss and slows it down.

God, he's so good that I could do nothing but kiss him constantly for the rest of my life and be satisfied. Until Black, I never knew kisses existed that could transport you from time and space and cause you to just lose yourself, but he manages it and does it without trying.

"I don't want you to go," I whimper, when we part to drag air into our lungs.

"I don't want to either, sweetheart, but I have to. I talked to Luka earlier today though and he's working on getting me off night shift at least most nights."

"He is?" I ask, unable to keep the joy out of my voice, so I don't even try.

"Yeah. I may have to work a stray night here and there, but it won't be often. You could see for yourself, it's not like we're swamped at night."

"Good thing, since you couldn't have helped anyone the other night, being locked up. I still want to die when I think about the fact we were having sex in the back with the front door to the department unlocked," I mumble, laying my forehead against his chest and holding him again.

"That wasn't ideal, but it was still the best night of my life," he says and I smile as I look up at him.

"I thought you said last night was," I say with a smirk.

"Well, I said it while your mouth was wrapped around my cock, so it probably was. We may need to try that again—just to make sure."

"Horn dog," I laugh, but I'm already more than ready.

"Around you, I am. I really have to go now, though. Luka took Petal out of town to celebrate their anniversary so I need to be there to oversee things."

"Would it make a difference if I told you that if you stay a little longer I'll give you my mouth again?"

"Christ woman," he groans, kissing me hard and fast and

taking my mouth with a hunger that leaves me weak in the knees. When it's done, I'm wet, my nipples are hard and my lips are bruised.

"That's probably a no," I tell him shakily, "But it's the best no I've ever had in my life."

"It's a hold that thought until I get home," he grumbles as we walk to the front door. "What are you doing today?" he asks, opening the door.

"Job hunting since I lost out to the other guy for the job I wanted." I got word on it yesterday. It made me sad. The competitive person inside of me doesn't like losing out. I want to excel and exceed in everything I do—especially when it comes to my career. It will happen however; I won't give up.

"I'm sorry, Addie," Black says, his finger, brushing under my chin. The street lamp outside outlines his body and his eyes are shining brighter than the stars. He truly is beautiful... inside and out, but the "out" makes my mouth water.

"It's okay. I'll find something. I have a few leads.

"Are you still looking to leave Mason?"

"I'll probably have to, Black. Though hopefully I can find some place relatively close and commute."

"We've got a lot to figure out," he says, his face pensive.

"We do, but we'll get it," I assure him. I only know one thing. I'm not giving Black up if I don't have to. I really do love him—even if I haven't told him that yet.

"We will. You, keep the doors locked, please?"

"Will do, Boss," I joke.

"Good to hear you admit it," he cracks and I roll my eyes heavenward again.

"Whatever," I say, shaking my head.

He kisses me again, only this time a small touch on my lips.

"One more thing, Addie," he calls out as he opens his squad car door.

"What's that?" I ask, busy thinking that this hunk of a man is really warming *my* bed at night.

"We weren't just having sex. We were making love, sweetheart. You need to remember that."

He gets in his car, waving as he drives off. I have no idea if he realizes that his words just caused my heart rate to kick into overdrive.

I close the door once he drives out of sight, locking it and walking over to the couch, like I'm walking on clouds. I pull Kong up in my lap and sigh happily.

"I'm in love, Kong. I can't remember ever being this happy." Kong probably doesn't understand anything I just said, but he burrows his little head against my hand, begging for petting and I pet him. He's just as commanding as his former owner... but then again, Black wasn't ever Kong's owner. *Not this Kong.* I need to find his dog... I couldn't imagine how painful it is to love your dog and not be able to find it or even know what happened to him.

I look up as there's a knock at the door, then I smile. Black's forgotten something... or came back for my mouth. I put Kong down on the cushion and scramble over to the door, opening it without thinking. It's not Black's face at the door, though. It's Lynn's.

"Lynn," I gasp, feeling guilty because I forgot all about her after she gave me a ride to the garage.

"You got back together with your boyfriend," she says, her voice sounding more than a little *angry.*

"What? I... yeah, I did. How did you know?" I ask her and small alarm bells are going off in my head.

"I just saw him leave," she says and I frown.

Has she been watching my apartment?

"Listen Lynn, it's nice of you to come and check on me, but it's late and I have to check into some job offers since I lost the one at Amour Fou," I tell her, anxious for her to leave. For a minute, I allow myself to grieve at the thought of losing out on that job. I can cook circles around the guy they hired. He got the job because he's good, but also because he's a man. There's a big problem in my profession in that it can be sexist, thinking a man can command the kitchen and other chefs better than a woman. It's depressing, the big dummies. It's a stupid name for a restaurant anyway.

I pull my thoughts back over to Lynn. The look on her face makes hairs on the back of my neck stand up. She's more than angry. I don't even know her, so this reaction is making me back away from the door, in preparation of slamming it shut.

"He's turning you into his whore," she sneers and that's it.

"He's my boyfriend and I love him. I don't know you and you have no right to talk to me like that!"

"I can talk to you anyway I want. I thought you had some brains, that you could see through the way he was using you, but clearly I was wrong. He'll leave you, you know." Her words hurt, maybe because somewhere in the back of mind, I'm afraid he will. Before I can respond though she walks off. "You'll regret this, Addie. You'll regret it more than you ever dreamed possible," she warns and then gets in her vehicle.

I don't wait for her to drive off. I close the door and I lock it, making sure to lock the deadbolt too.

For some weird reason Kong is hiding behind a pillow, his body trembling and he's growling too, but not as ferociously as he does at Black. Apparently Lynn set off warning bells inside of him too. I walk over and pick him up, cuddling him to me.

"There, there. It's okay. The crazy lady is gone and we'll never see her again," I tell him and he licks he side of my face. "Ew... dog germs," I laugh, petting the mutt.

Inside I'm praying I'm right and I never see Lynn again.

Chapter Forty-Six

BLACK

"Addie, are you calling to tempt me with phone sex, because I'm still hard from thinking about your offer earlier."

"What offer?" she asks, sounding a little preoccupied.

"Giving me your mouth if I stayed home?" I remind her.

"Oh... hah... I kind of forgot about that," she whispers.

"You forget about it and my dick won't go down. Doesn't seem fair, Princess."

"I'll take care of him when you get home in the morning."

"I like the sound of that," I tell her, and hell, I do. How Addie can make that damn apartment of hers feel like a home, I don't know—but, she does. I've been happier there the last two days than I ever was in Dallas, and I thought I had everything I wanted there. Now that Addie is in my life, everything has changed.

"Me too," she murmurs in a sleepy sounding voice that does nothing to make my dick soften. I'm going to be doomed with a permanent hard-on the rest of the night.

"Were you needing something, sweetheart?" I ask, when the line goes silent for a minute.

"Oh! Yeah. Sorry I forgot, I was thinking about you and giving you—"

"Addie, please. I'm begging you here. If you talk about giving me head right now, I'm probably going to come in my damn pants and I'm not going to be able to hide that from Tani who is already in the office."

"She working again tonight?" Addie asks.

"Just two more nights, then the regular girl comes back."

"Oh... Okay."

"You were about to tell me you needed something? Besides my dick that is," I joke.

"You're so full of yourself," she laughs.

"I rather you be full of me, but..."

"Whatever. Anyway. Remember my friend, Lynn?"

"Lynn?" I question, because at first the name doesn't ring a bell.

"Yeah, she's the one I met when shopping with Petal and CC and then later, she was at the store when my tire went flat?"

"Oh, yeah. What about her?"

"It's the weirdest thing, Black. She showed up outside, just a minute or two after you left."

"She did? She knows where you live?"

"Well, yes, she drove me home with my groceries remember? And then later to Hank's."

"Yeah, sorry. What did she want?" I ask, because I can finally decipher what I heard in her voice earlier... *fear*.

"She was angry..."

"Angry? At you? What on earth for?"

"Because you were staying here I think. It was weird, Black. She was like... over the top. She said you were turning me into your whore, even."

"She what?" I growl.

"I told you. Something about it just felt completely wrong and..."

"And what, Addie?" I ask when she breaks off. I'm mad as hell right now and I got a feeling whatever she says is only going to make it worse.

"She said I'd live to regret letting you... Well, I don't know what she meant, but her face was so cold. It has me on edge. Do you think she's... dangerous?"

"I'm not sure. I do know she doesn't sound stable. I need you to promise me something, Addie."

"What's that?" she asks and I hate that I hear that fear leak into her voice again.

"Keep all the doors and windows locked, just to be safe."

"Already done. Black, I'm sure it's fine. She was extremely nice the other day. If she meant to cause me harm she had the chance then."

"I know, but it's better to be safe rather than sorry. You call me if she shows up again, and whatever you do, don't open the door for her."

"I won't. You sure are bossy," she complains, but I can tell that talking to me has eased her worries a little bit and I'm glad.

I'm worried enough for both of us.

Things happened in Dallas that have taught me never to take things at face value. I've never been witness to anything bad happening in Mason, but I don't want to take the chance that Addie would be the first.

"I'm only bossy because I care about you, sweetheart.

"I... care about you too, Black," she confesses quietly.

"I know baby. I'll see you soon. You call me if you need me, okay?"

"Okay," she agrees. "Talk to you later."

"Later, Addie."

I click off my cell with a bad feeling in the pit of my stomach. Feelings like this, is what kept me alive as a detective. I look at the clock and it's late, but Hank is probably still in the garage. I pick up my radio to call into Tani.

"Dispatch," she answers over the static.

"Tani, I'm on duty, but I'm headed over to Hank's. I need to talk to him about something that happened. If you call and can't get me on my radio, I have my cell."

"Got it, Black. It's quiet so far, so you're good."

"Thanks," I answer, distractedly. Intent only on talking to Hank and seeing exactly what he thought about her tire and spare tire. Addie downplayed the flat, but now I'm just wondering. It seems like an awful big coincidence that both her flat and her spare were cut and Lynn just happened to be waiting for her outside...

And if being a cop has taught me anything, it's to not believe in coincidences.

Chapter Forty-Seven

BLACK

"Hello? Yeah, he's right here, hang on."

I hear Addie's voice through a fog, I grumble and pull her body back to me. I can't sleep if she's not snuggled against me. I may have only been living here a couple of weeks but it's time enough to know that I love her—even if I've been an idiot and not told her yet—and I can't live without her. Shit, I'm addicted to her. There's nothing else I can say about it. I'm addicted and I don't even care. I may have had fear before I caved and let Addie in, but there's no fear now. There's only need and an excitement to see what each day brings.

"Black, it's for you," she mutters, settling back against me. I open my eyes only to find hers are still closed. I duck, but don't quite make it as she slaps the phone next to my ear.

"Ow, damn it, Addie," I grumble.

"Sorry," she mumbles, kissing my chest. I doubt she has any idea what she's sorry about. Her breathing instantly evens out and I know that she's asleep. I'm not sure she was ever awake in the first place.

"Hello," I say into the phone, taking the time to bend down and kiss the top of Addie's head.

"Black, can you meet me out at your mom's?"

"Mom's? Why?" I ask, looking over at the bedside clock. "Jesus, Luka it's only five in the morning and this is my day off."

"We had a break in last night," Luka says and now he has all of my attention.

"At the farm? Was mom hurt?" I ask, worrying about her. Green is still staying there and Jansen got back a couple of weeks ago, but still...

"Not at the farm. This is just where I brought Petal and the kids for the day so I could investigate. I don't want her to be alone."

"Petal? Was she—"

"It was her new shop. It was broken into and ransacked."

"Fuck," I growl. Petal worked hard to open up her own shop and she was so proud of it.

"Yeah, I was hoping you could meet me over here and we could go check out the shop together. I could use another set of eyes."

"Sounds good, give me ten to get dressed and I'll head on out that way."

"That works, I'll leave my Jeep here for Petal and the kids and get you to drive me back for my squad car afterwards."

"On my way. You just take care of Petal."

"I am, but when I find out who did this, I'm going to kill them."

"You're the sheriff, you can't. I'll do it for you," I tell him, but he's already hanging up.

"Christ," I growl. So much for wanting to wake Addie up slow and easy this morning.

"What's wrong?" Addie asks, wide awake now.

"Petal's shop was broken into last night. Sounds like they fucked the place up pretty bad. Luka is pissed."

"Oh my God. Is Petal okay?"

"Yeah, just upset. She's at Mom's. I'm going to head over there and pick Luka up and go look at the place."

"I'm coming with you," Addie says, jumping out of bed.

For a second, I can't think because all I see is tits and ass—more specifically, Addie's tits and ass and my brain turns to mush. Then, I shake it off and walk over to the closet to find some clothes.

"Princess, I love you but this is police work," I tell her buttoning up my jeans.

"Not to the shop, idiot. I meant to the farm. I'll stay with Petal there. She's my friend. I don't want her to be alone."

"Have you seen the farm? There's no way she'll be alone."

"Still, I want to be there," she says pulling a long pink sleeveless dress on. She looks beautiful and she hasn't even brushed her hair. "Unless," she says stopping abruptly and there's something on her face that I don't like and haven't seen there in the weeks that we've really been together. A look I do not like.

"Unless," I prompt her, wanting her to get out whatever is bothering her so I can squash it before I leave. I don't want anything coming between me and Addie.

"Unless you would rather I not go out to the farm. I mean it is your family and I—"

"And you're my girlfriend," I tell her walking over and taking hold of her arms to hold her still. "You're mine, Addie. What we have is not temporary. You're a part of my life. I don't want you to ever doubt that."

"Oh, but you—"

"It's just that you were up late last night emailing your resume out and making a list of restaurants to take your resume to today. I thought you might want to sleep in," I tell her and then another thought occurs to me. "Shit, sweetheart. I'm sorry. I won't be able to go into Houston with you today."

"That's okay. I'd rather be with your family. You and I can do Houston tomorrow or even the next day. It's not like I haven't been out of work this long. A little longer won't hurt me, besides since you've moved in you keep insisting on paying all the bills."

"It's my job as the man," I grumble, knowing if I'm not careful this will be another argument and I don't want to fight with Addie.

Though to be fair, we fuss a lot, but mostly because I love how we make up.

"Whatever. One day you need to become acquainted with the present century," she laughs. "Let me go brush my teeth and throw on some makeup and I'll be ready to go."

"If you're sure," I tell her, making sure.

"I'm sure, but if you want to run into the kitchen and make us some coffee to go, I'll love you forever," she says carelessly, having no idea what affect her words just had on me.

"Hey, Addie?" I yell, as she starts to leave the room.

She stops at the bathroom door, still kind of rubbing sleep out of her eyes.

"Yeah?"

"I love you, sweetheart."

Surprise comes over her face. My heart rattles in my chest wondering if I did the right thing. I'm not much on making myself vulnerable with a woman. I'd like to say it's because of my past with Linda and maybe part of it is, but really, I think it's because I'm a man and it's engrained in our DNA.

She takes off running and hits my body in seconds. I catch her immediately, lifting her up, causing her dress to rise up to her thighs. Happiness is alive on her face, warming me in places I didn't know were cold.

"I love you, Black Horn Lucas—with all of my heart," she cries, kissing my face. I say my face because she's kissing me everywhere, peppering me with them. Lips, nose, jaw, eyelids, eyebrows, forehead... I'm not sure she misses kissing me anywhere. "I love you," she says again.

I pull away to look at her, using my hand to brush her hair and stare into her eyes, which have tears spilling out of them.

"Hey, no crying."

"I'm just... happy," she says.

"I am too, sweetheart. You make me happy."

"You make me happy too," she says, crying harder.

"I love you, Addie Harrington."

"I love you, too!" she cries and for some reason the way she just repeats what I say makes me laugh.

"You going to be okay?" I ask her.

"Are you going to stop loving me?"

"Never," I vow.

"Then, I'm going to be okay," she says and I kiss her... simply because I have to.

"We better get going," I tell her after the kiss, sliding her down my body and enjoying every second of it.

"Yeah," she breathes.

"You need to go finish getting ready."

"Yeah," she breathes again, just looking at me.

"I'll go make coffee," I murmur, leaning down to kiss her on the forehead. She's just too damn cute.

"Yes, coffee," she says and the mere mention of the word seems to bring her out of her trance. "Hey Black," she calls just as I'm about to leave the room.

"Yeah, baby?"

"I'm not going to stop either, you know. Loving you, I mean."

"I'm counting on it, Princess. I'm counting on it," I tell her and despite the shit start to the day and worrying over Petal, I go make coffee feeling more content and happy than I thought was possible.

Chapter Forty-Eight

BLACK

"I'll kill them."

"Luka, calm down," I tell him, because having him go off right now is not good.

"Don't fucking tell me to calm down. Do you see this shit?"

I rub the back of my neck, anger and frustration running through me because I do see. The place is a complete mess. The windows have been busted out, the cords on the blow dryers have been cut in two, there are combs and brushes, picks and probably twenty other things scattered all over the floor that I don't know what they are. All of the shampoo, conditioner and hair supplies have been turned upside down and spilled out onto the floor. The dryer tops have had a hammer taken to them and are broken into pieces. I know it's a hammer because it's stuck in the wall right beside some of the holes it made before getting stuck. Nail polish bottles have been crushed and are littered on the floor in an enormous array of colors. All of that is bad enough, but it's the huge red spray painted words that bother me the most.

Addie wanted to come with me and Luka, but Petal and Mom convinced her to stay at the farm. After seeing this mess... I'm glad. I don't want her exposed to this.

WHORE.

The word is everywhere, plastered on the wall with glaring red paint.

"I. Will. Kill. Them."

"We have to find out who it is first, man."

"I'll find out and then... *I'll kill him.*"

"I don't think it's a him," I tell Luka, looking over the damage.

"You don't?"

"Nah. Look at this? This much rage and the objects they took the time to destroy. I think it was a woman. A man wouldn't be this... frenzied."

"I've seen men do some pretty intense shit," he argues and he's right... but...

"Maybe, but their attacks are usually more personal," I tell him and I walk over to the hammer and after putting on a plastic glove I pull it out of the wall. It takes a little effort, but not that much.

"I've seen that look on you before, Black. What are you thinking?"

"That I got this hammer out pretty easily, but it took a bit of effort... effort the average woman might not have managed."

"Fucking hell."

"Pretty much."

"Who could hate Petal so much to do this kind of thing? You know as well as I do that she's loved in this town."

"That I can't answer, but we'll get some answers, buddy. That I know."

"We better, because until we do I'm not letting my wife out of my sight and you know how happy that will make her."

I sigh, because I do. Petal is about as independent as they come.

"It might be a good idea if you keep an eye on Addie too," Luka says and I frown. I had already mentioned to him my thoughts on Lynn and the fact that Addie's tires were pretty much slashed according to Hank.

"You think Addie's tires and Petal's shop are related?" I ask.

"I don't think we can rule it out."

I nod in reply because he's right, we can't.

"Addie was just here last night, Luka. This could be directed at her and Petal just got caught in the crossfire."

"It's possible, but it doesn't matter," he says and I nod agreement.

"Family is family." I answer along with him.

"We can get Addie to give a description of this Lynn's car. She doesn't know her last name, but maybe we can track her through the vehicle," I suggest.

"It's worth a shot. In the meantime, do you still have any connections with the Dallas P.D.? I'd like to have their forensics team go through this place. Fingerprints or DNA sure would be nice."

"I've got a few who will still help me out. I'll put a call through to them."

"Thanks, Black. I truly appreciate your help with this."

"Man, it affects me too," I tell him, still not believing the damage I'm seeing.

Luka grunts, and when I glance at him the look on his face probably mirrors mine.

There's trouble here... a lot of trouble...

I just wish I knew the source.

Chapter Forty-Nine

BLACK

"So, we're saying it's another dead end?" Luka growls. Petal curls up further on his lap and pets his hair like she's trying to calm an animal. Hell maybe that works for Luka, I'm not about to ask.

"Not exactly. We know that there is no Black Maxima with Texas tags registered to a Lynn that fits the description that Addie gave," I tell him.

"That right there is enough to make me stand up and take notice," Luka responds.

"Me too," I tell him. I was concerned before, but now I'm flat out worried.

"So, we think the vandalism at my shop was linked to Addie and whoever this Lynn person is?" Petal asks.

"I think there's a very good possibility. Did you see her that day you were all shopping?" I ask, hoping she might know something more than Addie has been able to tell me.

"No, it was weird. I thought I saw someone walking away when we got there, but she was literally jogging into the crowd, so all I saw was her back."

"Shit."

"You know, just in case it hasn't occurred to you two big fancy coppers and all, this *could* be Linda," Petal murmurs, studying my face.

At the mere mention of Linda's name my gut feels like there's something sour in there and my body goes tense. Petal's not wrong. It's been months and months since I've heard a peep out of Linda, but she's crazy so you can't really go by that. Still, there are a few things that don't line up.

"Linda doesn't drive a Maxima," I tell her.

"People do trade cars in, you know," Petal says.

"But you said she had black hair," I argue. "Linda was and always has been a blonde. She spent a fortune to keep it just the right shade."

"Who does?" Addie says coming in at just the *wrong* time.

"Linda," Petal supplies helpfully.

Addie's face goes to mine. I can't read it, but I can tell she's not happy.

"Why are we discussing Linda?" she asks.

"Now, Addie, there's no need to be jealous," I tell her and from the hissing curse that comes out of her mouth—that was probably the wrong thing to say.

"Do I look like an idiot?" she asks, just as my mother comes in behind her.

Someone should just shoot me and put me out of my misery.

"Who called my Orchid an idiot?" Mom huffs.

"No one," I groan. "I was just telling her there was no need to be jealous over Linda."

"So, you're the idiot," Mom says cheerfully coming deeper inside and putting a huge basket on Luka's desk.

"Mom—"

"Don't you mom me. Why would you think my Orchid would be worried about that psycho chick?"

"What? Well, I didn't just..."

"Addie is as smart as they come. She knows the only problem she's liable to have in your relationship is the fact that *you* can be an idiot."

"Thank you, Ida Sue," Addie laughs, walking over to me.

"Anytime, dear," Mom says, taking off this big floppy hat she wears to hide from the sun. She's discovered the sun is making these dark spots show up on her skin and she doesn't like it. So she goes around in that hat all the time these days.

"What's in the basket, Mom?" Luka asks as Petal slides off his lap.

"Thought my boys would like some fried chicken and potato salad. Then, my little Orchid came over and decided you guys would like some apple tarter—"

"A tarte tatin," Addie corrects.

"Yeah that," Mom says waving her off and making me grin. "Whatever, it's good. So, we decided to bring you lunch."

"Is there enough for me?" Petal asks, already looking in the basket.

"Yep, we made plenty," Ida Sue says.

Addie leans down and kisses me.

"Hey, sweetheart," I murmur against her lips.

"Hey, dummy," she whispers, but she's smiling.

"I'm sorry, you just looked upset when Petal mentioned Linda's name."

"Of course I did. That witch tried to destroy your life and she gave away your dog. I don't want you to have to deal with her."

"Fair enough. I am an idiot, just ask my mom," I admit, sighing.

"Only about some things," Addie giggles. "Are you hungry?"

"Starved, but not for food," I murmur, pulling her into my lap. She links her arm around the back of my neck and curls into me.

"Why did we bring up that wart on the ass of humanity anyway?" Mom asks.

"Petal thinks that Linda could be behind the break in at the shop," Luka says, his mouth full as he takes a bite out of a chicken leg.

"You really think it's her?" Addie asks Petal.

"It's possible. In fact, I'm wondering if she's not your mysterious friend, Lynn."

"But, I thought you said Linda was a blonde?" Petal asks, looking up at me.

"She is, that's what I was telling—"

"There's no way the girl I saw walking away from you had *that* black of hair completely natural. Her skin tone was too different," Petal says, interrupting me.

"I've seen black hair with light skin tone," Luka mutters.

"You have?"

"Well before I met you. I see no one but you now, Lo'," Luka wisely says.

"That's a good one, honey," Petal laughs.

"I try."

"The point is, at least in this I'm an expert and I'm telling you that hair wasn't natural."

"That's crazy though. Why on earth would she come all the way down here to cause trouble. She has to know by now it's over. I would have thought getting rid of your dog was her final insult," Addie asks, shaking her head.

"You're acting like Linda is normal," Petal argues. "She's nutty as a fruitcake," she mutters. Dishing up a paper plate of food.

"Petal's right about that one, dear. If brains were gasoline, some folks couldn't run a piss ant's go-kart one lap around a watermelon seed."

"It would have been helpful if you guys would have told me how you felt while I was living with the woman. Could have saved me a hell of a lot of trouble," I growl.

"You were thinking with the wrong head at the time," Mom answers and Addie's body starts shaking against me.

"You laughing at me, Princess?"

"You can punish me for it later," she murmurs and just like that, all of the irritation that comes with talking about Linda disappears.

"Count on it," I tell her and she leans in and kisses me.

"Holy shit, Addie! This is good," Petal murmurs over a mouthful of Addie's dessert.

Addie blushes.

"I'm glad you like it," she answers, shyly.

"Well don't hog it, give me some," I tell her.

Addie slides off my lap, her fingers playing in my hair.

"I'll get you some."

"Okay, sweetheart," I tell her, unable to take my eyes off of her. I don't know how it's possible, but I love her more every day. When she grins at me I can see the same feeling on her face. I may have made a hell of a wrong turn with Linda, but Addie... Addie is my forever.

Chapter Fifty

ADDIE

"I got a call back!" I yell excitedly into the phone.

"What?" Black says, clearly startled.

"Amour Fou," called! The guy they hired didn't work out. They want me to come in and cook tomorrow! Isn't that great?"

"Yeah, it's good, sweetheart."

"Well don't sound so excited," I complain.

"I am... it's just..."

"Black?" I ask, hearing something in his voice that makes me nervous.

"We haven't really discussed it, Addie."

"Discussed what?"

"I should have realized that it's what you wanted. For some reason I just didn't," he says and I'm more confused than ever.

"Maybe you could explain to me what I want? Because, sweetheart you have me confused as heck."

"To leave Mason and move back to the city," he says and I get this funny feeling in my stomach.

It sounds silly, but I haven't really thought of it in those terms before. I've grown to love Mason. Heck, now that Black is there I even love living in the apartment. I love being close to his family and my dad. It feels like home and I haven't had a home in a long time. Still, I want to be a chef. I love being in a kitchen and feeling the accomplishment of giving people food they might not have tried before. I don't want to give that up. I have a dream that someday I will own a restaurant. I don't want to let go of that dream.

"Addie? Are you there, sweetheart?"

"Yeah, I'm just thinking. I guess we have a lot to talk over."

"Probably."

"Black? Is it a deal breaker if I do?"

"Deal breaker?"

"I mean, you're happy in Mason and your family is here. You have a job you love. I would understand—"

"Addie I'm not going anywhere," he says quietly.

"But—"

"I love you, Addie. I'm in this for the long haul, not for a month or two. If you get a job you love in the city, then we'll adapt."

"You mean commute?"

"Maybe at first, at least until I can find a job and move there to be with you."

"I don't want to be apart from you," I tell him. Even the thought of that idea makes me hurt.

"I don't want that either, Princess. At all."

"Damn," I whisper, because I'm completely at a loss.

"We don't have to decide all this at once, Addie. We have time. As long as we're together in our decisions, it will be okay," he says, making me smile.

"You're a smart man."

"I'm getting there," he cracks. "It's taken a while. We have dinner with your dad tomorrow night. We'll turn it into a celebration. I'm proud of you, Addie."

"You're starting to sound like my dad," I grin.

"He's growing on me. I'm still not happy with the way Tina was treated, but knowing your father was on the board and voted against the foreclosure helps a little. I thought he called the shots back then."

"Good. Now for the reason I called," I tell him, almost forgetting with everything else we've been talking about. "I've got to run by Petal's and then I'll meet you back home. I just didn't want you to get worried when I wasn't there."

"Why are you going by Petal's? You know I don't like you going places alone," Black grumbles.

"Listen, I doubt very seriously it's Linda causing all these problems, but if it is I *can* take care of myself you know. I lived overseas on my own without a problem."

"Addie, Linda can be psychotic. She's toxic. Don't underestimate her. What if I take off work early and drive you to Petal's?"

"What if you relax, a little. Petal told me to come over around six. She's closing up around four to have dinner with her family, but she's going to meet me there and she's going to color my hair and give me a fresh cut to doll me up for when I go to Amour Fou next week."

"Addie—"

"Will you relax? I'll be fine."

"You better check in and doors locked on the shop *and* your car."

"Yes, sir."

"And park in front of the shop where you guys can see your car at all times."

"Oh Lord."

"I'll talk to Luka about having a squad car patrol through there after six too."

"Black—"

"Got to go, Addie. I'm going to call and arrange that now. Be safe, I love you," he says and before I can even respond he hangs up.

I stare at the phone for a minute, but I do it smiling. He can be annoying, but it feels good knowing he cares about me and worries.

Now, if I just knew how to stay in Mason and still keep the job of my dreams.

Chapter Fifty-One

ADDIE

"I'm so sorry, I'm late! Rain needed Mommy cuddles. River rarely wants to be seen with me anymore, he's all about his dad, so it's nice to get that."

"You're not that late. This isn't urgent you know, we can do it some other time," I tell Petal as I get out of the car. She's got her hair pulled back in a messy bun and she's wearing a loose fitting blue maxi dress that looks so pretty on her. She's gorgeous without trying, but what makes her truly pretty is that she's just so genuine. I truly like her.

"No, now that I've got the shop opened back up I'm booked. I want to do this."

"If you're sure," I tell her, still feeling guilty that I'm taking her away from family time.

"I'm sure. Besides—and don't tell Luka, I feel weird leaving the shop. Now that it's fixed, I'm afraid crazy Linda will break in and destroy it again."

I feel bad for her. She wasn't out of business long. All of us pitched in to do the initial clean up and then her insurance had contractors come in and do the rest, but this shop was her baby and it hurt her to see the damage and to be closed as long as she was.

"You really think she's the one behind all of it?"

"I do. I can't say why I do, but I do. Just a gut feeling."

"Still, you can't stay at the shop 24/7," I tell her as we make it to the front door.

"I keep telling myself it will get better. Luka is having some big shot company out of Dallas come by at the end of the week to install new security measures. That will help."

"I bet that's costing a pretty penny."

"All of this is. We had insurance on the place but it had a deductible and since we were basically having to remodel, I wanted to add a few things I didn't have before. Shit..."

"What is it?" I ask, hearing the alarm in her voice.

"The door is unlocked. I made Tilly promise to lock up before she left for the night."

"Maybe she forgot?" I respond, though I'm worried too.

"Maybe," Petal says. "Stay behind me, Addie," she orders, opening the door slowly.

"Bullshit, we will go in together," I argue. What is it about these Lucas's that make them think they have to protect everyone?

We enter slowly and Petal reaches up to turn the light on. The place looks clean and is completely empty. I relax a little.

"I need to check the back," she says, distracted, her eyes darting around to take in the entire shop.

"Let's lock the door and I'll go back there with you," I tell her, remembering my promise to Black. I click the lock into place and we walk to the back quietly. Petal switches on a light and again, everything looks fine.

Petal lets out a huge sigh.

"Damn it, I keep looking for boogey men everywhere."

"That's understandable, honey."

"Maybe, but it's damn annoying," she says with a wry smile. "Why don't you get settled in a chair. I've got a sample thing here to show blonde ranges..."

"I love my original color, but I wouldn't mind trying some of those caramel tones mixed in you were talking about."

"Deal. Love a woman who knows her own mind. I'll get the color together and you get in the chair closest to the door. That's mine and all my stuff is there that I like to work with," Petal orders.

———

"There, that's it. Now we wait for a bit. I'd like to put you under the dryer for a bit, and bake that color in."

"I'm yours to command," I joke.

"If only I could get Luka to agree to that," she laughs.

"You're not fooling me, girl. I've seen you two together. You like it when he commands you."

"Maybe, a little," she giggles. "Speaking of which, you and my brother seem to be really happy."

"We are," I admit. "I love him. I wasn't expecting it, but I do... *completely.*"

"Good. Black needs someone to love him. Of all of my brothers, I'm probably closest to him. He jokes and plays a good game, but he's a romantic at heart you know."

"I don't know. He sure didn't want a relationship," I tell her, as she settles the top down on the dryer.

"Linda had him messed up. It just took him a little bit to pull his head out of his ass. I'm glad he managed it before he lost you."

"I couldn't make myself give up on him," I confess.

"I'm glad. I'm going to leave you under this for a bit. I'm going to go in the back and check in with Luka before he shows up."

"I'll text Black too," I laugh. I pull out my phone. The heat from the dryer seems to be hitting the chemicals different than they have in the past. My eyes are watering. It'd be just my luck to develop some kind of allergy to hair coloring. I push the thought aside and take out my phone and pull up my ongoing texts with Black.

"Hey, just letting you know I'm safe and sound."

"Thanks, sweetheart. How are you doing?"

"Currently under the dryer letting the new color bake in."

"I like your natural color."

"Quit pouting."

"Don't cut much off. I like the way it wraps around my hand, when I'm fucking you from behind... or when you are going down on me."

"LOL! If you keep it up. I'll cut it extremely short."

"Shutting up now. I have a surprise waiting for you when you get home."

"Gee, wonder what that is."

"Cum and see."

"You're such a goof. See you soon. Love you."

"Love you too."

I put my phone up grinning. I have no doubt the surprise is him. A couple of days ago, I got out of the shower to find him lying on the bed, naked, with a big red bow tied around his cock. He's such a goofball.

I frown because the top of my head feels like it's burning. I've had color before, although not at regular intervals. But, I've never had it burn like this before.

"Petal?" I call, wondering if I'm just being a big baby and over-reacting.

"What's up?" she says coming out of the back, the phone still in her hand.

"Something doesn't feel right. Did you use something new, maybe something that I don't normally get when I color?"

"No... why?"

"It's burning and my eyes are watering," I tell her and the longer I sit under the dryer, the more intense the feeling gets.

Petal's face instantly goes concerned.

"Luka, I'm going to hang up. Something's going on with Addie's hair," she says into the phone, hanging up before I'm sure that Luka could respond. Something on her face makes me even more worried. She all but throws the phone down and lifts up the dryer. She unrolls one of the foils and it's when I hear her softly whispered, "Fuck!" when I really start to panic.

Chapter Fifty-Two

BLACK

"What's going on?" I growl, entering the opened door of the shop. Luka is already there with Danny, one of the other deputies.

I look around and I see Petal, crying. Nothing looks out of place though, except for the fact that I don't see Addie.

"Black!" Petal cries and she comes running to me.

"Sis, what's going on? Where's Addie?"

"She's in the back, still washing her hair. It wasn't me, Black. I don't know what happened, but this wasn't anything I would have done!" she cries, and I'm so confused and worried.

Luka comes over and takes Petal out of my arms.

"Luka?" I ask, because I don't know shit. All I got was a phone call from Danny telling me I was needed at the beauty shop. That's it. Nothing else. All the way over here I kept having visions of Addie dead, or something happening to Petal. I could kill Danny— and I still might.

"When Petal and Addie got here the shop door was unlocked—"

"Hold up, Addie didn't mention it when she texted and she seemed fine."

"They decided to inspect the place themselves and didn't see anything wrong," Luka murmurs.

"*Motherfucker,*" I growl. It's not a word I use often, but right now it about sums up everything I'm feeling.

"I'm so sorry, Black. I didn't think. It all looked okay," Petal cries into Luka's chest. The words muffled, but I can still make them out.

"What happened to Addie and *where in the hell is she?*" I roar, tired of having this overwhelming fear surging inside of me.

"Black."

I hear this weakened, quiet voice that sounds like my Addie, but different. My gaze darts around the room searching it out with all the chaos and that's when I see her. She's standing over in the corner, holding onto the door of the back room. She looks fine. My eyes scan her quickly. She's got on jeans and a buttoned up, loose shirt. Her hair is wrapped up in a towel like she just got out of the shower. She's perfect... except... *she looks sad.* I don't see tears, however. I practically run to her, relief washing over me so instantly my damn knees are weak.

"Addie! Sweetheart, you're okay," I exclaim, picking her up and holding her tightly against me.

"Black," she whispers again, but this time I can hear tears in her voice. I pull back to look at her face and sure enough there are tears just silently running down her face, I try to swipe them away with my thumb.

"Don't cry baby. You're alright, we're together now. Please, don't cry."

"I can't help it," she wails. Her body trembling as the sobs take over and she clings to me as if her life depends on it.

Frustration is surging through me. I can't fix something when I don't know what's going on.

"Tell me what's wrong, Addie," I urge her because I'm one step away from screaming like a madman, until someone tells me what is wrong with my woman.

Addie pulls away from me and I let her go, even if I don't want to.

She looks up at me and slowly takes the towel off the top of her head that she was wearing.

As she takes it off she clings to it, holding it tightly to her chest. At first, I think I'm seeing things. I blink to just clear my eyes, in case I'm wrong... *but I'm not.* Addie's beautiful blonde hair is now a bright florescent pink and has a little orange mixed in. It's also short... really short... and frizzy. Addie's hair was always long and silky.

What the fuck happened? I'm about to take heads off, and if my sister did this I may take hers too. Before I can, Addie breaks down. She slides to the floor a complete broken mess.

"I look like a troll doll!" she cries and I swallow my anger down. However this happened, it wasn't Petal or anything Addie did... I have a sneaking suspicion that this came from Addie's stalker, Lynn.

And now, I'm convinced that Lynn is...Linda.

Fuck.

Chapter Fifty-Three

ADDIE

"I look hideous," I cry, throwing the comb down.

It's been four days since the incident at Petal's salon. My hair is still a freaking mess, but I'm lucky. The forensic team did a search and though the color Petal used is still being tested for its components—they're pretty sure it did contain trace amounts of Drano clog remover. They do know that the finishing conditioner had traces of boric acid. If Petal hadn't pulled me out of the dryer and immediately started rinsing me, who knows what would have happened.

I don't really care at this point. All I know is that my hair is cut short all over my head. Petal did manage to wash it enough that the harsh pink has died down to a bright neon pink, which is still bad, but at least a little better. Petal and I were both afraid to add more chemicals to it right now. My hair needs to recover and we're afraid something we use might react worse, since we're not all that sure what Linda used. I'm pretty sure Linda is the culprit too, because Black pulled up her picture on the computer. The hair has changed but the face is exact. I don't think it's a coincidence that she dyed my hair the same color that Little Kong had at first either.

"You do not, you're beautiful," Black says and I sigh.

I turn around to look at him.

"You love me, you have to say that," I grumble.

"I do love you, that's true. I'd even love you if your hair was green."

"Thanks... I think," I half-laugh. "I guess worrying about your hair is kind of stupid. There are worse things to happen, right?"

"Exactly. You could look like my brother Green," Black says, with a fake shudder.

"I don't know, Green's kind of sexy."

"I'm going to pretend I didn't hear that," Black grumbles.

I giggle, I can't help myself.

"I wouldn't want to make love to you if you looked like my brother..." Black says, leering at me.

"I really should be going over my notes for tomorrow's try out at Amour Fou," I tell him. "They moved up the appointment and I couldn't tell them I can't come because I'm having a bad hair day."

"You could have," he shrugs.

"And kissed the job goodbye," I agree. "I mean, I don't think they're going to be too thrilled when they see my hair as it is, but if I cook well enough it may make up for it," I respond with a shrug. "At least I'll have a shot."

"That's crazy. Women have those haircuts all the time.

"Not in conservative restaurants with bosses like these," I sigh.

"I think it's kind of sexy."

"Black—"

"It makes me want to fuck you," he growls.

"You're a pervert," I laugh.

Black picks me up and before I can even settle against him he tosses me on the bed. I wasn't far away from it, but it's been a long time since I've sailed through the air. I bounce on the bed a couple of times before I finally stop.

"Now, let's see if I can fuck the nerves out of you."

"You think you can manage that?" I ask.

"I'll do my best. Now strip."

"I'm too tired," I tell him.

"Too tired for sex? What's this bullshit I'm hearing?"

"Too tired to undress. I'm afraid you'll have to do it for me," I tell him, smiling up sweetly.

"Just remember you asked for it," he warns, then he grabs the collar of his t-shirt I'm wearing—because let's face it, lately when I wake up I'm wearing one of three things. It's either his t-shirt, Black himself, or nothing. If I had to pick a favorite, it would definitely be when he's over me and his cock is deep inside.

That's the best way to wake up in the mornings.

"What are you doing?"

"Undressing you, Princess."

He's barely finished the words when he rips the shirt apart, baring me to him.

"I really liked that shirt."

"It was mine," he says.

"I know but it was my favorite of yours to wear," I pout.

"I'll give you your other favorite thing of me to wear instead," he says thoughtfully, and as he grabs his cock and starts stroking it over me, there's not a doubt to be had about what he's talking about.

"That's nice of you," I grin.

"I'm a nice guy," he says.

I watch as his hand moves up and down his hard cock. Pre-cum is already drizzling from the head and sliding down his shaft. Some of it drips down and makes its way to my chest.

"I thought nice guys finished last," I respond.

"Not this time," he grins.

I lean up to lick the head of his cock and take some of his pre-cum into my mouth.

He lets me do that, but then he pushes his hand on my chest and firmly pushes me back down onto the bed. Black knows what he wants and I decide to let him have it. If there's one thing I've learned about him—he will reciprocate... *excessively.* Which, it must be said, I *really like.*

So, like a good woman, I lay back and let him have his way and as jet after jet of his cum splashes against my chest, and runs down my breasts, I have to agree. This is another favorite thing of his I like to wear.

Chapter Fifty-Four

ADDIE

"You have less than ten minutes," the guy says, sticking his head in the kitchen. I want to tell him to kiss my ass, but I don't. I nod and smile and go back to working on my roux. Ever since I got to the restaurant it's been a complete disaster, so I'm not holding out hope that this is going to work.

First I arrived and setup. I learned then that the kitchen was still going today and I'd essentially be running the kitchen and overseeing the orders as well as cooking. It's not so much as trying out for the job, as giving them one day of free labor to see if they like me. I'm pretty sure that kind of crap is illegal and it doesn't fill me with warm fuzzy feelings about working here. I suck it up though.

I'm out to prove myself—not only here, but in my industry, so I shake it off. Then the owner keeps walking around, watching every move I make. I mean, that's his right but it's starting to get on my nerves. It wasn't so bad until he had the audacity to comment on my hair.

"I hope you cook better than you choose your hairstyles," he murmurs.

His words cut, because I'm still mentally trying to recover

from everything to do with my hair, but I suck that up too. I'm frazzled, but everything seems to be going really well and by that I mean in ten minutes I've completed an entire shift and I've not had one issue and no real complaints. By this time, I'm feeling like the job is mine. I'll admit that I'm starting to wonder why I want to work for these guys, but all the same, I'm feeling accomplished.

"Chef Harrington," one of the waiter's holler.

"Yes?"

"You have a call."

I frown. Very few people know I'm here. Black and his family and my father. That's it and none of them would call unless it was absolutely necessary.

"We don't allow personal calls during working hours," the owner says, his stern face looking down at me with disdain. I've felt like he's judged me all day and this doesn't help.

"No one would bother me here unless it was an absolute emergency," I tell him, but I can tell that he doesn't believe me.

I dry my hands on a dish towel, after instructing one of the line cooks to continue stirring the roux. I hustle over to the phone, my eyes on the clock overhead and I'm pretty sure I'm about three steps away from panic—not only about my cooking, but I'm afraid something has happened to Black or to my father.

"Hello?" I hold the receiver and wait for an answer. I hear nothing. "Hello? Is anyone there?" I ask, but again no one is there. It's just a second later that I hear a recording.

"If you'd like to make a call, please hang up and try your call again..."

I frown, but hang up. I rush back over to my station, but there are two waiters already heading out the door with orders.

"Wait! I didn't get to check the plate," I cry, but it's too late, they've already entered the dining area.

Crap.

"I gave orders that nothing leaves the kitchen without my approval," I mutter.

"You were tending to *personal* business on company time. My patrons can't wait for you to get off the phone. *I* gave the order," the guy says, coming up from behind me.

I jump, because I wasn't expecting him to be there.

"Did you check the plates?"

"That's not my job. That's yours," he dismisses, and my mouth goes tight as I bite my tongue and don't tell the guy what I think of him.

I try to put the plates out of my head and instead, go back to dishing up the last plate of the day. I'm feeling even more confident until the unexpected happens.

"This was returned," a waitress says, bringing back one of the plates that I didn't get to oversee.

"A hair!" the owner gasps. Just the sound of his voice makes me wince.

"There can't be, or at least if there is, it didn't come from the kitchen," I defend.

"I don't think you can be so sure."

"But I can. The entire staff has the proper netting in place and their hair pulled completely away. I made sure of that," I argue.

"Be that as it may, there's a hair in the food, obviously," he replies.

"Well it didn't come from the kitchen. If there's a hair it came from the waitress or perhaps the customer themselves!" I argue stubbornly, crossing my hands at my chest.

The waitress shoots me a dirty look, which I could understand, I've pretty much thrown her under the bus.

"Open the tray and let us look," the owner says haughtily.

"I can assure you it's not mine," the waitress says, lifting the top.

"How can you be so sure?" I ask.

"Because it's not... hot pink," she responds once the lid is clear. I look down at the food and sure enough there's pink hair beside the steak. Worse, there's more than one. There's like four.

I close my eyes. When I look back up at the owner, I know it's over.

The worst part is, I'm not upset at losing the job. I'm more upset because I know that the hair didn't fall off my head. I go straight to the double doors that lead to the dining room. I fully expect to see Linda there.

"Where are you going?" the owner asks, the waitress right beside him. I stop long enough to turn to them.

"Show me the customer. I want to offer an apology," I lie. If it is Linda, I don't want to apologize, not at all. I want to strangle her, jump up and down on her and possibly cut off her hair even shorter than mine—and that's just the start. Mostly I just plain want to kill her.

"She left. She was highly upset," the waitress says.

Crap.

"I just bet she was," I mutter.

"You need to clean your filth out of my kitchen," the owner says and it takes everything in me not to slap him.

In the end I don't, but I'm fuming. All the way home I wish I could go back and make him eat that damn chef hat on his head.

Chapter Fifty-Five

BLACK

"What do you mean there's no sign of Linda? It's not like the bitch could just disappear!" I growl into the phone.

"Buddy, we're doing all we can. It's not like we even have proof Linda is behind all of this. We've basically got nothing. All we can do is question her—and that's *if* we can find her."

"Then, we need to put out—"

"I can't put out anything. She's innocent in the law's eyes right now. I can't have state police out searching for her.

"Fucking hell," I mumble, understanding what Luka is saying, but not liking it one damn bit.

"I know you're upset," Luka starts.

"I'm beyond upset. I can deal when it's my life she fucks up. I figure that's what I get for tangling up with the bitch in the first place, but this is Addie's life she's messing with."

"I know you're not happy, but we really are doing everything we can. Addie's father is even using his connections to have the Dallas P.D. on alert for her."

"He told us, but it's like I told him, I doubt Linda is in Dallas. It wouldn't surprise me if she isn't hiding out here in Mason somewhere."

"We're checking that out too, Black, I promise. We can't do it officially, but we are doing it."

"I know," I sigh, knowing that taking my anger out on Luka isn't going to accomplish anything. "It's all just so damn frustrating."

"I get that. Petal isn't exactly too happy these days either," Luka says and I know he's right. I scratch my forehead and do my best to rein in my anger. It's not Luka's fault.

It's mine.

I'm the one that allowed that toxic woman into my world, and to affect my family.

"You still coming back to work tomorrow?"

"Yeah. Addie's demanding it. She says I'm smothering her."

Luka laughs in response to that. I wish I could find something funny. The truth is, since she came back from her job interview I've stuck by her side like glue. I want to protect her from Linda and until I locate her, I need Addie in my sight at all times. I didn't want to go back to work, but she insisted. She said that her and Mom are going to can tomatoes tomorrow—which is what they were doing today when she shooed me away like I was a pest. She loves working in the kitchen with my mother and it's a good distraction for her—so I guess I should be thankful. Part of me is, I guess. Another part wishes she was with me right now. Which would be bad. I'm on a top secret mission and I'm doing it in hopes of surprising Addie.

I just hope she sees it like that...

"I'll talk to you later, Luka. I've just pulled into the old Collins building."

"Good luck, buddy. Hope it works out."

"Me too," I tell him and then quickly hang up the phone.

"Mr. Lucas, I'm glad you could make it," Peter Graves says, reaching out to shake my hand the minute I get out of my truck.

"Mr. Graves. I appreciate the call. I didn't realize it would be you I was meeting with," I respond, feeling a little uncomfortable.

"Please. When Ida Sue called me and told me what you were

looking for, I just had to show you first hand. It's a beauty, isn't it?" he asks, looking up at the building like it was a work of art.

I study it for a minute. It has always been one of my favorite buildings. It's outside of downtown, but it's within ten minutes of the bowling alley, and the city park. It used to house Stampede, a popular steak house. The business shut down when the owner died. The building itself is covered in white brick and is two stories. The entire lower half—which is huge—is mostly glass in the front and there's a large deck to the side for outdoor eating. The landscaping is non-existent but with some work it could be just as nice as any of those fancy restaurants in Dallas.

"How big is it?" I ask, my mind working now to try and see it in Addie's eyes.

"The restaurant dining area—not counting the kitchen is around eighteen hundred square feet, so for fine dining that's around ninety give or take and that doesn't count the outdoor area."

"I see."

"It's more than big enough for our area—if that's what concerns you," Mr. Graves says.

"What about upstairs?"

"It's a complete home really. There's even a deck off the back that leads down into a yard. It's an open floor plan, so you feel as if there is more space. It's a great starter home. "Shall I take you through the tour?" he asks when I don't answer right away.

"You're positive this place is mine, if I want it?"

"I wouldn't have called otherwise, Black. Your family and I go way back. And to be quite frank, this property has been bank owned for three years. I'd like to get it off my records *and* I'd consider it an honor to help you purchase your home."

"Can I call Addie and Mom to come over and look at it?" I ask, suddenly feeling better about things than I have since this whole mess with Linda started.

"Sounds good," he smiles. "If you're wanting your young lady to be a part of the decision you can't hardly buy it until she gives her approval. I actually thought she'd be here with you," he says as I take my phone out to dial.

"I wanted to make sure it was okay and that there wouldn't be any issues if she fell in love with it first. I don't want Addie to have any more disappointments."

"That happens when we fall in love," he says, smiling and I don't argue... because it's true.

"Hey Mom? Can you bring Addie over to the old Collins Building?" I ask the minute she says hello.

"That I can do my boy. Especially if this means what I think it does."

"Yeah... Well if Addie likes it," I tell her grinning into the phone.

"Praise Jesus, I guess miracles still happen," she says and if I wasn't too busy grinning and thinking about Addie's reaction I'd grumble at her.

"Mom—"

"My boy finally stopped dragging his di—"

"Mom, Mr. Graves is waiting with me," I remind her, cutting her off.

"We'll be there in two shakes of a lamb's tail. We just finished the last of the tomatoes."

"Thanks, Mom."

I hang up the phone and look at Mr. Graves—still smiling.

"Maybe I could see the upstairs, since that's the part I'm most concerned with," I tell him.

"Sounds good," he says walking me toward the entrance. "I must admit, I am curious about one thing," Mr. Graves says, ushering me back towards the kitchen where there's an entrance door that leads to a stairway.

"What's that?" I ask, taking in the old oak stairwell and liking everything about it. If Addie and I decided to move out into a house later on, we could rent the upstairs out for extra income, maybe even convert it into apartments which might entice staff to live there...

"Why didn't you ask Ms. Harrington's father for help when it came to finding a place. He does own several banks, after all."

"It's really something I wanted to do on my own. I don't really want my future father-in-law helping me find a home. It's my job to provide for Addie now," I tell him. "It might be old-fashioned, but that's who I am."

"I like that," he says. "The world moves too fast these days," he adds just as he opens the entrance to the home. I take one look at the open living area and large kitchen with marble counters and I know Addie is going to love it. I love it...

Most of all I love that I've found mine and Addie's home. Things are definitely looking up.

If only I could close the book on Linda...

Chapter Fifty-Six

ADDIE

"You're sure about this?"

I snuggle up to Black, my ear pressed against his heart, listening to it beat. The sound makes me happy.

Black makes me happy.

"If I wasn't sure, sweetheart, I never would have shown you the place."

"Living over top of a restaurant isn't an ideal home. It's not good for babies or dogs or..."

"Addie, we've discussed this. You want this. Your own restaurant might not be what you had in mind. I know you were set on working your way up with a prestigious name. But, you can build this one to whatever heights you want. You have that ability."

"You have that much faith in me?" I ask, more than a little awestruck.

"Sweetheart, I have all the faith in the world in you. Plus, I eat a lot of your cooking. Trust me, if anyone can put Mason on the map as *the* place for culinary excellence... It is you."

"It's a lot of money, Black," I remind him and it is.

The building itself might be a bargain, but we'll be taking out loans for renovations, and staffing... so much that it makes my head spin.

"It's an investment," he argues and looking at him, I feel his confidence in me and it makes me feel powerful.

"You don't have to do this you know?" I'll be fine working for a small restaurant. I don't even care if it has a big name. As long as I have you to come home to, I'm fine."

"I know," he says, kissing along the side of my neck. "I want you to have a restaurant, Addie and to be honest, I kind of want to remain in Mason."

"You do?"

"Yeah. I love it here, I love being close to my family and I enjoy my job. This is where I want to raise a family and this is where I want to grow old with you."

"Me too," I whisper.

"Then we're doing this right? We're buying the building and my woman is going to be the most kick-ass Chef this side of the Pecos."

"We're doing this," I giggle, then I flip so I'm straddling him and kiss him. It's a kiss of hope, promise and love... *definitely love.*

"I only have one question," he asks.

"What's that?"

"Did you say that tomorrow is the day that Petal is going to take the pink out of your hair?"

"Yep, by this time tomorrow night you will be sleeping with a blonde again," I tell him. "It's starting to grow again too, thank God."

"Then, I guess I better get busy," he says.

"Busy doing—" I never finish my question; it breaks off into a squeal instead. "What are you doing?" I laugh as he flips me over on my back and then he straddles me, a knee on each side of me.

"I'm running out of time," he says, grabbing the ends of his t-shirt that I'm wearing and pulling it over my head. I help him get it off—it's not like I have much choice... *or that I want one.*

"For what," I ask, still laughing even as he wraps his hands under each of my breasts, kneading them.

"To have wild sex with a girl with pink hair. It's on my bucket list."

"Then I guess you had better hurry," I smile, as I reach down and circle his cock in my hand.

"I'll see what I can do," he grins, right before he sucks on my breast.

Heaven.

"Do we really have to go over this tonight?" I groan, looking at the different waiter/waitress uniforms that Addie has in pictures. They're strung out over one of the new tables in the restaurant.

We've been in our new home for two months. We're in the middle of renovations and the expense is making my head swim. Addie's father insisted on giving us a big chunk of the renovation as a housewarming gift and Addie asked my mother to help her in the kitchen and organizing the restaurant. I didn't think my mom would want to work outside the farm, but her and Addie have become super close and she jumped at the chance. Which means, my mother also put in on the renovations. We're still spending a huge chunk of change, but it could have been much worse.

Life has been good. Every day with Addie just keeps getting better and better. We still haven't heard from Linda. I keep hoping that means she's given up, but somewhere in the back of my head I know she'll show up again. It's just the waiting for it that's driving me insane.

"This is important, Black," Addie says, looking up from the pictures.

"I'm tired, sweetheart. I want to go to bed."

"Then—"

"In our bed, with my woman."

"It's not even dark outside, crazy man."

"Is this what we've come to, Addie?"

"What?"

"A couple who can't go to bed and have sex until it's dark outside."

"You said you were sleepy, not that you wanted to have sex," she laughs.

"Would it have made a difference?"

"Damn straight. Let me just lock the door and—"

"Jesus, it's hotter out there than a hooker's doorknob on nickel night," Mom says coming in like the hurricane that she is.

"Hold that thought, Princess," I whisper to Addie.

"Hey, Ida Sue," she responds, giving me a sneaky grin as Mom comes over and hugs her.

"Hey, Orchid. What are we doing tonight?"

I hold my head down, because if Mom's here to work there's one thing clear. I'm not about to get sex tonight.

"We're deciding on the wait-staff uniforms. Black's being zero help."

"Why doesn't that surprise me? Hey son, how are you?" she says, hugging me.

"Hey, Mom."

"So have we picked our favorites?" she questions, sitting down beside me.

"We've just started," Addie explains. "These are my four favorites and Black was just about to tell me his."

"I was?"

"I'd like to finish this before bedtime tonight," she says, giving me a pointed look.

Score!

"I like this one," I tell her picking one out without really looking at it.

"Good Lord! That's a no, son. We want couples to come in for food—not a divorce."

"What are you talking about?"

"Those shorts are so short on that girl that I swear you can see parts of her hairy critter."

"I swear, Mom," I laugh, because I can't stop myself. "Hairy critter?"

"Exactly. We don't want none of that in my Orchid's restaurant. It needs to be classy not a petting zoo free for all."

"Petting zoo?" Addie asks, but I shake my head no. You really shouldn't encourage my mother.

"These outfits will show off the girl's barns. You make the barn look that enticing and everyone will want to pet the…"

"Hairy critters," Addie finishes for Mom.

"There you go," Mom answers.

"Okay, these are out of consideration," Addie giggles.

"Either of the three remaining works. You figure out which one you like, Orchid. That's what matters."

"I'm too tired to think about it right now," Addie sighs. "I'll tackle it again tomorrow. I have to be up early. The ceiling fans are coming in and I have to sign for them."

"Oh! I know a guy who can put them up," Mom says cheerfully.

"He needs to know what he's doing. I have a number for a certified electrician and—"

"Pfft. That's a waste of money. My Chocolate Thunder can do it and he won't charge a dime."

"Titan?"

"He's amazing at this kind of thing, Orchid. You take my word for it," Mom croons, patting Addie's hand.

"Jensen will not be happy if he comes over and finds you staring at Titan without a shirt again, Mom."

"Then he can punish me later and it will be a win-win," Mom laughs.

"Shoot me now," I moan, putting my head down on the table, hearing Addie's laughter.

"Not yet. I kind of like having you around," Mom responds with that sly grin she gets sometimes. "I am wondering, however, what you're doing to find that psycho-ex of yours."

"Not a damn thing. I have people everywhere looking for her and it's like she's just dropped off the face of the earth. We're finding nothing."

"I think that's good. Maybe she got afraid and decided to cut her losses and go—hopefully to another country, but at least another state," Addie says cheerfully.

"You're being too optimistic, Orchid. No, with that kind of crazy you know they're not going to give up easily. I think she'll rear her head soon."

"You do?" Addie asks.

"She wants to make you pay for taking what she deems as hers," Mom says and I frown.

"Bullshit. I was never hers," I growl, still pissed at myself over even being with Linda in the first place.

"Not the way she sees it, boy," Mom corrects me. "In her eyes, you were her property and she'll want you to pay for leaving, but she'll want Orchid to pay more."

I know she's right. Anger and fear mix inside of me. I'm running out of time to find Linda. I feel it.

"You think she'll attack when she can hurt me the most," Addie says, frowning.

"Yeah, I'm afraid so, Orchid."

"Then the most likely time will be the opening of the restaurant," Addie says.

Mom looks at me and we're both thinking the same thing.

"Or sooner," I murmur along with Mom. *Shit.*

Chapter Fifty-Eight

ADDIE

"Let's go, Lovey," Jansen practically orders.

Jansen has a hold of Ida Sue's hand, practically pulling her out of the restaurant. I'm standing by the entrance with Titan and Faith, doing a really bad job of holding in my laughter. Titan has been putting up the new ceiling fans and Ida Sue—along with Faith and I—have been enjoying the show. Hey, what can I say? I'm only human and he's a fine specimen of why God created men.

Tonight was the first night Ida Sue got really upset with me. I wouldn't turn the heat up to eighty-five. Now I admit, the urge to do it was there, but I'm not about to give myself heat stroke to admire Titan sweating.

"CT, you promise to bring my sweet little Faith over to see me with that precious Eris Sue?" Ida Sue asks, sounding entirely too sweet.

"You got it, CL," Titan says easily and I have to giggle then— which was probably a mistake.

Ida Sue narrows her eyes at me and if I didn't know her well enough to know that tomorrow she'd love me again—I'd be worried.

"You and me, Adelle. We have problems. Don't think we don't. You broke my heart."

"What happened to Orchid?" I can't help but ask.

"That name has been revoked," she huffs. "No child of mine would break my heart like you did. There I was just freezing and you refusing to turn the heat up. I'm old. These bones get settled into the cold and I could die of pneumonia. Of course that's probably what you want. You want me to die of—"

"That's it," Jansen growls and he picks Ida Sue up and throws her over his shoulders—a pretty impressive feat for the man. I hope Black is that athletic when he hits his sixties, because Ida Sue isn't exactly small. She cooks good and enjoys it.

Jansen doesn't bother saying goodbye, he just starts walking away. Ida Sue practically raises her upper half up, instead of resting on Jansen's back. The three of us step closer to the door so we can watch them walk up the street.

"I'll see you tomorrow CT!"

"What about me?" Faith asks her.

"Oh you too, darlin'," she says, but her eyes are glued on Titan. "Bye CT!"

"Bye, CL," Titan says, rubbing the side of his face and hiding his smile.

"Bye, Ida Sue," I call out and she sniffs at me, not bothering to answer.

"Children, Jansen. They walk on your feet when they're little, but when they get older they walk on your poor feeble heart," she moans.

"I wasn't around you when I was little to walk on your feet," I call out.

"If you had been, you would have!" Ida Sue yells back as they round the corner and disappear out of sight.

"White people are damn crazy," Titan laughs, his arm wrapped around Faith.

"Hey now," Faith giggles.

"You're crazy too, Babe. It's just I like your kind of crazy."

"Don't lie, you like Ida Sue's crazy," I laugh at Titan.

"Can't lie. That woman is as whacked as they come, but I love her deep. She's got soul."

"Does she know that CL stands for Crazy Lady?" I ask out of curiosity.

"She don't care, but yeah. Thinks it's sweet we have pet names for one another. Thanks, by the way, for not turning the heat up. Faith always goes along with her."

"That's because I like it when my man sweats," Faith giggles.

"How about we get home and I'll see what I can do to help you out?" Titan asks.

"Like that's going to happen. Eris never sleeps through the night," Faith moans hugging me. "Will you be okay, Addie? Do you want us to stay a little longer?"

"What? No. You get home to your girl. I'm not sure how long I'd trust Cyan to babysit," I joke.

"He's a wild one, but surprisingly around babies, he's the best, so sweet and tender."

"I like him," I tell her, just in case she thinks I don't.

"You like the whole family. You're one of us now," Faith grins.

"I do feel like I've been adopted by everyone, that's for sure," I laugh.

"It's a good feeling," Titan says. "If you're sure you're okay, we'll head out. What time does Black get home?"

"In about four hours, which is early for him, but he wasn't happy about having to work tonight, so Danny said he'd come in and let Black come home early."

"That's good. You make sure you lock your doors, though," Faith says as her and Titan go outside.

"Will do. Thank you again for all of your help. I truly appreciate it. Hopefully Ida Sue will forgive me in time to help me do the last minute touches in the kitchen this week and we'll be ready to open Monday."

"I don't think you have to worry about that," Titan says. "But, thanks again for having my back," he adds and I wave goodbye and then lock the door.

I turn around to look at the dining area and I feel a sense of pride and accomplishment. The ceiling fans really just set the whole place off. The pendant lights are white with a brushed antique look to them and have two small gold lines around the bottom and the insides are gold with a steel wire guard. They look like something you'd find in a country home in France and I'm in love with them.

I'm in love with the whole place really. I'm nervous about the opening, but I know in my heart it's going to be okay. I'll work my tail off to make sure it succeeds and if it doesn't... the one thing that will always be okay is me and Black. He's with me now and somehow even my dreams take a backseat to that.

He's my world.

I turn out the lights in the dining area and follow the glow of the hall lights to the kitchen. I need to make sure the door is locked there too, since we used that door to bring in all of the fans earlier. I just clear the counter, when I hear a scream.

I turn to see what's going on, not really having time to react.

Before I realize it though, Linda is standing behind me and she's got a bat in her hand. I hold my hands up as the bat comes down. Pain blooms on my head so intense my vision goes white— and then everything goes black as I hit the floor.

Chapter Fifty-Nine

BLACK

I'm staring at the clock, counting down the hours until I get home. I have paperwork to catch up on, but I'll be damned if I can concentrate long enough to do it.

I'm on edge tonight. I'm trying to write it off as just being away from Addie, but I know in my gut it's something more. At least I think I do. Jesus, all this worrying about Linda has me so keyed up that I see ghosts where there are none. I need to get myself under control. I stare at the phone and then at the clock. It's late, but I need to hear her voice and know she's okay. I had a patrol go by there a couple of hours ago and he said everything looked fine from the outside, but I just can't shake this feeling.

The phone startles me and I jump like a damn fool. I'm definitely too wired up for this crap.

"Hello?"

"Hey, bro', just thought I'd give you a heads up. Faith and I just left Addie. She was locking up when we left," Titan says. Titan's a good man. He's married to my cousin Faith. They had a rough start of it... but that seems to be the way with our family. Addie and I didn't exactly have an easy go of it. I smile when I think back to the day she almost plowed over me with a lawnmower. I should have known then that she was the one.

"So, she was good?" I ask. Breathing a little easier.

"Yeah. She pissed your Mom off pretty good, but she was laughing when we left."

"Mom? How'd that happen?"

"She refused to turn the heat up while I was working," Titan laughs and I groan. "Anyways, just giving you a heads up, you might give her a few minutes and call just to make sure she made it upstairs okay."

"Will do, thank you, man."

"Anytime. Later, Bro'."

I'm feeling a little better about things, but I know I won't rest until I hear Addie's voice.

I dial the phone and sigh when I get a busy signal. She's probably talking to her father. They normally call each other every night once we lock the place up for the night.

I rub the back of my neck after putting the phone down and walk back to grab a cup of coffee. I pace around the room for a bit, but nothing is calming me down and I guess the coffee doesn't really help that either. I try Addie a couple of more times and it's still busy.

That feeling in my gut gets worse.

Finally, I give it up. I'm alone in the office tonight, we couldn't find anyone that would work nights and not call in all the time. It was working Tani to death, so we've just been channeling everything through the new 911 office. I lock up and get in my squad car, use my radio to let dispatch know where I'm at and head home. Addie will hand me my ass for checking up on her but I can't help it.

Something is just telling me I need to go to her, and it's the same feeling that kept me alive as a detective in Dallas.

Chapter Sixty

ADDIE

I'm groggy as hell when I come to. I'm in a fog and it feels like there are a herd of elephants running in my head. I do my best to shake it off, however. I know Linda is here and I need to be alert.

The first thing I notice is I'm in the kitchen still... and I'm alone. The second thing I notice is that there is entirely too much noise going on in the dining room. The last thing I notice is that I'm bleeding.

I reach up to touch the side of my head and moan, because even that small movement hurts. When I pull my hand away there's blood on my fingers. *My blood.* I shake my head slowly. I can't give in to the pain. There's a bitch in the front room I need to contain.

I can't believe she just left me in here alone and not tied up. She probably thought she killed me the way she hit me with the bat. I guess I should send up a thanks to my guardian angel she didn't. My thought is that putting my arms up must have lessened the blow. God knows my arms sure are sore.

I get up slowly—mostly because I don't have a choice. I hold onto the counter to help pull myself up and once I do, I go light-headed and dizzy. If I give into the urge, I would sink back on the floor. The noise in the dining area is getting louder though and I don't see the bat anywhere, so I know Linda is out there destroying my restaurant. That pisses me off, because so many of us have put in money and hard work. It's not just me at this point. Black has insisted on naming the place Adelle's but he hasn't seen the tweak I made on the sign we're unveiling in a few days.

That's if there's anything left to unveil...

I look around the room for a weapon of any kind—something to defend myself. There are knives, but I'm not sure Linda would respond to a weapon in the first place and in the second, I'm not sure I could stab anyone. There's a gun in the safe upstairs that Black keeps, but I doubt I could bring myself to shoot another person, even Linda. I'm running out of options and time, so with a whispered, "What the hell," I grab the largest knife in my kitchen and take off toward the dining room.

I wasn't prepared. I really should have taken time to prepare myself. Black is right. Linda is crazy and we're talking *'One Flew Over The Cuckoo's Nest,'* crazy. Actually, since I'm on the Jack Nicholson theme, I think *'The Shining,'* might fit better. She smashed a few things—like all of my table centerpieces—but, it looks like she dropped her bat in favor of some bright pink paint that she obviously brought with her.

Seriously! What is it with this woman and pink?

She's currently spray painting the word whore all over my walls. Not the most original word, but at least Linda is consistent.

"You thought you could steal my man, my life. He would have come back to me! You *whore!*" she screams as she writes the word on the wall again... Shit! Right over that picture of the French countryside that I paid five hundred bucks for! *Now*, I could probably shoot her—too bad I don't have time to go and get the gun.

"I followed you and made you pay! You even lost your damn hair and you couldn't leave! *I hate you!*" she screams.

I sneak over—although, she's so crazed with her spray painting I doubt she could hear me—to the baseball bat and grab it. I hide the knife on one of the booth's chairs. I might not be able to use it, but I have no doubt she would against me if I give her the chance.

"Yo!" I yell out channeling my inner Dwayne Johnson, because I'm pretty sure if the Rock was here right now he could handle Linda pretty damn easily."

"You whore!" she screams, coming at me with a still spraying, paint can.

Damn it! I didn't think this through and Linda seriously needs another word to use. I duck, to avoid having my face painted. I've just gotten used to having blonde hair again and I have no urge whatsoever to go back to pink—at least hot pink.

I hold onto the bat and choke up on it like I've seen the big leaguers do. It's not that easy and I'd like to think it's because I'm keeping my head down, but it's probably because I'm not that athletic. But, right before the screaming-banshee-ex-girlfriend-from-hell gets to me, I swing hard. It connects with a loud thud and she doubles over. A second later she falls to the ground and I think I've won. I should have known better.

"You whore! I warned you to stay away! You refused to listen! I thought once your precious father's place burned to the ground and you lost all your stuff you'd leave, but you didn't!" she screams and I feel sick to my stomach. "You ruined everything! Black would have eventually come back to me if you had just stayed away!" she yells and then she grabs a serving tray she apparently tried to destroy earlier and throws it at me. I move so that it misses me and my stomach protests. I'm dizzy and breaking out in a sweat, but I fight to keep focused. Realistically I figure I have a concussion and I hope that's all. I don't have time to give into it right now, though.

"He wouldn't come back to you," I tell her. "He hates you."

"He loves me! He craves what only I can give him! That's why he keeps coming back to me!"

Coming back to her? Maybe Black and I should talk more about Linda after all!

"You nearly destroyed him," I tell her. "You took his dog from him!"

"That freaking dog! I hated the bastard. I drove him all the way to Oklahoma to a kill shelter and I laughed all the way home!" she laughs hysterically now and she tries to get up.

Yeah... I could shoot her.

"It's safer for you if you stay on the ground. That's the only warning you're going to get," I tell her, huffing. It's hard to catch my breath for some reason.

Linda ignores me, probably because she's dumb as a bucket of rocks. So, I do the only thing I can. I swing the bat again and it hits much harder than before and this time against her knees. She goes down instantly. That skater chick—I forget her name—would be proud of me.

"You—"

"Whore," I interrupt with a sigh. "I've heard you the first million times. If you're lucky the state prison has courses you can enroll in to help your vocabulary, because you really need to broaden your horizons," I huff out.

"Addie!" Black screams, opening the door all at once and so hard that it springs back against the outside of the building. With my luck the door will need to be replaced now, too.

"About time you got here, honey," I tell him, trying to smile, but now with Black here and Linda curled up crying and holding her knees, I feel myself fading.

Black is running to me. I don't know why. Maybe he can see that I'm about to go under. He catches me about the time my knees give out. At least this time when the blackness pulls me under, it's Black's face I see last. I like that better—even if he does look scared to death.

Chapter Sixty-One

BLACK

"Will you let me down?" Addie complains. "I can walk, you know."

"I know, sweetheart," I tell her, my chest still tight.

I kiss the top of her head and ignore her plea. I'm not going to let her down. I'm not going to let go of her. Not right now and I'm not sure I ever will again. She's been in the hospital for the last twenty-four hours for observation. She had a major concussion and a couple of broken ribs. The doctors assume Addie was hit once on the head and then again on her side. Addie doesn't remember, so the doctors figure she was already out when Linda hit her again. The thought of my precious Addie that defenseless while Linda was wreaking her special brand of crazy everywhere terrifies me.

"I forgot how horrible the place was," Addie whispers, looking around the restaurant at the chaos Linda left behind.

"We'll fix it back up," I assure her. I take her over to the sofa and chairs that she had placed in front of the window for people to sit on while waiting for a table and I sit down, keeping her in my arms.

"Not in time for the opening Monday. There's no way. We'll have to postpone and we already paid for so much advertising," she says dejectedly. She doesn't sob, but silent tears start streaming from her face and it breaks my heart. Somehow I think sobs might have been easier to take.

I bend down and kiss the tears, taking them into my mouth and trying to banish them from her face.

"Stop that crying, Princess Addie. Everything will be fine. I promise."

"I know. I'm being a big baby. It's just that I was looking so forward to opening the doors next week."

"You think you'll be able to cook?" I ask her, curious. I don't want her overdoing it.

"I think so. I hired a few line cooks and then your Mom will be here helping too."

"Then we just have to get the place cleaned up," I tell her. "Honestly, Addie, I need you to hear me when I tell you this."

"I'm listening," she says with a muted sigh, holding her head close to my chest.

"It doesn't matter if we open today, tomorrow, next week or even next month. Adelle's Bistro is going to be a success. *You* are going to be a success."

"I love you, Black."

"And most importantly, my beautiful Addie, you're still here with me and we're together."

"Yeah," she whispers, with a smile.

"Yeah," I agree and I lean down to kiss her carefully. I don't want to hurt her more, but I need this from her. I need to constantly reassure myself that she's alive, she's okay and that she's here with me. "I love you, Addie."

"Is this a private party? Or can anyone join?"

"Daddy!" Adelle smiles, sitting up a little, although I still won't let her out of my lap.

"Hey, Princess. How are you doing?" he asks, walking over to us and leaning down to kiss her.

"I'm okay, I promise. What are you holding?"

"It's a couple of buckets of paint. Thought we could use it on this place. It's the same color of pale blue you used before *and* it has primer to help cover," he winks.

"No offense, Dad. It's going to take more than two buckets of paint and you and the two of us to get this place back in shape," Addie says wistfully.

"That's why he brought reinforcements, Orchid baby," Ida Sue says coming through the open door carrying buckets that seem stacked full of cleaning materials.

"Ida Sue?" she whispers.

"There are advantages to being part of a huge family, Addie. We can be aggravating, but one thing we Lucas's do," Petal says, as she comes through the door carrying buckets too.

"We stick together," I finish, kissing the side of Addie's head, just above her bandage.

"Oh my God," she whispers as Luka comes in behind Petal, Jansen is there with him. Next, Blue, Cyan, White, and Gray come in, with Kayla and CC right behind them. Titan and Faith are next and right behind them is my cousin Hope, with her man, Aden. Maggie brings up the rear smiling.

"Mary would have been here too, but God help her soul, she's watching the kids," Maggie says.

"You're all..." Addie seems to lose all words and she's crying again, but I figure these are happy tears. "This is too much," she says finally and it's my brother Blue who comes forward.

"This is family, little sister and that's exactly what you are," he says kissing her forehead. That might be as many words as Blue has spoken at one time to Addie, but the thing about my twin is... when he speaks, it's worth listening to. "Love you," he whispers into her ear and that makes her cry a little more.

"Who's in charge? Where should we start first?" Gray asks.

"I am," Mom pipes up. "We'll start stripping the walls down and painting. You boys do that. Us girls will start cleaning out the debris and putting it in the dumpster the Mayor had delivered. CT honey you're with me. I have some paint stripper I'd like to try on Addie's big fancy painting. It says it can only be used in a well ventilated area. I know it's over a hundred outside, but there's nothing we can do. I hope you don't get too hot."

"Ida Sue!" Jansen growls. "*I'll* help you with that painting."

"Hey! Is this a private party or can anyone join?" Green asks standing at the door with his son, Allen.

"Oh my God!" Addie cries. "Black! Green Lucas is going to work at my restaurant. *The* Green Lucas!" she giggles.

I see the mischief in her eyes and if she was able, I'd spank her ass for it.

"You'll pay for that one, soon, Princess," I tell her, whispering, as I kiss her lips.

"I was hoping you'd say that," she responds when we break apart. "I guess this is as good of a time as any to show you my surprise," she announces, not only to me—but to all of us. Everyone stops what they're doing and she looks over at Blue. "Could you open the closet by the entrance and pull out my surprise. It's wrapped in a white packing blanket." Blue immediately goes to do as she asks. "It's heavy! You might need some help," she adds and Jansen immediately goes over to help. They get it out and Jansen takes off the blanket and I read it with a grin.

Lucas Family Bistro.

"Well, hell," I mutter, completely shocked.

"Do you like it?" she whispers as everyone gives their shouts of approval, before going back to work.

"I love it. There's just one problem," I tell her.

"What's that?" she asks, but she looks nervous.

"Mayor, could you sit with Addie for a minute while I run in the back?"

"Sure thing," he says, as I carefully sit her in the chair.

"Are you happy, Addie-girl?" I hear her father ask, as I jog away.

"Ecstatic," she assures him and that one word lodges in my heart and I know that's what I always want.

I make it up the stairs quicker than any man has ever climbed stairs in his life and I go straight for my lock box that I keep my pistol in. Addie doesn't like guns, so I knew that would be one place she'd never look. I grab the ring box, take out the ring, leaving the box, pistol and all on the bed.

I'm winded by the time I make it back downstairs, but the room is quiet. My family knows what's coming next. I've told them. I even asked the Mayor's permission first. It's old-fashioned, I know, but I wanted to do this right.

"Black?" Addie asks when I come back into the room.

"The problem with the sign, Addie, is that your last name isn't Lucas," I tell her, just as I get right in front of her.

"Oh, well... I..."

She looks flustered, and before she can second guess herself I go down on one knee.

"I want to fix that," I tell her holding the ring up.

"Oh my God," she gasps.

"Will you marry me, Addie?"

Addie looks at me, and then back to the ring. Then she squeals so loud it has to hurt her, but she's smiling and happy.

"Yes! Yes! I'll marry you!" she cries, holding out her trembling hand as I slide the engagement ring on her finger.

Once the ring is in place, I take her in my arms and kiss her, cementing the promise. My family's talking and celebrating around us, but I don't care. I have my woman in my arms and she's just agreed to be my wife.

It doesn't get any better than that.

EPILOGUE

Addie

Almost Two Months Later

"Why are you breaking into your own house?" I laugh at Black as he opens up the door at the back of our home.

I can't really call it a house, after all there's a restaurant below us. A very successful restaurant that I love. We've been open almost two months now and since our opening, the Lucas Family Bistro has had a steady stream of customers. The best news is that those only seem to be increasing with time. I have a cook and wait-staff in place that I adore and every day seems to be a new adventure. Dad always eats there and we're both in agreement that my mother would be in the kitchen with me and be on cloud nine for me.

Life is about as near perfect as it can get. We managed to open on time with everyone's help and the only hiccup we had was Linda's court hearing. Luckily she pleaded guilty and in a court plea deal is receiving treatment in a medical facility in Maine. I figure that's far enough away she might not try to come back to Texas. On my days when I remember the hell she put us through, I might wish a small case of frostbite on her—because I hear the winters in Maine can be rough.

"It's not breaking in, if you have a key, Princess. Give your man a kiss," Black grumbles, that vibrating voice sending electricity through me, just like it always does.

His lips connect with mine and I open for his kiss, swallowing down a groan as I taste him. Kissing Black is always so erotic. It's like I can taste sex with just his mouth on mine.

"God I've missed you," I breathe as I curl deeper into his arms.

"I've only been gone since this morning, sweetheart," he murmurs.

"I don't like being without you at all," I tell him and it might be pitiful, but it's true.

"That mean you aren't going to hyperventilate because I'm seeing the bride the night before our wedding?" he grins, picking me up and carrying me over to the sofa.

"Not in the least, it wasn't *my* idea that you leave this morning, remember?"

"I remember. When my mother gets a bee in her bonnet you have to let her have her way."

"This is true. Ida Sue is a force to be reckoned with when she gets an idea in her head."

"You've got too many clothes on," he complains, pulling my t-shirt up and over my head.

"I wasn't exactly expecting you. How did you get away anyway? I would have thought your mother was watching you like a hawk."

"I'm supposed to be staying the night with Blue. He's covering for me," Black groans as he unlatches my bra. "God, you have the prettiest tits in the world."

"Have you seen them all?" I laugh, helping him get my bra untangled from my arms.

"I can't remember any but yours," he says, working on my pants next.

"That's a good answer, Black," I giggle and now I'm the one taking his shirt off.

"See, I'm the perfect husband. You're very lucky to marry me tomorrow," he brags, pulling his shirt over his head.

"Don't I know it. Now take your pants off," I order.

"Is this what we've become, sweetheart? Am I to spend the rest of my life being your sex object?" he asks, yanking the rest of his clothes off—including those jeans—which means he's naked in front of me and with that look in his eyes, I just want to stretch and purr.

"You have any complaints?" I ask him, licking my lips as I watch him palm his cock.

"Only that you still have your pants on," he says, watching me.

I'm about to take my pants off when there's a thud coming from our bathroom.

"What was that?"

"I'm not sure," I lie. "It was probably a bird hitting the window or something. Now where were we?"

The noise happens again and I sigh. This is not the way it was supposed to happen.

"That was *not* a bird, Addie. You stay here and I'll go look," he says already turning to leave the room.

"Wait!" I cry and he turns around.

"What?" he asks.

"Maybe it was just Little Kong. You know how he gets bored being alone."

"I'll go and check just the same," he says and I sigh.

"Shouldn't you at least put some pants on first? You're kind of *vulnerable* like that... Don't you think?"

He rolls his eyes heavenward like he doesn't know what to do with me.

"Please?" I ask.

He doesn't answer. He lets out a sound like a bear foraging for food and finding none. In other words, he is *not* happy. He does however, put his pants on, or half on, he doesn't bother buttoning them, just uses the zipper to hold them in place. I figure that's good enough.

Since I *know* what he's going to find, I hurry and take off my jeans and throw on his shirt, rolling the sleeves up as I quietly make my way into the bedroom. I get there just as he opens the bedroom door.

I climb on the bed and Little Kong immediately jumps up in my lap. He's still my dog, but at least he doesn't try to bite Black any time he gets around him now.

"I thought I told you to stay in there," Black hisses.

I just grin at him.

"Stay there!" he orders so sternly my nipples go hard.

I watch as Black opens the bathroom door, anticipation filling me. There's some quiet noise and I think I hear an awe filled "Fuck!" in there too. The best sound is the deep sound of a bark... a happy bark.

"Addie..." Black says and there's shock all over his face when he comes out holding a huge, and very fat—but *very happy* English bulldog.

"Please, please, *please* don't tell me that it's the wrong dog. Blue swore it was Kong and he answers to the name! Don't you big guy?" I croon, making kissy faces at Kong—to which he barks.

"I... he's my dog... how did you...."

Black sits down on the bed with his dog and Little Kong immediately jumps off and goes and hides.

I let out a sigh.

"It's going to take a little bit of work getting Little Kong so he's not terrified of his big brother," I tell Black, thinking in my head of the best way to make this work.

"Brother?" Black asks me and when I look at him, I swear there are tears in his eyes and my heart constricts.

"Well, the four of us really are a family. They'll have to learn to get along. Do you like your wedding present?" I ask him, when he doesn't say anything for a few minutes. He's just petting Kong and holding him. The big guy is soaking it in and even rolls over onto his stomach. I reach out and scratch him just like Black is doing.

"How did you find him?" Black asks, quietly—not looking at me, just looking at his dog.

"Whack-a-doo Linda let it slip that she drove Kong to Oklahoma to a shelter to have him put down..." I stop when I see the shudder that rolls through Black. I reach out and touch his face gently and Kong flops over and licks his arm, demanding more petting. Black happily gives that to him and even bends down and kisses the top of Kong's head. I watch for a minute because in that moment I think I do the impossible.

I fall even more in love with Black. I would have thought I was already as in love as a person could get—apparently I was wrong.

"But he's still here," Black answers, saying it more to himself than to me.

"I had to search through a shit ton of shelters and talk to them directly, but I finally found a small one and the owner knew right away what I was talking about. She said the woman was adamant the dog be put down, but she couldn't bring herself to do it. So, she sent Linda on her way and told her to come back in an hour and when she came back she gave her ashes—just not of Kong."

"I can't believe it. I'm staring at him and I still can't believe it," Black says.

"When I explained what had gone on, she told me to come and get Kong. She kept him at the shelter running free as the facility's mascot."

"I can't believe it."

"Does that mean you like my wedding gift, Mr. Lucas?"

"That means I love my wedding gift... but..."

"But?" I ask, confused.

"I love you so much, Addie. I put you through hell in the beginning until I—"

"Stopped dragging your dick in the dirt?" I supply helpfully.

"Yeah," he says bashfully. "The point is, I don't deserve you, but I swear I'm going to do everything in my power to make you happy for the rest of our lives. I love you with everything inside of me, Adelle Harrington—soon to be Lucas."

"I love you even more than that, Black Lucas," I tell him lying down. Kong lays his head on my stomach and I scratch his ears, hoping my dog doesn't get too jealous.

"Not possible, woman."

"Is too, possible," I reply.

Black picks Kong up and puts him on a rug by the bed. He whimpers, but scratches around until he gets comfortable.

"I didn't get you a wedding present, Addie."

"You'll have to remedy that," I tell him, pulling his t-shirt off. Black is still standing, but he slips his jeans off and climbs on the bed.

"I guess I will," he says, lying over me and taking me into his arms.

We hear Little Kong padding across the floor and I tense, sure we're about to see a doggie murder and my little guy being the victim. He sniffs around Kong and Kong barely raises a doggie-eyebrow before he puts his head back down to sleep. Little Kong moves in and Black and I both look down at them as Little Kong finally decides to jump on Kong's back and lay there.

It's the craziest thing I've ever seen, but Big Kong doesn't even move. It looks like they're both just going to go to sleep.

"See," I grin up at Black. "We're just a happy family."

"That we are, Addie, and all because of you," he says, those blue eyes full of love and promise.

In the beginning I wasn't planning on staying over a couple of days in Mason. One chance meeting with a grumpy cop with eyes bluer than the Caribbean waters changed that. He changed everything. Now I never plan on leaving Mason. I may have been mad at my father for taking away my home, because even without my mother it was the only home I'd known. What I could have never guessed is that he didn't.

He just helped me find an even better one—and I know my Mom would agree.

THE END

Not had enough of Addie and Black, or that crazy Lucas family? Would you like to read all about their crazy wedding? You have two options! You can head over to Books & Main and find me there, or you can check out my webpage!
The scene is completely free. Below are the links.

Jordan's Webpage: Exclusive Content

Books & Main

ALSO BY JORDAN MARIE

Doing Bad Things Series

Going Down Hard (Free On All Markets)

In Too Deep

Taking It Slow

Savage Brothers MC—Tennessee Chapter

Devil

Diesel

Savage Brothers MC

Breaking Dragon

Saving Dancer

Loving Nicole

Claiming Crusher

Trusting Bull

Needing Carrie

Devil's Blaze MC

Captured

Burned

Released

Shafted

Beast

Beauty

Lucas Brothers Series

Perfect Stroke

Raging Heart On

Happy Trail

Cocked & Loaded

Pen Name Baylee Rose & Re-released

Filthy Florida Alphas Series

Unlawful Seizure

Unjustified Demands

Unwritten Rules

FOLLOW JORDAN

Links:

Here's my social media links! Make sure you sign up for my newsletter. I give things away there and you get to see things before others! I also have a blog on my webpage you can subscribe to and besides my strange ramblings I'll update you on my work in progress.

Newsletter Subscription
    Books & Main
    Facebook Page
    Twitter
    Webpage
    Bookbub
    Instagram

Text Alerts (US Subscribers Only—Standard Text Messaging Rates May Apply):

Text *JORDAN* to 797979 to be the first to know when Jordan has a sale or released a new book.

Made in United States
North Haven, CT
14 January 2024

47452230R00166